"Why did you agree to come here and help me?" Drury asked.

She propped her chin on her hand, elbow on the table. "Was it a sense of duty? You're from Alaska, but I still don't understand why you took this case."

Why did his reason matter? "Duty. Anger. If I could stop all cop killers, I would. But I have to settle for one case at a time."

What had led him into show business differed from what had driven him from Alaska. That old, haunting darkness threatened to surface. Brycen wouldn't let it. He'd put that part of his life behind him long ago.

"I don't want my story told on your show," she said. "Period. It's too real and it's a private matter."

As her beautiful, striking blue eyes shifted to him in fiery disagreement, shattering glass interrupted.

Brycen stood in an instant and drew his gun from its holster at his hip, hidden by his jacket. Drury sprang off the chair and rushed to her son.

A rock with a piece of paper fastened to it with a rubber band rolled to a stop against the refrigerator.

* * *

Be sure to check out the next books in this miniseries. Cold Case Detectives: Powerful investigations, unexpected passion...

* * *

tell us what you
omantic Suspense!
msuspense

D1051562

Dear Reader,

My Cold Case Detectives series is in full swing. Dark Alley Investigations is growing. For the first time, Kadin Tandy has to recruit detectives. One of those recruits is Brycen Cage, a sexy, hard-core homicide cop and television celebrity who never fails a case, no matter how cold.

Cold Case Recruit is an Alaskan adventure. I find the remote islands and villages romantic and wild, and love writing about places not often traveled. The setting complements my secretive hero and native heroine.

Drury Decoteau isn't afraid of much. She comes from a line of doers and has what it takes to break through Brycen's boundaries. These two take DAI to the next level.

Look for the next book in the series—you're in for a surprise! Kadin's team of detectives is getting really interesting...

Jennie

COLD CASE RECRUIT

—

Jennifer Morey

HARLEQUIN® ROMANTIC SUSPENSE

Recycling programs
for this product may
not exist in your area.

ISBN-13: 978-0-373-28195-4

Cold Case Recruit

Copyright © 2016 by Jennifer Morey

Printed in U.S.A.

www.Harlequin.com

Two-time RITA® Award nominee and Golden Quill Award winner **Jennifer Morey** writes single-title contemporary romance and page-turning romantic suspense. She has a geology degree and has managed export programs in compliance with the International Traffic in Arms Regulations (ITAR) for the aerospace industry. She lives at the foot of the Rocky Mountains in Denver, Colorado, and loves to hear from readers through her website, jennifermorey.com, or Facebook.

Visit Jennifer's Author Profile page at Harlequin.com, or jennifermorey.com, for more titles.

For all those who made it possible for me to work from home. I am grateful.

Prologue

With another episode of Chicago crime recorded for the archives, Brycen Cage walked off the set of *Speak of the Dead* and headed backstage. Fans loved the chilling, grisly, terrible stories. He'd discovered a talent for reproducing them in a much lighter tone than their reality, the darkest side of humanity twisted into entertainment. Ten years ago, if anyone had told him he'd end up somewhat of a celebrity showcasing murder, he'd have laughed.

He greeted a stagehand on his way down a dimly lit hallway toward his dressing room. Outside the double doors, two security guards waited. A few other crew members busied themselves closing out the program and prepping the stage for tomorrow's schedule. Brycen liked the social aspect of the show. It beat interacting with the dead.

His agent let five or six people into his dressing room

after every live taping. Good PR, he'd said. Entering the clean, white-walled, well-lit room, he saw the fans waiting for him just inside, five women and one man. The man seemed out of place in a casual business jacket with a cowboy hat shading his gray eyes and black hair sticking out from the rim. Men rarely came here for an autograph.

He focused on the women, one tall and slender, one short and chesty, one average but great-looking blonde, another taller blonde and a fifty-something librarian stereotype.

"Hello, ladies." He inserted himself in the middle of the women and took the first pen offered him. His agent made sure they all brought their own pens. The women giggled breathlessly—all but the fifty-something. She watched with an entertained smile, or maybe a fond smile best described that look. The man stepped back and waited. He didn't have a pen and paper ready. If he wasn't here for an autograph, what did he want?

"I *love* your shows," the great-looking blonde said.

Who could *love* murder stories about real people? A living, breathing human being had suffered horrifically at the hands of a perverted monster and people *loved* hearing about it?

"Thanks." He gave her his standard charmer of a grin. Had she demonstrated more intelligence, he would not be opposed to spending some personal time with her.

"Are you still a detective?" the chesty woman asked, waiting to hand him her paper and pen.

She came off as shy and a little innocent. Sweet. With a nonstandard, genuine smile for her, he signed the blonde's autograph. "I don't work for the Chicago police anymore, no." He came to this studio and recorded shows on cases he'd solved over the years. Talking about them was much easier than having them front and center in his face.

He handed the great-looking but not-so-bright blonde his autograph, and one of the security guards ushered her out the door.

"I love your shows on Alaska," the chesty woman said, handing him her pen and paper.

She ruined his opinion of her by bringing up Alaska. "Thanks."

"Do a lot of criminals go to Alaska to hide?" she asked.

"Some." He handed her the autographed plain piece of paper. "Thanks for coming to my show."

She looked disappointed at the brevity of their chat. This wasn't supposed to take long. The other security guard ushered her out the door as the first one returned.

"I'm Carol," the tall and slender woman said, thrusting a pen and pad of flowery stationery paper toward him. People handed him all sorts of media to sign. The oddest one so far was a giant wall clock. The visual still made him want to chuckle. What made that woman decide on the clock, and why have his name so prominently displayed? Did time have some meaning? The short time humans had to live? Or had she been fascinated by murder and got a thrill every time she saw his name? Maybe both. Who knew?

"Will you write *great to meet you, let's get together sometime*?" Carol flashed her pretty brown eyes with a big smile, all in fun.

He admired her courage. "I'd be glad to." He began to write.

"Do you mean it?" she asked excitedly.

Finished writing, he handed her the pen and stationery back. "Of course. Now you can show all your friends." He always got uncomfortable when the groupies came to see him. He wasn't a rock star, after all.

Her smile deflated a bit when she noticed his neutrality, or lack of interest, as she might interpret.

"Right this way," the security guard said, guiding her away.

She looked back over her shoulder as though lamenting the failure of this one attempt to hook up with someone famous. Well, not *famous*. His show was popular, that was all. And he did like his privacy.

"Is it true that you don't believe in marriage?" the tall blonde asked, handing him her piece of paper.

A magazine had done an interview with him once, a few months ago. Promotion, his agent had said. He hadn't enjoyed it at all. Talking about his personal life always set him on edge. "I'm a skeptic."

"Haven't you ever been in love?" She smiled flirtatiously.

"Once, but it wouldn't have worked out anyway." He handed her the pen and paper and nodded to the other security guard.

Her flirty smile vanished at his easy dismissal. She didn't look back as she was taken through the door.

The fifty-something handed him a photograph of himself. She'd patiently waited, like the man hanging back in the shadows. Brycen glanced over at him watching the exchange as he likely had done with all the others, nothing revealing on his face or in his eyes. Who the hell was this guy?

"It's so refreshing to know there are people like you left in this world," the fifty-something said.

Her sincerity brought his attention right back to her.

"My daughter was murdered eleven years ago and her case was just solved a few months ago, thanks to one of your shows," she said. "She was murdered by that serial rapist you put away in Chicago a few years ago. The detectives didn't put it together until your show aired. A DNA test linked the killer to my daughter's rape and murder. I flew down here to meet you and to thank you in person."

He had not expected gratitude from a woman whose daughter had been murdered. Touched, he took the pen she offered and the photograph. "I'm very sorry for your loss, Ms...."

"Lynden. Molly Lynden."

He wrote, *For Molly Lynden and her daughter. I wish I would have caught him sooner.*

Handing her the photograph and pen, he asked, "How long are you in town?"

His question seemed to startle her, but she said, "I'm staying with a friend until the end of the week."

Turning to the waiting security guard, "Tell my agent to arrange a dinner for me and Ms. Lynden." And then to her, he said, "I'd like to know more about your daughter. That is…if you don't mind." Some people didn't want to—or couldn't—talk about the ones they'd lost.

"Oh, why, that isn't necessary, but such a nice gesture, Mr. Cage." She took the business card he handed her. "I'd love to have dinner with you. And get to know you. You can't know what solving my daughter's case has done for me and my family."

"It's not a gesture, and I do know, Ms. Lynden. Many times over, I've seen what losing loved ones to heartless killers does to people. You have my highest respect and regard. It will be my pleasure to have dinner with you."

"Thank you. I… I don't know what to say."

"Say goodbye for now." He leaned in. "Security won't let you stay long."

"Of course."

He gave her a casual hug.

When she moved away, she said, "Thank you so much."

"We'll be in touch."

"Okay." Her eyes glistened with emotion as she looked back with a wave.

Watching her leave the room, he could put himself in her shoes. He could experience what she experienced. Feel what she felt. The anxiety. The despair. Several years of solving homicides had given him that dark insight, his experience in Alaska especially. A man could stand up to that only for so long before he began to break. He'd reached that point. He could no longer endure the gore, the brutality and, most of all, the senseless injustice. Call him a bleeding heart, but meeting people like Molly always brought him to his knees.

Several seconds passed before he realized the man was still waiting for his turn.

"I never got used to it, either," the man said.

Brycen had forgotten he was there, so caught up in Molly and her murdered daughter.

The man moved to stand beside him as Molly left the dressing room.

"You're a detective?" Brycen asked.

"Kadin Tandy." The tall, piercing-eyed man handed him a business card. "I'm not here for an autograph."

"I didn't think so." Brycen took the card and read.

Dark Alley Investigations. He grunted. "Are you my competition?" As Kadin's hand moved back to his side, Brycen caught sight of a double holster and two pistols. "Or not…"

Something about the name and the man was familiar. What was he doing here and how had he gotten by the network's security?

"Not everyone knows who I am," Kadin said, not at all put out that Brycen didn't recognize him. "I run a private detective agency out of Rock Springs, Wyoming. I've got five good detectives working for me and all of them are on assignment except one, but he's expecting a baby with his new wife, so I'm scouting for more."

And he'd traveled all the way to Chicago to talk to… *him*? He must have researched many detectives. To single him out struck Brycen as both odd and a compliment. The sense of familiarity grew. He'd heard of this man before.

"DAI's workload has more than doubled since word got out about us," Kadin said.

Still stunned that the man had found him, Brycen didn't respond.

"We solve cold cases," Kadin said. "Sometimes families of the victims come to us. Sometimes we go to them."

Brycen began to recall a story about a New York detective who'd gone private. "Wait a minute…you're not…"

"Several years ago, my daughter was kidnapped and murdered in New York. There was a lot of publicity on it. I moved back to Wyoming and opened DAI to fight back against criminals who've gotten away with murder."

Kadin Tandy *was* the man who'd opened a private investigations agency in Wyoming. Brycen couldn't believe it. "Yes. I remember you now. You don't stop until you catch them."

"No. Never. And neither do you."

Now Brycen understood why he'd come here, and he didn't like it. "Did." He started for the door.

Kadin followed, catching up to walk beside him.

Brycen waved off the security guard when he stepped forward to intercept Kadin.

"At least listen to my offer."

"I got out of that line of work."

"I'm aware of that. I know all about you."

That stopped Brycen. He let go of the door handle and faced him. How much did he know? "You researched me? Why?"

Kadin extended his hand toward the doors. "Let's go somewhere we can talk."

Why did he want to talk alone?

"Here's fine." If this went the way he suspected, he'd tell the guard to escort Kadin out of here. But what if he knew about Alaska…?

Well, he couldn't possibly know all of it. Brycen hadn't told a soul about the worst of it.

Kadin glanced back at the guard. "We need some privacy."

Brycen debated whether to ask the guard to escort Kadin out or not. Not facing this would be like running, avoiding whatever Kadin would bring to light. And he'd rather not have the guard—or anyone—hear this conversation.

"You can go now," Brycen said to the guard, who promptly obeyed.

Kadin closed the dressing room door after the guard left. Putting his hands on his hips, exposing the guns and appearing to choose his words carefully. "I need you to join my team."

Or maybe *not* choose them carefully. He'd come right out and said what he'd come to say. Brycen wasn't sure if he should be relieved or not. Why did this man want him to join his team of detectives?

"I told you. I got out of that line of work," he finally said.

"No, you haven't." Kadin made a show of glancing around the spacious dressing room, over the desk and lit mirror, the tall chair for the makeup and hair prep, and racks of clothes lining one wall. The polished concrete floor gleamed and pictures of cities had been handpicked for a specific reason. The single window, tinted with one-way transparency, offered a sparkling view of downtown Chicago. He loved the city. It didn't remind him of mountains. Looking at mountains depressed him.

"I'm here to recruit you," Kadin said.

"Why me?" The man might be confident, but this took it to the extreme.

Kadin wandered back into the dressing room, going to bookshelf filled with binders. "I believe you'd make a valuable addition to my team. I need you."

What he offered did seem exciting, and for the good. What better way to utilize his talent?

But to go back to that…

"Well, I don't need you, Mr. Tandy. As you can see, I have a job. A *good* job. I make lots of money, I drive a nice car and I live in a nice house. Why would I leave all that and go back to dealing with crime scenes and victims' families?"

Kadin twisted to look at him. "You just made dinner plans with one of those family members."

He did, and that would always be his weakness.

When Brycen had no comeback, a half smile curved up on Kadin's calculating face, more of a cat-got-the-mouse grin. He'd just confirmed whatever had made him come here with this insane offer.

Facing the binders again, he said, "Nothing satisfies you more than catching sadistic killers who hurt the innocent without remorse and ruin the lives of those who loved them."

Nothing like driving his point home.

Brycen shook his head. "You don't understand. I—"

Kadin cut him off. "The ugliness wore you down. I get that. But the detective in you will never die. You wouldn't have started this show otherwise. Detectives—good detectives—don't give up. Some may have a breakdown and need to step away for a while, but they always come back to what they were born to do."

Every word rang true in Brycen's heart. Sometimes he did miss the chase, the puzzle-solving and the satisfaction of sending violent criminals to prison. But he did not miss the horror…or the darkness that had begun to swallow him.

"Look," Brycen began, not feeling full conviction to stay his course and apprehensive over the temptation he faced, "I'm flattered you came all this way, but I'm not your man."

"You're not the only one I'm seeking out." Kadin slipped out a binder, cradling it as he opened to the first page.

Brycen had kept all of his case files. He used them to create shows.

"I'm recruiting others based on their suitability to

specific cases," Kadin went on, turning pages and seeming to read.

Brycen wondered how much was a show, a way to appear nonchalant, so as not to alarm Brycen to the full extent of his determination to sway him. "What case do you have in mind for me?"

"What made you decide to become a detective?" Kadin asked instead of answering.

He would ask *that* question. Homing in his sharp weapon and taking aim at Brycen's soul. Brycen walked to the bookshelf and lifted the latest murder mystery he was reading. "I loved reading when I was a kid." He held up the book. "That doesn't mean I was *born* to be a detective." He dropped the book with a slap onto the desk. "Fiction is not the same as reality."

"We all learn that when we go to our first crime scene." Kadin put the binder away and turned to face him fully, his eyes too certain for Brycen's comfort. "But you *were* born for this, Brycen. You must know. You must feel it right here." He pressed his fist to the center of his chest. "I felt it. I still do. Even though I lost my daughter to a killer, I do it because I was born to. And in a way, I honor her by helping others. How can you feel good about yourself if you aren't helping those families who desperately need you? The Molly Lyndens of the world."

"Oh, now you're going to try and guilt me." Brycen nodded, thinking it might work.

"Why did you leave southern Colorado?" Kadin asked abruptly, and then for emphasis, "For Alaska?"

He had a feeling the man already had an explanation. No point in answering, he just let him go on.

"You were inspired by the books you read. And you *knew* you could make a difference in a city where the crime rate is high. In a state that has many dangerous places to live. You had the ambition in your heart."

All true, for the most part. But that didn't lessen the toll it had taken on him.

"Do you know how many families whose loved ones are still missing? Whose killers still walk free?"

He knew it when he worked homicide and he still did now. And it bothered him.

"This show is a waste of your talent," Kadin said. "Think of the families. Molly Lynden."

"I thought of nothing else when I worked in Anchorage and then the CPD." That and solving the crimes, the mystery, the challenge to outsmart killers. The reward of feeling like a hero. As a young man, he'd felt satisfied most by that.

"Yes, but…why did you leave Alaska?"

The deliberate question put Brycen on edge. "People do horrific things when they have mountains and water separating them from law enforcement." He had told everyone that was why he'd left. Although some might speculate, no one knew the real reason. Except this man, it would appear.

"And you thought Chicago would be better?"

Few could rattle Brycen, but Kadin did.

He didn't respond, moving away from the man who pushed all the right buttons. He'd done some thorough research. Brycen stopped at the racks of clothes, wishing he could put one of the outfits on and go back onstage. But that would be running, wouldn't it? Was that what he'd been doing? Running? And not from Chicago or Alaska per se. From something in particular.

"You know all about feeling responsible for that, don't you?" Kadin pushed some more, following him across the room. "About feeling responsible for the life of some-one loved by their family?"

Brycen turned to face him. Had he meant something by that? He looked hard into the seasoned detective's eyes and found only intelligence. Cutting intelligence.

"Tell me…" Kadin subtly, but with powder-keg precision, said. "What's the real reason you left Alaska?"

A shock wave singed him. A man like Kadin could dig up what Brycen had buried. All he had to do was look.

"You're good," Brycen said. "I'll give you that."

"If you join my team, I'll give you exclusive rights to the cases you're authorized to use. As long as the families agree to you doing a story about their murdered loved ones, you can use them for your show."

Kadin was right. Brycen didn't have an exhaustive list of shows. He could solicit other cases, but that wasn't the premise of his show. Its popularity stemmed from the fact that all the cases were his. He had solved them all. The Alaska programs received the highest reviews. Some of the cases were in remote areas—and there were plenty in Alaska—in villages that didn't have law enforcement. That made for entertainment. He'd moved there from Colorado because of that, because Alaska offered a challenge, as Kadin had pointed out. Alaska had also offered other things, things he'd like to forget, things he almost had forgotten until this man had come to see him.

"You can work for me when you aren't working here," Kadin said. "You won't even have to move. Just travel to the sights of the cold cases when you need to until they're solved. A man with your experience won't take that long."

"I'm done with that line of work," Brycen said, much more feebly than before.

"Are you?" Kadin pinpointed Brycen's weakness, his thirst to solve crimes. After holding his gaze a beat longer, Kadin added, "Give it some thought. I'll be waiting to hear from you." And with that, he left the dressing room.

Brycen went to the dressing table and leaned over, bowing his head. Now what?

Plaguing regret spread its poison. Again. Every time he managed to erase the life he'd left in Alaska, something or someone rekindled the nightmare. "Damn you, Kadin Tandy."

Chapter 1

Filming ended for the season of *Speak of the Dead* and Brycen found himself with too much time to think. Everything Kadin said kept going through his mind. That, and his dinner with Molly Lynden. Talking to her reminded him of what had brought him satisfaction as a homicide detective. Solving crimes, yes, but people like her made the biggest difference. After he'd grown up and learned his love of fiction didn't compare to his work, he'd found other things to love about crime-solving.

Even with all Molly had lost, she still had forgiveness in her heart, and an ability to move forward. That was why he walked into Dark Alley Investigations today, unannounced, with a reporter taking a shot of him. News would get out that the host of *Speak of the Dead* had returned to work. And in a big way.

Inside, the receptionist's desk was empty, but Kadin

stood in the open doorway of his office. He stepped aside as Brycen approached. "I've been expecting you."

Brycen disregarded the teasing statement and entered the office.

Kadin passed him and went to his desk, picking up a folder and going to a table in the adjacent corner. Brycen took the bait and joined him there, glancing at Kadin as he opened the file. Neat handwriting spelled Drury Decoteau on the folder tab.

Brycen sat down and opened the thick file. The first page was a summary of Kadin's first conversation with the woman.

"She called a few weeks ago. A year ago her husband was gunned down as he came out of an Anchorage coffee shop. He was an Alaska State Trooper."

Brycen stopped at Anchorage. He flipped the file shut and stood from the chair. "I can't believe I fell for this." He'd asked what case Kadin had in mind for him back in Chicago and he hadn't answered. He'd known Brycen would refuse outright if he knew sooner.

Kadin planted his hand on Brycen's chest and stopped him. "I had to get you here."

"So you could fool me into taking a case in Alaska?" He had to know his history there.

"You're the best detective in the country for this case." Kadin dropped his hand. "I've had to calm Drury down on numerous occasions and ask for her patience while I recruited you."

"You told her about me?"

"I told her you were the best detective in the country for her husband's murder case."

In other words, he hadn't told her about his history outside of his detective work in Alaska.

"Read the file."

Brycen didn't move at first. But then that old curiosity overcame him, excitement over solving a new case. The need. He could not walk away from this.

Going back to the table, he sat again. The trooper, Noah Decoteau, left a coffee shop and walked to his vehicle. Before he reached the vehicle, a gunman shot him three times, once in the head, twice in the chest from an alley across the street. Ballistics came back with a 9-millimeter bullet, probably from a Ruger SR9c. Detectives spoke with patrons and neighboring shops. No one saw the shooter.

"Noah answered three calls for help the week of the shooting," Kadin explained as Brycen turned pages.

"An attempted rape in Anchorage, a domestic violence call in a remote island village and a burglary," Kadin said.

"Was there an arrest in any of the cases?" Brycen asked.

"The perp of the attempted rape was never found. Burglar was arrested, and no charges were filed in the DV call. The wife refused."

As they often did, out of fear their husbands would retaliate. "What happened in the attempted rape?"

"Cocktail waitress left work after two and someone tried to get her into their pickup truck. She fought hard and got away. It was dark, so she wasn't sure she could recognize the man. He also attacked her from behind. Some hunters came in and gave her a hard time a few nights prior. She got them kicked out and one of them wasn't very happy. He was a person of interest for a while."

Brycen read that the man had been questioned and his

wife vouched for him the night of the attempted rape. That didn't mean she hadn't lied for him. Some women would do anything to maintain peace in their home, especially with a violent man.

Next, he found the report on the DV call. The call came in from the woman, who had hidden in the bedroom closet. She said her husband had been drinking and struck her when dinner was late. It took some time to reach the house, and by the time the trooper and his partner arrived, the woman had changed her story, saying she made a mistake. Her husband didn't really hit her. With no visible signs of abuse, the troopers had left.

He went back to the description of the crime. The trooper had been gunned down in cold blood, without ever being aware someone had him in their aim. Something the trooper had either seen or done had earned him three bullets.

He searched the report for prior arrests. The abuser didn't have any. The burglar had a rap sheet. The hunters were clean.

Four other criminals the trooper had put away were still in Alaska and now free. All had been checked out. All but one had a solid alibi. In an interview, the prostitute claimed she'd been home at the time of the murder. Maybe she'd lied, since her profession was illegal. There were no more details on her. The rest of the criminals the trooper had arrested and who were listed in the report either had left the state or were still in jail.

After reading the report all the way through, Brycen put the last page down and looked out the window. Whenever one of their own died in the line of duty, Brycen took it personally. He just got mad that the trooper hadn't even had a chance. The gunman had taken the cowardly way and targeted him, hidden in the shadows and taken down an innocent, good man. He'd turned a wife into a widow. DAI's newest client. She'd called them, desperate to find the man who'd destroyed her life.

When he finally turned back to the office, he saw Kadin standing at the side of his desk, leaning there with his feet crossed and his hands resting over the edge.

"I'll do it, but I'll make no promises that I'll work for you permanently." He could not let a cop killer go free. He wouldn't be in Alaska long. Then he could return to Chicago and the city life he craved.

The smell of jet fuel and crisp northern air soaked into Drury Decoteau as she stepped down from her De Havilland Beaver. She'd finished another day of flying tourists and business professionals to wherever they needed to go in the great and vast Alaska. Today that involved a trip to Prudhoe Bay. Flights to places like that invigorated her. Weather could turn in a heartbeat. She'd been stranded in remote locations before. Not today. Late summer, the weather had cooperated, although fall seemed to be approaching faster this year than last.

She couldn't wait to get home to her nine-year-old son, Junior. Sometimes they watched a movie or played a video game. Sometimes she read stories out loud. Sometimes they had a barbecue, even after winter sank its teeth into Anchorage. It was a Decoteau family tradition. Drury tried to keep up on all of those things. While not the same as with a whole family unit, the festivity did hold them together.

Crossing the tarmac on her way to the terminal building, Drury looked around. Not many ground crew members worked right now. She didn't see anyone suspicious.

Last night the doorbell rang and while she never answered the door after dark, when whoever had left, she'd
discovered a dead cat on her doorstep. Someone didn't
like her taking Noah's homicide investigation into her
own hands. All very horror-movie style for shock value,
but the message had been clear.

Had the killer done that? Who else would have? Proof
that her husband's killer was still so close unnerved her,
but angered her more. Yeah, he should be scared. When
her detective arrived, that scourge of society wouldn't be
free much longer. Getting past the worst of the grief led
to anger. Someone had taken her husband from her, disrupted her life and her family's life. It was so unfair. No
one should get away with taking a good man's life. And
she'd make sure whoever had done so paid. She'd have
her justice and then she'd move on, satisfied with closure.
She wouldn't have it as long as Noah's killer ran free.

She spotted a man in jeans and black leather jacket
leaning against the front fender of a deep blue Yukon.
More than his towering height and solid build made him
stand out from the ground crew that had begun to work
on her plane. He didn't move, just watched her approach,
mysterious and acutely observant. Dark hair showed no
sign of receding and sunglasses hid his eyes. She slowed
her steps on her way to the private airport's main terminal building entrance. He wouldn't be on the tarmac
without authorization. He had to be here on business.

He pushed off the fender.

That must be him.

Excitement and gladness surged forth. Kadin had told
her he sent a detective. For the amount she paid, he'd
better be worth it. Dark Alley Investigations had a flexible fee structure. Those who could pay did. Those who

couldn't didn't. Kadin ran his business like a nonprofit organization, relying heavily on donations. Drury was no millionaire, but she had a sizable nest egg from her husband's life insurance and an uncle who'd left her an inheritance. And, of course, her job as a bush pilot.

The closer she came to him, the more she saw of his rugged good looks. Her husband had looked like that. Not as tall, though. This man was a giant. Noah's ruggedness had attracted her. He hadn't been the wild, backwoodsman like so many other men in Alaska, especially the more remote areas. He'd had clean-cut hair and masculine angles. Why the comparison struck her threw her off a bit. The man before her now had that same appeal, ruggedly handsome, but she shied away from admitting to herself that he attracted her.

"Drury Decoteau?"

Noah didn't have that deep a voice, either. The rich, gravelly sound tickled her senses. That and his general aura of power, a dark energy cultivated from his experience as a homicide detective and the reason Kadin Tandy had handpicked him for her dead husband's case.

"Yes."

He removed his sunglasses and revealed hard, light gray eyes that warmed when he smiled.

"Detective Cage?" She shook his hand, which ought to be rougher on a man like him. She also wondered if manly interest delayed his own introduction.

His smile changed, richer and more of a sexy grin. "Brycen. Do I stand out that much?"

She found it both refreshing and captivating that such a big man who dealt in gory murders for a living would be so approachable. Never mind the sexy part. "You do stand out, but I've been expecting you. Kadin told me you'd be coming. He also told me you were the best in the country for my husband's case."

The grin smoothed, more professional now. "I worked in Alaska for many years."

"He didn't say you were humble, but that's a nice quality." Or was it bittersweetness that made his grin fade? Maybe he didn't like the reminder of his work in Alaska.

A plane rolled up to the terminal, the engines wining, and another ground crew worked quickly to service the private flight.

"Kadin's been more communicative with you than me." He nodded toward her plane. "He didn't mention you were a pilot."

"I'm a pilot," she said happily. Glancing back at her high-wing, blue-and-white De Havilland with conventional landing gear, she felt a familiar pride come over her. She'd loved flying ever since she was a kid. "I wasn't one of those people who had a hard time deciding what to do for a living."

He admired her plane with those light gray eyes, glimmering and intelligent. They shifted to her, lasers penetrating. A pleasurable zing stunned her for a second.

"Why Alaska?" he asked.

"Um…" She cleared her throat in discomfort. What was the zing all about? "I'm… I'm from here." She tugged the ends of her thick, wavy black hair, needing humor to get her past this awkward moment. Next, she pointed to her blue eyes. "Native American even with these. My mother is from New York. I inherited her attitude, too."

He laughed low and breathy. "Where did you learn to fly?"

"I joined the air force and would have been a fighter

pilot, but I was too petite for the g-force." Yes, focus on that and not her reaction to him. Bush piloting had saved her after Noah's murder. She'd gotten much more daring since then.

She saw how his gaze lost professionalism as it roamed down her body and back up again. "You still are."

The zing heated into unmistakable attraction. Any single woman would notice this man's good looks. Add strong, manly confidence and hotness oozing from every one of his pores.

Flashes of Noah, glimpses of times passed—anchors of grief that had been her constant companion in the days and months following his murder—swallowed her. Noah, laughing with her the morning of his death over a cute kid in a commercial. They'd talked about having another child, maybe trying for a girl. Noah, holding her during a dance at a local festival, looking at her with all his love in his eyes. She had often marveled over her luck in finding him, wondering why her. And then he'd been ripped from her in the most horrific way. Something so beautiful and pure, slaughtered.

It had been a year, long enough to be on her way healing, but not long enough. She needed more time. She couldn't let go. Not yet.

"So…" she said, "about the file…"

Wearing his professional face again, Brycen said, "The police did a standard job collecting evidence and questioning witnesses and anyone your husband came into contact with prior to the shooting." Was he being a detective or did he wonder how deep her feelings ran for a dead man? Deep. She didn't have to tell him.

Relieved he'd recognized their unexpected chemistry

and how that might crowd her while she searched for her husband's killer, she said, "Standard?"

"They asked all the expected questions. Did they ask you if he had any enemies?"

She nodded. "They did, and he didn't. Not that I was aware. He was a good man. Well respected by everyone who knew him."

"What I found missing was a closer look into those who came in contact with him prior to his murder. They were all questioned and leads checked, but I saw no further investigation."

She wasn't sure what he meant. How much further could those who'd come in contact with Noah be investigated? If they had no involvement, they couldn't be charged with murder.

"Tell me about the attempted rape," he said. "Your version."

The attacker had gotten away, but he must know that. He must be looking for inconsistencies, something that might change the investigation. "Noah didn't mention anything to me, but his partner said she tried to keep them from getting out of control and they kept coming on to her. Eventually they were asked to leave. A few nights later, she was attacked leaving work. She fought and got away."

"Did your husband's partner make any observations about the people he questioned?"

"You mean, like habits or appearances?" She shook her head. "No. He stuck to the case."

"And the domestic violence call?" he asked. "What turned up there? Your version."

"Carter." In case he didn't recall or know yet, she added, "Carter Nichols was Noah's partner."

Brycen nodded once.

"He didn't mention anything significant. The wife refused to press charges and there was no evidence of abuse—no visible evidence. Not only that, but the Cummingses live on a remote island, and there doesn't seem to be any motive for Melvin Cummings to travel all the way to Anchorage to shoot Noah outside the coffee shop."

"I agree," Brycen said. "Why kill a trooper who didn't arrest you?" He looked past her where passengers had deboarded the private plane and the crew worked to finish up. The crew working on Drury's plane had finished and now the plane rolled toward the airport apron, where it would be parked until its next flight.

"Do you think things are missing from the files?" she asked, much more interested in this than the status of her plane.

He tucked his sunglasses into an inner pocket of his jacket, revealing a gun holster. "Nothing other than what I suggested, no notes on impressions. No observations on reactions or relationships. Just evidence gathering. Information gathering. Data."

Unless the observations were on the killer, Drury didn't see how those would make a difference. But he was the hotshot detective, not she.

When she'd first heard about Dark Alley Investigations, she had been skeptical, but after reading about a few of the cases the agency had solved, she changed her mind. Kadin led an aggressive agency, all geared toward justice for cold cases and a reputation for never quitting. But she was curious of one thing.

"So, what makes you so different than other detectives?" She wasn't afraid to ask direct questions.

He laughed shortly, eyes crinkling at the corners and disarming her once again. "I'm not sure."

Another plane took off down a runway and she waited for the sound to die a bit. "Kadin said you had a zero unsolved case rate. How do you do it?"

He didn't seem uncomfortable, stood relaxed and answered straightforward. "Experience. A talent for looking at the crime from multiple angles. And the evidence. A person's outlook and circumstances in life are important, too. Circumstances can drive people to do things they ordinarily wouldn't. On the other hand, people who seem normal can be the most dangerous criminals of all."

He must have a keen eye for evidence and how it tied in with a person or a suspect, how all the information told a story. She hoped he could see one for Noah.

"Excuse me, Mrs. Decoteau."

She turned to see the driver of the touring company she worked for, standing in the doorway of the terminal building, holding the door open. He picked her up on the tarmac and drove her home after her days of flying, a perk the company offered its pilots. That saved her parking fees and the company from having to reimburse her. But she just now noticed the van was not on the tarmac and he'd come through the terminal building.

"My van broke down," he said. "I'm afraid you're going to have to take a cab."

That would take a while this far outside Anchorage. "Oh." She had to go pick up her son. She checked her watch. By the time she made it home to get her car and back out to the school, she'd be late. Even if she took a taxi to the school, she wouldn't make it.

"I can take you," Brycen said. "We can further discuss the case on the way."

How nice of him to offer. "I have to go pick up my son."

Seeing him blanch slightly at the mention of her son, she wondered what had caused it.

"Kadin didn't mention you had a son."

She smiled to cover her wariness over his reaction. "He left out a lot about me." The fact that she had a son shouldn't be significant for what he'd come for. "Didn't fill you in on the personal details, huh?"

"No." He walked to the passenger door of his Yukon, seeming angry that he had not been told. Had Kadin deliberately left the detail out? But why? He must know personal details that Drury didn't, details that may have prevented Brycen from coming to Alaska to take the case. She found herself much more curious about him.

She climbed into the passenger seat. As Brycen drove off the tarmac toward the airport exit, she caught sight of a man smoking a cigarette in the gravel parking area, near the entrance to the tarmac. Wearing a hoodie and sunglasses, he leaned against a light post, a few spaces from where Mountain Ridge Air Taxi's shuttle van had parked—or broken down.

"Someone you know?"

Startled and impressed by his sharp observation, she turned to him. "No. Just nervous, I guess. I didn't get a chance to tell Kadin that someone left a dead cat on my doorstep last night."

He drove a few beats as the news registered. "I'll take that as a welcome back."

Noah Decoteau Jr. walked out of school, saying something to one of his pals before parting ways. He used to interact with a lot more enthusiasm and the number of his friends had dwindled. The light had gone out after Noah's death and Drury couldn't find a way to turn it back on. His resemblance to Noah didn't help. Arrows of happier times stabbed along with immeasurable love. His head full of dark hair, the way he walked, even some of his expressions were mini versions of the adult. Would she ever get past the heartache? Did anyone who lost someone they loved to murder? Many times she'd felt guilty for living when he died. Or that she hadn't grieved enough. She hadn't told anyone that. But it was one of the reasons she'd called DAI. She hoped to find closure.

Glancing over at Brycen, she felt a lighter arrow pierce her, Cupid's arrow. His rugged face and thick hair, big body taking up the seat without an ounce of fat. His eyes watched the kids and then turned to her. She'd only just met him and already felt a strong connection. Intimate curiosity. How could that be? From the moment she'd seen him leaning on the SUV, keenly observant, he'd struck something buried in her. He'd rekindled an interest in the opposite sex. What frightened her most, not just any man could have done that.

She must be excited to catch Noah's killer, that's all.

Opening the door, she got out as Junior searched for the Mountain Ridge shuttle van. Spotting her, he started to walk faster. Brycen got out on the other side and Junior saw him, staring a bit before looking back at his mother.

When he reached her, she messed up the top of his hair. "Hey, kiddo."

He grumbled something and lowered his head.

"What's wrong?"

He squinted up at her, sunlight streaming onto his face. "Gatchel Maxwell is *stupid*."

One of the kids gave him a hard time today? "What did he do?"

"He said single moms don't make any money and boys with single moms grow up to be crack-eds."

He meant *crackheads*. "Well, I think boys with names like Gatchel are more likely to grow up like that."

That sprang a smile onto Junior's face, followed by a lighthearted laugh. A real kid laugh that reached his young brown eyes. Drury loved it. He'd withdrawn a lot since Noah died, but she could bring him out of it every once in a while.

She faced the SUV to see Brycen had gotten out and headed toward them.

"Who's that?" Junior asked.

He stepped onto the sidewalk and came to a stop beside Drury. "Brycen Cage." He held out his hand.

Junior eyed the hand and looked up—way up—at Brycen's face.

"This is the detective I told you about." Why had he offered his hand as though Junior were a professional business contact? She stopped a laugh. "This is my son, Noah Jr. I call him Junior."

"Junior." Brycen nodded once in acknowledgment, stuffing his hands into his front jean pockets. When Junior didn't respond, he looked from the boy to the area surrounding the school, and she went to the back door of the SUV to let Junior in.

"Where's Mac?" Junior asked.

He and the van driver had become fast friends. "Van broke down. We have a different ride today." She gestured for him to get in the back.

Junior didn't move as he sized up the big stranger. He'd gotten shy around men she encountered. Mac had taken a while to warm up to him. Drury often wondered what went through his little mind. Did he compare them to his dad? In a blue button-up shirt that matched one she'd gotten Noah, Junior looked a lot like his father.

"Why is *he* driving us?"

"He met me after work. He's kindly offered us a ride home." What was it about Brycen that put off Junior? Yes, Junior was shy around men, but he seemed defensive. What was different? Had he picked up on the man's awkwardness? Big, imposing stranger who stiffened around kids? Probably.

And what made Brycen so anti-kid? Was it his lack of experience? Or did he dislike them? She couldn't be sure which or if it was something else entirely, something personal that Kadin had left out.

Junior lowered his head and kicked at the concrete sidewalk.

"Junior?" She noticed he held something in his hand, a piece of folded paper. "What's that you've got?" She went to him and held her hand out.

He looked sullenly up at her and handed her the paper.

She opened it and saw it was his report card. Seeing several unsatisfactory marks and long notes from his teachers, Drury quelled her sinking disappointment. "Junior, what happened here?"

He kicked at the concrete again and shrugged as though he didn't care. Drury knew he did care.

"How many times do I have to tell you to keep up your grades?"

His head lifted and defiance sprang from his eyes. "I try."

"Not hard enough. You used to be at the top of your class. Why are you still letting your grades fall so much?"

Drury put her hand on Junior's shoulder. "That's not the Decoteau way. We give everything our all."

Junior jerked away. "Then I'll just stay here! I don't want to go anywhere with you anyway!" He started marching back up the sidewalk toward the school.

"Noah Jr.!" Drury trotted to catch up to his small strides. She put her hand on his shoulder and stopped him, turning him to face her and bending to his level. He pouted at her.

She took in his adorable face awhile. "You're going with me and that's final. Got it?"

His pout plumped up his lower lip some more.

Drury ran her forefinger down the tiny bulge. "Brycen is the detective who's going to help Mommy. You don't have to like him, but you do have to get into the SUV." She straightened, taking his hand. "And you have to get your grades back up." She walked with him back to the Yukon.

Brycen leaned against the front bumper, ankles crossed and phone to his ear.

As she and Junior returned, she heard him say, "Thanks." Before putting his phone away and impassively surveying Junior and then her. "Everything okay?"

He seemed like a completely different man than the one she'd met on the tarmac. Distant. All purpose.

"Yes."

He looked down at Junior with the same detachment.

Junior angled his head as he returned the look with defiance. "Are you going to find my daddy?"

Drury wasn't sure Junior fully understood his father had been murdered, or what it meant when a person died. He asked when his father was coming back every so often. Even though she said he wasn't, Junior didn't seem to compute.

"I'm going to catch the man who hurt him."

Relieved that he had found a gentle way to answer, Drury saw how Junior wavered over what to think of this stranger.

"You promise?" Junior asked.

Brycen pushed off from the bumper and said, "I promise."

The absolute certainty in Brycen's tone made Drury stop from opening the back passenger door. In Junior's young mind, his father would someday come home. She'd tried to explain Noah would never come home, but she hadn't been able to say it in adult language, to expose her son to such brutality and darkness. She hadn't had the heart. Protecting him might preserve his childhood, to allow him to be a kid until he grew up. But that didn't seem to work. Junior missed his father and he understood enough to know something terrible had happened to him.

It meant a lot to her to know Brycen had picked up on the boy's trouble. He might not like kids, but he had a way with them. Interesting.

His gaze moved from Junior to her, communicating without words and heating her up. She didn't remember feeling this with Noah, these instant sparks so early on. Disturbed by that revelation, she opened the back door. Kadin had sent a top-notch detective. That was all he was to her. She had a mighty thirst to avenge Noah's death. When his case went cold, she'd gotten angry, not at law enforcement's failure, at the killer. He could not get away with what he'd done.

Wasn't that why she'd called Dark Alley?

Certainly not to find love again.

"Hop in, Junior."

Junior did, head low. Closing the door, she faced Brycen, who'd opened the front passenger door. "What hotel are you staying at? We can start working tomorrow morning if you're ready. Maybe I could meet you for breakfast after I drop Junior off at school."

"I canceled my hotel."

"You…" She hurried to follow his thinking. That was who he must have called when she went after Junior.

"If you don't mind, I thought I'd sleep on your couch… in case someone does more than leave something on your front porch. Whoever left it didn't like you digging into the case, and I'm guessing they'll like me showing up even less."

She appreciated him leaving out the detail of the dead cat. She hadn't told Junior and had disposed of the poor animal before he saw anything.

"All right." She got in and he went around to the other side.

He drove off the tarmac and into the parking area, passing the van.

Drury waved to Mac, who stood talking to the tow truck driver.

As they left the parking area, Drury noticed Brycen looking in the rearview mirrors. Only his eyes moved. She leaned forward just a little to look at the mirror on her side. Two cars trailed them.

"The Subaru Outback," Brycen said. "It was at the airport."

There weren't a ton of cars parked, but enough to make it impossible to remember all of them. "How do you know?"

"It's got a dreamcatcher hanging from the mirror. I saw it parked in clear view of the shuttle van."

He had a vigilant eye. Someone didn't want her investigating her husband's death. But why risk exposure by tailing her so blatantly? She looked back at Junior, who stared out the window, oblivious in his young innocence. The stalker hadn't attacked yet, but maybe things would change now that she had her own detective working her husband's case.

Without driving recklessly to lose the man, Brycen pulled over and parked along the street. The Subaru passed, the driver not looking their way. The hoodie and sunglasses disguised him enough to avoid recognition.

Brycen drove back into traffic, making the stalker the stalked. He trailed behind the Subaru, making no attempt to conceal the fact that he did so.

"What if he's armed?" They had Junior in the SUV.

"If he was going to shoot at us, he'd have done it by now. I'll just send him a message."

Brycen turned a corner when the Subaru did. And another.

When the Subaru reached the two-lane highway that followed the coastline to the south, the driver sped up, and not just to reach the speed limit. He hot-rodded the Subaru, springing into top speed in a matter of seconds.

The driver did not want to be caught. And instead of attacking, he ran. Had he been sent for surveillance only, or did Brycen and Dark Alley Investigations' reputation scare him off? Either way, the driver would not slow and, more importantly, would not lead them to whomever sent him.

Drury watched as Brycen slowed, confirming her assessment. Patience was one of the ingredients to his success. Let the man run. He couldn't hide forever. If she was that driver, she would be worried right now.

Delight tickled her insides. She had a great detective sitting across the vehicle from her. Maybe a great something else, too…

As soon as that thought floated giddily into her head, she struggled to squash it. Falling for her detective was not part of the plan.

Chapter 2

Brycen let the blinds close after peering through the crack he'd opened. Nothing stirred in the street. Still, Drury had a stalker before he'd even begun his investigation.

"Junior, what's it going to be tonight?" Drury called from the kitchen.

"I dunno," Junior answered absently, hands busy with a video game.

"You want to go play catch for a while before dinner?" She seemed to slip that one in.

Didn't Junior like to play ball, or play outside? Brycen found that curious.

"No."

"You're not doing homework." She'd slipped that in, too.

"Don't have any."

Drury frowned as though not believing him but didn't

press as she flipped a grilled cheese sandwich in the pan. "Then come in here and sit at the table. Dinner's ready."

Junior grumbled but got up and came into the kitchen. She deposited a plate of grilled cheese in front of him. A glass of chocolate milk came next.

Brycen hadn't had a grilled cheese sandwich since he was about Junior's age and wasn't sure he wanted to break the drought. He was a cute kid, but Brycen would rather not have any kids around while he investigated a murder. And not because they disrupted the peace and quiet.

Going into the kitchen, he sat before the plate she'd set out for him, a glass of chocolate milk tapping down afterward. He saw her silky black hair float down from one shoulder, dark lashes covering what he knew to be striking blue eyes. She sat down with another glass of chocolate milk, oblivious of the fact that not everyone would consider this meal ordinary.

Junior drank his milk and set the glass down, looking at Brycen, or more like dissecting him. When Brycen didn't look away, Junior twirled a superhero figure over his plate and then flew him toward Brycen, going back and forth in front of his face, leaning over the table to get as close as he could, which only reached halfway across the table.

Putting the superhero down and wearing a smug scowl only a kid could pull off and still be cute, he took a few big gulps of the chocolate milk. When he put the glass down, a chocolaty rim covered his upper lip. Then he dug into the basket of crispy french fries, all the while making sure Brycen still watched. Showing up the adult.

"So, Brycen. Why don't you tell us a little about yourself?" Drury asked with a peculiar glance at Junior. "Since you're going to be staying on our couch, we should get to know you."

He supposed he forfeited his right to keep things professional when he invited himself to stay in her house. "What would you like to know?"

"Why'd you leave Alaska?"

She would have to start with that question. "I applied for a job in Chicago." And that was about all he'd say. Kadin had earned more of his respect having not said anything about what he'd uncovered.

She stopped chewing a fry. "You just applied for it?"

"I got a call from an old friend. The climate is pretty close to Anchorage. Days are longer here in summer." He watched Junior fly the superhero over his plate and out across the table toward Brycen, probably imagining clipping his nose.

"The climate is what made you move?" Drury asked, clearly accustomed to her son's play tactics.

Junior shoved french fries into his mouth, eyes on Brycen, seeing if he'd get a rise out of him.

"No, the job made me move," Brycen said to Drury.

"Do you like Chicago?"

"I like the big city. It's a nice change."

"No family? Wife? Kids?"

"No."

"Pets?" She smiled.

"I'm gone too much. Crimes don't happen on a regular work schedule."

Junior stuffed a giant portion of his grilled cheese sandwich into his mouth and chewed with his mouth open. When he finally regained control of the mass, grease oozed out from the corners of his mouth.

"Noah Jr., use your napkin." Drury picked up the

crumpled cloth napkin and handed it to him. "You're getting grease on that superhero."

Putting down the figure, Junior laughed as he wiped his mouth and looked at Brycen. Besting him. Gaining attention through what he perceived as funny but shocking behavior. He didn't know nothing shocked Brycen anymore.

"It laughs," Drury said, smiling.

Junior made a face and then resumed stuffing more fries into his mouth.

"If you had a job in Chicago, why did you start your crime show?"

She sure asked a lot of pointed questions. "The opportunity arose."

Lifting her sandwich, she paused with his short, uninformative answer. "Were you born in Alaska?"

She must have gotten the hint that he didn't welcome talk about his reasons for leaving Alaska or what had sent him into show business. "No. Colorado. Moved to Anchorage after college when I started working law enforcement." There. That ought to be enough to tide her over.

Taking a bite of her sandwich, she studied his face while whatever thoughts she had about him danced in her mind.

"Have you ever thought about getting out of Alaska?" he asked.

The blink and lowering of her eyes revealed that she'd considered it and maybe the issue caused her some trouble.

"No. My family is here. Junior's grandparents…" She got a faraway look, turning her head and abandoning her sandwich. "It wouldn't be so bad if I wasn't alone. I mean, I'm not alone, just…I miss the companionship."

A murderer had torn her family apart and still held her hostage. She didn't have the heart to move Noah Jr. away from his paternal grandparents. He was their only living link to their son.

"Would you move if you could?"

She took some time to think on that. "No, I don't think so. It's like I said. Sometimes I feel so alone."

He could relate to that. He just would not engage in a discussion over why. "Do you have a big family?" They didn't need to talk about death.

"Not so big. My parents live here and I have a sister. She moved away. California. She's a lawyer."

"A lawyer and a bush pilot." Interesting combination. He chuckled. "I bet you have proud parents."

"They could have done worse. What about you?"

"My parents still live in southern Colorado. They're divorced." After almost thirty years, they finally decided they weren't good for each other. "I'm an only child." Probably the only time they'd had sex was when he was conceived.

Junior began making grunting, singing sounds as he ate, swinging his feet and bobbing his head while he flew his superhero. "Uh, uh, uh-uh-uh-uh…"

"What's it like not having any brothers or sisters?" Drury asked with a glance at her son and slight elevation of her eyebrows.

"What's it like having them?" he countered.

She laughed. "Active. My dad flew. Not professionally, though. He runs a local hardware store, one of the oldest in the city. My mother inherited it when her parents died. My dad worked there, so he ran it from then on. Some of the old-timers still call it a sporting goods store. He sells a lot of that still, to this day." She kept smiling with the good memories that must bring. "He took us many places. Haven't been to Europe, though. That's one place I'd like to visit someday."

Brycen had never thought about where he'd like to travel before his end came. Travel wasn't important to him. He liked to read or watch documentaries about the world. He used to love the mountains, but that all changed when he left Alaska. If he had to pick somewhere he'd like to go, he'd choose a beach, he supposed. He'd taken a woman to the Caribbean once. That had been okay. Women loved beaches.

"They like to stay active. They're older now, but they still hike and camp and go on trips to fun places."

"How did they meet? You said your mother was from New York."

"She went on a cruise. She always wanted to see Alaska, so when she was in college, her parents helped her scrounge up enough money. The ship docked in Anchorage and she went in my dad's store. They stayed in touch after that. When my mother graduated, she moved here and the rest, as they say, is history."

He smiled, wondering if her parents' relationship was as storybook as she made it seem.

"We all joke that New York must have made her the active spitfire she is, or was. She was a white tornado when I was a kid. I think that's what my dad loved about her. He worked hard, but on his time off he liked to pick up and go, usually somewhere remote."

"Is that what drew you into piloting?" Her dad had been a pilot. That must have influenced her.

Junior had stopped his grunt-singing and chewed on a fry, eyeing his superhero. Apparently he'd given up trying to shock Brycen.

"I wanted an education, and at the time, I didn't consider bush piloting very professional. Air force had a nicer ring to it, and serving the country had a certain... I don't know..." She lifted her face in thought. "Noble appeal."

"What do you like most about flying?" He never understood why anyone would want to fly a big metal tube through the air.

"The freedom," she said, looking upward dreamily. "Soaring through the sky. Everything looks so different from up there. You can see so much more of the land than your own little patch of it in everyday life."

"Freedom?" Did she mean nothing but air could stop her? No train tracks, no other cars...?

"Yeah. The freedom to go wherever I want, to not follow any roads. To see more of the world. It's hard to explain. Maybe what I really love is the thrill." She laughed a little.

"Like the air force would have been?"

"Yeah. I dreamed of flying a fighter jet when I was in high school." She lifted her eyes in mock wonder.

Maybe he could see her as a fighter pilot. More likely she'd thought doing so would be cool as a teenager.

"And then reality stepped in?" he asked.

She breathed a short laugh. "It's a far cry from solving crimes." She sipped her chocolate milk. "Is that what made you decide to start a crime show? The reality? It had to be more than a good opportunity."

She had a quick mind. Sneaky. "Yes." But then, it wouldn't take much to figure that out. Detectives were human. Murder wasn't cheerful.

Junior had finished eating and had taken to staring at Brycen. He had his head on his palm, elbow on the table, idly twirling his superhero. Brycen didn't look away and Junior showed no sign of backing down. He decided to have a little fun with the kid.

"Do I have something in my teeth?" Brycen asked, baring his pearly whites. "A piece of spinach?"

"No," Junior said. "We didn't have spinach."

"Something in my hair?" He fingered his hair. "Horns?"

Junior laughed. "No."

"Oh, good. You had me worried there for a second."

"You're weird." Junior got off his chair and asked his mother, "Can I go play my game now?"

"What about your homework?"

His head dropped to one side in annoyed frustration. "I don't have any."

"Noah Jr...?"

"I don't," he whined. "I did it at school. I don't have any, Mom."

"All right. Go ahead, then." She watched him go to the floor in front of the TV. Crossing his legs, he picked up the controller and began playing.

Then she turned to him. "You were pretty good with him just now."

"Asking if I had horns in my hair? What else can you do when kids stare?"

"I didn't expect it, that's all."

Why hadn't she? He didn't want to know. That might lead down a path he'd rather not take.

"His grades are slipping?" Brycen said, not really a question.

Drury sighed, her full, sexy lips pinched a little, forming a dimple on her right side. Then those blue eyes pierced him with a confessing look. "They have been for a while now. I might have to hold him back a year."

He didn't have to state the obvious. The poor kid missed his father and didn't understand why he was gone.

"He used to get top grades. He used to play catch with his daddy almost every day. Sounds so corny, but it's true. He did homework and played Little League. Now... he isn't interested anymore."

Losing a dad would do that to a kid. Not unusual as far as Brycen was concerned. But he wondered if Drury felt left out because her son didn't want to play catch with her the way he had with his father.

"I wish there was something I could do to help him deal," she said. "I've taken him to counseling, but that didn't seem to help. He just misses his dad so much. They were very close."

Brycen would be close to his son if he had one. What father wouldn't? "Maybe you should try doing things differently instead of trying to keep everything the same."

Drury leaned back against the chair, drawing his attention unwittingly to her breasts pushing the material of her shirt tighter. "Like what?"

He had to regain his aplomb. "Like not playing catch."

"How would not playing catch help his lack of enthusiasm?" She continued to scrutinize him.

"You're not his dad. That's something he did with his dad, not you."

Her mouth opened and whatever she'd have said she didn't. "Are you saying I should start baking brownies with him?"

He grinned. "Why not?"

"Wait a minute. Are you criticizing me?"

Analytical by nature, he didn't include criticism in

the talent. "No." He wasn't sure why he'd spoken his thoughts. Normally he engaged as little as possible with children or their mothers. "You don't seem like the type who likes to bake brownies."

She smiled. "No?"

"No. More like…bush pilot who makes grilled cheese sandwiches and french fries for dinner."

"You don't like grilled cheese?"

"I do. It's just a kid meal, especially with the chocolate milk."

"It's too much work to make something different for me. Sorry. I should have asked what you wanted."

"You like kid meals, just admit it."

She sipped more of her chocolate milk, watching him with light in her eyes, telling him she responded to him as a man. Their banter had warmed the kitchen.

"Would you have taken this case if you knew I had a son?" she asked.

He should have seen that coming. She could see he had an issue with kids, one she didn't understand and one he wouldn't explain. "Your son, or any other child, had nothing to do with my decision."

Flattening her hands on the table, she rubbed the surface, unaware she'd done it. She must be contemplating how to ask him something. "Why did you agree to come here and help me?"

"Your husband was an Alaska State Trooper. Law enforcement."

She propped her chin on her hand, elbow on the table. "So it was a sense of duty?"

Why did his reason matter? "Duty. Anger. If I could stop them all from killing cops, I would. But I have to settle for one case at a time."

What had led him into show business differed from what had driven him from Alaska. He'd gone into law enforcement because he wanted to make a difference. He'd only made a mess of his personal life in Alaska. That old, haunting darkness threatened to surface. Brycen wouldn't let it. He'd put that part behind him long ago.

"You didn't come here for a good story to put on your show?" Drury asked.

"Every case I solve is good for my show." He didn't include that every show kept him from witnessing death and the reminder that no matter how many cases he solved, he'd never feel he'd won. Justice was done, and that made it rewarding. When he first became a detective, he'd believed what he stood for. Now he wasn't sure. Ever since he'd left Alaska, his purpose seemed to have blurred.

"Not mine." When he looked closer at her, she said, "I won't agree to go on TV to tell my story."

"You wouldn't personally have to appear on the show."

"I don't want my story told. Period. It's too real and it's a private matter."

Brycen calmed his initial disappointment. Her story would make a good episode for his show. But he couldn't—and wouldn't—force her or coerce her. At least, not aggressively.

"Most people who've gone through what you have benefit from telling their story. Sharing it helps them heal and it also helps others." Not those who craved the entertainment, those who had gone through something similar.

"Not me. I could never go on air and talk about Noah's murder, and I couldn't bear to hear it told." She pushed her plate away and folded her arms on the table with a sigh.

"If I solve his murder, that's what I'd like to do. Take his story to my show. Featuring solved cold cases could make another criminal think twice before killing someone." He held back the nagging thought that more than his show and avenging a State Trooper drove him back to Alaska. He'd left to forget some things, but he couldn't deny they had influenced his decision to take this case, more than solving the murder crime of a trooper, more than a story for his show. He'd left something unfinished. Kadin had rubbed a raw nerve coercing him to take the case, but deep down, maybe he wished he could put his past to rest.

Shattering glass interrupted.

Brycen stood in an instant and drew his gun from its holster at his hip, hidden by his jacket. Drury sprang off the chair and rushed to her son, grabbing him and taking him to the protection of the living room wall.

A rock with a piece of paper fastened with a rubber band rolled to a stop against the refrigerator.

Drury told Junior to stay put and moved back into the kitchen, going to the rock.

"Don't touch it." He held out his hand to stop her from reaching the rock. "Stay here!"

Brycen ran to the back door and raced into the backyard. It was still light out but drizzling. He saw movement in the trees that bordered Drury's house on a quiet street not far from the coastline. He ran after the moving figure, dodging thick vegetation.

In a clearing, the man aimed a gun and fired. Brycen ducked behind a tree trunk and then peered out. The man vanished in the trees.

Brycen chased after him, catching a glimpse of a hoodie. When the man veered to the right, he cut a path straight to him. The man glanced back, seeing him gaining. He unsteadily moved the gun over his shoulder while he ran at top speed. His aim was off.

Crouching, Brycen heard the bullet hit a tree. He dove for the man's feet, tackling him.

The man rolled and Brycen knocked the gun off just before it fired. The man had painted his face black. More disguise than his hoodie. The man swung his foot, and the heel of his boot clipped Brycen on his forehead. He fell backward, rolling in time to miss the next bullet.

Brycen drew his own gun.

The man turned and ran.

Brycen fired twice, missing both times through the thick stand of trees. Climbing to his feet, whipping blood from his forehead, he ran after the man. He was very familiar with Anchorage but not this particular neighborhood. There was a park nearby. Possibly the man had left his car there and hiked to Drury's house.

At the park, he saw no one. The weather had chased everyone away and the man hadn't parked his car there.

Getting wet from the steady rain, Brycen jogged toward the street. Nothing stirred except the squeal of tires in the opposite direction from Drury's house. Brycen turned in time to see the Subaru that had tailed them earlier swerve around the corner. Brycen would never catch him.

He jogged back to the house.

Drury opened the front door for him.

"He got away."

Junior stood behind her, staring wide-eyed up at him as he entered. Drury scanned the neighborhood before closing and locking the door. Passing Junior, he went into the kitchen where the rock still lay. "Do you have a plastic storage bag?"

While she went to go get one, he used some cooking prongs to move the rock. The paper banded to it said "Stop before it's too late."

He met Drury's worried face as he put the rock in the bag she held open. "We need a safer place to stay."

"Where can we go?" Drury asked.

Brycen looked over his shoulder. "I have a cabin. Close enough to town but remote and secure." It was the only piece of Alaska he'd held on to. And the only reason he had was that he'd bought it just before things turned sour for him.

"You're hurt." Drury touched his arm, seeing his face.

The cut stung where the stalker had kicked him.

She took his hand and led him to the bathroom, Junior following, no longer scared and now curious.

Drury indicated Brycen should sit on the closed toilet seat. He did and she bent to retrieve a first aid kit from under the sink. Opening the lid, she dug out an alcohol wipe while Junior's small hands took out a Band-Aid.

Holding the Band-Aid out for his mother, Junior eyed Brycen, undecided as to whether he'd welcome him into his circle.

Drury finished dabbing the small cut and threw that out before taking the Band-Aid.

Junior stuffed his fingers into the front pockets of his jeans and stared at Brycen, a much different stare than at the table. "Looks like you get Captain America."

"I can do Captain America." He winked at Junior, whose eyebrows went down in distrust.

"Don't worry, I don't bite," Brycen said. "I might seem like I do, but I don't." Did he sound like he was trying too hard? He felt like he was. He didn't understand why Junior liking him was so important.

"You don't smile very much," Junior said.

Drury paused in her care of his cut to look at Junior through the mirror. "Junior…that wasn't very nice."

With a sullen look up at her, he said, "He doesn't."

Brycen smiled then. The kid had a way about him. Just now he felt he'd gotten a glimpse of the boy he'd once been, before tragedy crumbled his young world. A more talkative boy. A more curious boy. And something about Brycen had him very curious.

As Drury smoothed the bandage over the cut, her soft touch made him aware of other soft parts in contact with him. Her leg against his. Her breast as she leaned to throw out the paper from the bandage, long, shiny hair falling forward.

When she rose, her face passed in front of his. Their gazes locked. Heat quickly followed. A mounting sense of dread came over him. This wouldn't end well if he continued to desire her. He had more than one compelling reason to steer clear of women like her. He shifted his gaze to the boy. And that.

Drury straightened. "Junior, why don't you go pack?"

The boy didn't move, still eyeing Brycen uncertainly. "Junior?"

The boy looked up at her and then reluctantly turned and went up the hall.

"It usually doesn't take him this long to get used to people," Drury said. "He seems especially guarded with you. He responds to you, but then he withdraws."

"He hasn't decided whether he likes me or not."

"Why is that? Do you think he picked up on your stiffness when you first met him?"

He didn't say what he really thought. Junior sized him up, measuring him against his idea of a father figure. He might not be aware he did this, but Brycen felt it. Acknowledging that would take him down that dreaded path. The "what if" path.

"Maybe."

"Do you like kids?" She moved to stand directly in front of him.

"I've never had kids of my own." He wished she'd leave this topic alone.

Leaning over the sink, she washed her hands. "You don't have to have kids of your own to like them."

"What makes you think I don't like them?"

Drying her hands on the towel hanging from a hook on the wall, she shrugged. Then she scrutinized him through the mirror. "Why were you so uncomfortable when you met him? What is it with you and kids?"

This conversation was over. Brycen stood. "Let's get going."

Turning from the sink, she frowned her confusion as he passed and followed him out of the bathroom. "Touchy subject?"

He stopped and turned and she bumped into him. Bounced, really. All her soft parts against his harder chest and abdomen. And her hands had landed on him. She pulled back as though startled.

He felt it, too. The sparks came out of nowhere and set them both on fire. Of all the women he'd met and considered dating, Drury didn't fit the mold. She represented what he most sought to avoid. Single mom. Serious baggage. How could he compete with a dead husband? One she'd hired an elite investigation agency to solve his cold case.

"Look." He dove right in. He had to stop this from heating up any more. "I've picked up on some attraction between us and I just have to get something off my chest."

"Okay." She took a step back.

"I don't do marriage and I don't do kids. You should know that up front."

"Wh…what?"

Clearly, she hadn't expected him to say something like that. "You need to understand that about me before this goes any further."

Outraged, she put her hands on her hips. "Before *what* goes any further? You're jumping to conclusions a little, don't you think? *Marriage*?"

Maybe, maybe not. "I just want it out in the open." And he didn't want to talk about his past in Alaska.

She gaped at him, slack-jawed. "That you don't do marriage or kids."

"Yes. This is a business relationship. We don't get involved. And if we…you know, then I've warned you."

No marriage. No kids. That included Junior. He had nothing against the boy; he just couldn't be part of her family unit.

"Well, for your information, I don't want a relationship anyway. My husband was *murdered*. What makes you think I'd want to get involved with you?" She passed him.

Maybe he'd spoken too soon. Maybe he should have waited. "I'm sorry. I just thought I should tell you. I mean no disrespect."

With a peculiar glance back, she went into the kitchen and started cleaning up before packing for their trip.

He helped her clear the table in awkward silence until

she calmed down. He could tell she'd calmed, because she stopped slamming dishes.

"Why don't you think you'll never get married?" she asked at the sink.

"I don't think. It's a choice I've made because I don't believe in it. Marriages never last. My parents were married almost thirty years and should have divorced after ten. Humans aren't meant to stay married to the same person their entire lives. So why bother getting married?"

"You base your decision off your parents' marriage? Did they love each other?"

"Sure. My mother loved that he worked and she didn't have to and then she loved the alimony payments until she remarried. My dad loved a woman who didn't complain and always had dinner ready and the laundry clean."

She loaded a dish into the dishwasher. "You don't make them sound very likable. Do you ever see them?"

"Every Christmas." He threw out some trash, finding an automatic lid trash container by the counter.

"I bet you aren't this charming on your TV show."

He chuckled. She meant the exact opposite. He came across as an ass when he talked about marriage. Some people didn't like hearing the truth. "My mother wasn't happy. My father wasn't happy. They convinced themselves early on that they were. And maybe they were at first. They liked each other. But then after a few years, they wasted too much time trying to make their marriage work. I just wish they wouldn't have waited, that's all. When they could no longer convince themselves they were happy, they should have ended it."

She worked as she absorbed what he said. "You must feel like every memory of them together was a lie."

"Some of them, yes. They basically played roles for my

benefit. The good, loving mother who doted on her husband. The steady, kind, disciplinary father who took care of his wife. Now that I can see what phonies they were, it makes me bitter. I'd rather they fought and threw things. At least it would have been real." He handed her a glass from the sink, which was full of about a day's worth of dishes.

She took it from him. "You must not like your parents much."

"Oh, no. Contrary. I love them both very much."

She breathed a laugh. "Really."

"Yes, especially now that I know who they really are."

"Is that what you think you have with women? Real relationships?" She put the glass in the dishwasher.

"Unconditionally." He truly believed in sticking with the truth no matter how ugly or harmful. Maybe that was the homicide detective in him. Maybe he'd learned from his parents.

With the water still running in the sink, she rested her hands on the counter and turned her head toward him. "Do you believe in love?"

This qualified as personal, but he didn't object. She needed to understand. "I believe we're meant to love lots of people, not just one. And I don't mean that it's okay to be unfaithful. Monogamy is important while the relationship lasts."

"That's not love."

"It's a form of love." He rinsed a plate and handed it to her.

She took it. "No. That's impulsively going from one relationship to the next and not holding out for the one that really matters."

But the one that really matters didn't exist. To him, every woman he was with mattered, not just one, exulted one. One, superior woman was the stuff of fairy tales. Like Cinderella. Pure fantasy. A wonderful, magical dream. She walked into that ballroom alone and everyone stopped just to watch her come down the stairs in her fairy godmother gown that outshined all others. Something like that would never happen in real life. A man didn't find a woman who made all others seem plain and insignificant.

But he didn't think he could make Drury understand.

"It's love to me," he said.

She put the plate in the dishwasher. "No. That is not love. Clearly you've never *been* in love."

"I only know what works for me." He handed her another plate.

"Well. Thanks for the warning, then." She put the plate in the dishwasher and glanced at him from behind a sexy curtain of hair.

He didn't say she likely idolized her husband in death and merely *thought* she had true love with him. He wouldn't argue over this. He wouldn't have a chance with her. He'd scared her off. Well, good. He didn't need his ideals put to any kind of love test anyway. Especially since he also had to put aside the nagging feeling that his attraction to her rose above anything he'd ever experienced before.

His Cinderella…?

Chapter 3

Carter Nichols stepped out into the reception room of the Division of Alaska State Troopers, Bureau of Investigations Unit. A tall, burly man with close-cropped medium brown hair and light gray eyes, he wore a state trooper's uniform, blue shirt with an insignia, and black pants with a gun on his belt. He must have left his hat at his desk. Drury had seen some of the other officers wearing them and Carter had always gone without whenever he could. Seeing him reminded her of Noah, but this time the sight of him seemed strangely less impactful. With Brycen by her side, she had to wonder if he had anything to do with that.

Carter went straight to Drury. "Hey, Drury." He took her into a hug and leaned back. "How are you doing?"

He hugged her every time she came to see him since Noah's murder. It had comforted her knowing he'd worked so closely with her husband.

"Good." She stepped back to put space between them. "This is Brycen Cage." Why she felt awkward introducing him, she had to wonder. Was her attraction obvious? Although she had tried to subdue her reaction to Brycen, nature kept bringing her closer to that point when she could no longer resist. The strength of the temptation made her feel guilty. She wasn't betraying her dead husband. The guilt came from knowing and not wanting to face that she couldn't recall feeling the same degree of desire with Noah. Theirs had been more of a comfortable companionship, a close friendship that had grown into love.

"Brycen." The trooper offered his hand with no sign of animosity.

They shook hands briefly, Carter noticing the slight cut on Brycen, who'd removed the bandage shortly after it had been put on.

"I heard you were on your way. It's an honor to have you, and if there's anything we can do to help with your investigation, just let me know." He turned to Drury. "We did our best, but we've reached a wall."

"You did a thorough investigation. I read the report," Brycen said. "But maybe fresh eyes will see something new. In my experience, it's sometimes all a case needs. I distance myself from a case for a while, just so I can come back to it later with a new perspective."

Carter gave a single affirmative nod. "If you find something to crack open my partner's case, I'll forever be in your debt." His head bowed with the heavy weight of his failure to find a friend and partner's killer.

"I'll catch his killer," Brycen said. "But I'd appreciate some assistance from your office. Access to resources and a crime lab if we need one."

Carter gave another nod. "Whatever you need." He took out his wallet and removed a card. "That there is my cell phone." He pointed to the third number listed on the card. "You can reach me anytime. Or just call here and someone will radio me." He grinned as though he had a confession. "Service is patchy once you get away from the city."

"Of course." Brycen put the card in his back jean pocket. "On the sexual assault call that Noah responded to, did you happen to interview any other suspects than the hunters?"

"When I questioned the victim, she didn't report any other suspicious contacts. We spoke with her ex-boyfriend, but he broke up with her several months prior. She had a falling-out with a friend, but that led to nothing, and her coworkers said she was nice. I didn't find anyone else who'd fit the profile and could place none of them at the scene. My other thought on that was that it could have been random."

Drury agreed a stranger could have singled the victim out and attacked. "Have there been any rapes reported since then?"

"Almost every day." Carter grunted sardonically. "This is Alaska. In the cities there's more control, but law enforcement can't always reach the remote areas in time."

"The report said you have no fingerprints or other evidence," Brycen said.

"No, only a vague description from the victim. It was dark and the man wore gloves and a mask. All she could say is he fit the body type of the hunter who came in to the restaurant and started harassing her."

"Can I see the evidence?"

"Sure. I arranged for you to get in the room before

you got here." He started walking back toward the way he'd come. "Follow me."

Carter had always worked hard to find Noah's killer. At first he'd been ridden with guilt and grief, wishing he could have stopped the shooter somehow. But he hadn't been there.

Passing through two hallways, Carter stopped at a metal door and used his badge to enter. The evidence room wasn't large, but it had a decent capacity for the allotted space. Rows of shelves took up most of the room, with a small space for a table and an officer behind a desk up front.

"I've got your evidence ready over there. The smaller box is for the assault vic. The larger is from Noah's scene."

On the table, two cardboard boxes sat open. Brycen went there and started with the smaller one, lifting out a clear plastic bag containing the victim's clothes and the forensic psychologist's report.

"I tried to get her to confront the angry hunter with a wire, but she refused," Carter said. "A lot of times, a rapist might start talking about the incident and he implicates himself. But she was too scared."

Drury could hardly blame her. Although she had never been through something like that, she didn't think she'd have refused to help the police. A predator still ran free to hurt other women.

"I'd like to talk to her myself," Brycen said. "Would you have a problem with that?"

Carter folded his arms and shook his head. "None. Why would I?"

Brycen smiled slightly. "Some law enforcement types are threatened when someone from Dark Alley Inves-

tigations shows up. Or so I'm told. I'm new to the organization."

"I confess I hadn't heard of the agency until Drury
said she called you, but I've done a little reading and
threatened isn't a word I'd use. Hopeful is much more
appropriate."

Carter did have one of those easygoing personalities.
People liked him. But Drury wasn't sure what Brycen
thought he could gain from talking to the assault victim
again. The hunter's wife had claimed he'd been home in
northern Washington the night of the attack. He had a
solid alibi and had never been arrested. He had no motive
to kill a cop other than the altercation at the restaurant,
which had no connection in Drury's opinion.

"I'll just confirm there's no one else Noah crossed
paths with who may have been involved with the victim." Brycen glanced at Drury and she wondered if he
thought she'd be insulted if he told her what kind of path
that could mean. Some kind of love triangle? Did he think
it possible Noah had an affair with the victim before her
attack and that maybe the hunter who'd given her the
roughest time was the third party?

"Noah didn't have an affair and he was a clean cop,"
she said. "That's going to be a dead end."

"You think Noah may have been involved in something?" Carter asked, new interest alert in his eyes. Light
from overhead in the evidence room cast deepened shadows under his brow.

"I'm not assuming anything." He moved to the bigger box. "Just checking every angle." He said the last
to her before turning back to Carter. "I'll need contact
information on the prostitute Noah arrested prior to the
shooting, as well."

"Of course."

Drury glowered at Brycen. Surely he didn't think Noah would cavort with a prostitute? Checking every angle…

Brycen removed the bagged bullet. "And the domestic violence call. I'd like to talk to the wife again."

"Do you think Noah had an affair with her, too?" Drury asked with a bite in her voice.

"No. But he may have crossed paths with someone associated with her. There are many ways he could have encountered someone with something to hide. These people might lead me to them."

Carter observed him thoughtfully, clearly not having thought of that in his investigation.

And Drury chided herself for being so narrow-minded. She refused to believe Noah had an affair, but something or someone connected to one of his calls could have led to his death.

"I'll have a clerk write down the addresses and contact information we have," Carter said.

Drury watched Brycen check over the evidence, putting the bullet back and taking out blood and fiber samples and copies of photos and lab reports.

"Have there been any other calls from the woman who reported domestic violence?" he asked as he worked.

Carter shook his head. "None. She only called that one time. If she'd called again, I'd have put it in the report."

A year had passed since the domestic violence call— the one and only that the woman had made. Did that mean the violence had stopped? Drury doubted that. She looked forward to talking to the woman. Maybe they could help her get away. Except the woman had to *want* to leave her husband on top of mustering the courage.

Brycen looked at the photos taken of the area where the fatal shot had been fired. The alley could have hidden the shooter. There was a pharmacy and an antique shop with apartments above across the street.

Next, he took out photos from security cameras at the pharmacy. Nothing or no one suspicious had been captured, but the shooter could have known the locations of the cameras and avoided them.

"Did you check out these apartments?" Brycen asked.

"Yes. I talked to the managers at both places. No new tenants were reported, and no break-ins."

The gunman could have known someone in one of the apartments, but the shots had come from the alley.

"What about cameras at the other end of the alley?" she asked.

"There were none," Brycen said, and then to Carter, "That's what I read in the report anyway."

"That's correct. No cameras. The commercial spaces on that street are vacant. One was recently leased, but the tenant hadn't opened its doors yet."

"What about across from those spaces?" Brycen took out his phone and brought up a street map.

"Houses," Carter said as Drury viewed the satellite map version on the phone screen with Brycen. "We questioned all the residents in the area. In a six-block radius."

Brycen put the evidence back in the box and moved back. "Thank you again. I appreciate your willingness to help."

"Noah was more than my partner. He was my friend."

Brycen didn't react to that declaration. He remained neutral. He must go into that mode when he delved into investigations, not making assumptions, just gathering information and keeping his initial assessment to himself.

"If anything comes to mind that you may not have explored in the case, let me know," he said. "No matter how insignificant you think the detail is, it may be important enough to lead to more."

"I've been through that case so many times I doubt I'd be capable of seeing anything new." Carter seemed to need to explain or cover his tracks if he ended up having missed something.

Which in turn explained why he welcomed Brycen's involvement. Carter had worked tirelessly to find Noah's killer. As with anything too close to a person, details sometimes were lost. He'd shown Drury the same support when she told him she'd gone to Dark Alley Investigations.

"Let's hope you have better luck than me," Carter said.

"I'll see what I can find."

Carter gave another of his nods. Habitual? Or was he nervous?

"We'll need a helicopter to visit the domestic violence victim," Drury said. "It's a remote location."

Carter turned perplexed eyes to her. "You're going with him? You're investigating with him?"

She glanced at Brycen.

"There's nothing in the rules that say you can't," Brycen said. "Dark Alley only requires putting together a solid case come time for an arrest."

"Isn't that dangerous?" Carter asked.

"Don't worry about me." Drury smiled. "Not only am I an adventurer, I'll be with one of the best." She patted Brycen's right biceps—which felt deliciously hard. "Besides, I want to be part of the investigation now, every step of the way."

"You could get hurt, Drury," Carter said.

She angled her head. "You should know me by now. I don't sit on the sidelines."

"She wanted to be a fighter pilot," Brycen pointed out.

Carter contemplated her while she noticed Brycen looking at her in a not very professional way. Her adventurous spirit attracted him. He might say no marriage, no kids, but did he really want that?

"Nothing much does scare you, does it, Drury? All right," Carter conceded. "Let's go get a helicopter arranged." He turned and headed for the door.

Brycen followed him out of the room, Drury behind, glad Carter hadn't changed his position in the year he'd been investigating Noah's death. He might have given up hope in himself to find the killer, but he hadn't given up hope entirely.

Cora Parker lived in an apartment building in downtown Anchorage and walked to her job at the restaurant, a log structure with Old West charm next to a new shopping center. The report said the hunters had stayed at the hotel across the street from the shopping center and had flights home to Washington State the next day. Even more proof that none of them could have attacked Cora. They would have had to travel back to commit the crime. But Brycen had learned when a criminal wanted to kill badly enough, he'd find a way, and northern Washington wasn't that far from Anchorage.

He and Drury stood at her apartment door. Cora wasn't home.

A door across the hall opened and an old woman with curly white hair and thick glasses appeared. "She's at work. Who are you?"

With no security in the building, Cora made easy prey

for a rapist. With the police onto him, the man must have decided not to risk going after her again.

"We'll find her at work," Drury said. "Let's go."

He walked down the hall with her. "We can wait until she gets off."

"Can I tell her who stopped by?" the old woman called after them. "We keep an eye on her after she was attacked last year."

"Thanks, we'll find her at work." Drury pushed Brycen toward the elevator.

"Let's just wait for her out front." He'd rather not spend too much time in public. The fewer people who recognized him during his stay, the better. That was why he preferred staying at his cabin.

"I'm hungry anyway. Let's grab a bite to eat. I heard the Lodge has pretty good food for a pub."

"I'll find a drive-through, then."

She grunted indignantly. "I'm not eating fast food. Come on. Let's just go to the Lodge." She stepped out of the elevator and Brycen reluctantly trailed behind.

Noticing his lack of enthusiasm, she asked, "Do you have something against restaurants?"

"People will recognize me."

"Ah," she said as she drew her own conclusion. His popularity with the show would get him noticed.

He let her think that was the reason, even while an inner urging told him it might be good to be seen. It might lead to putting his past behind him. He would just rather avoid any unwanted encounters.

Brycen opened the heavy wood door, which had no windows. Inside, the smell of cedar hit him. Pool tables and a bar took up a tidy and clean right side and the dining area with pine tables the opposite. A sign said Please Wait to Be Seated. He waited in the front entry for someone to notice them. Drury stopped with him.

A few minutes later, a woman in her sixties approached with a well-used black apron around her, tickets stuffed in her ticket holders.

"Right this way." She took two menus with them.

"Would you tell Cora we're here to see her?" Drury asked the woman.

"Of course. It'll just be a minute." She indicated a table for them.

Brycen sat across from Drury, who eagerly read the menu. He caught sight of another table where two women were talking and looking right at him.

They smiled.

"Uh-oh," he said. "I've been caught."

The women stood as Drury lowered her menu and turned, watching with him as the admirers approached.

"You're Brycen Cage, aren't you?" the blonde said.

Her plainer, brown-haired friend stuck out a napkin. "Can I have your autograph? My name is Amy."

He took the napkin and looked for a pen. Drury produced one from her purse, a silent participant so far. He couldn't tell what she thought of this.

As he wrote something flattering on the napkin, the blonde said, "We just love your show," and chattered on about one of the episodes involving a stripper and a health club manager. When she finished she said, "Oh, and we saw you on the news. How you were planning on coming here to Alaska to solve a case, and how you joined that agency. You must be so brave."

"And smart," her friend said.

He saw Drury look from the women to him, still unreadable.

"And available." The blonde laughed, her friend joining in. Then the blonde looked at Drury. "Oh…sorry."

Drury held up her hands. "It's all right. We aren't together like that."

The blonde, missing that Drury might very well be involved in the case that had brought him here, opened her eyes wider, thrilled. "Well, then, you *are* available."

Some women didn't know when they made a spectacle of themselves. Brycen handed the napkin to the plainer girl. "Not for socializing, I'm afraid. I'm here on business."

The blonde's mouth parted and she looked at Drury. "Ooooh."

"Will the case you're investigating be on one of your shows?" the other woman asked.

Brycen looked over at Drury. "We'll have to see."

Drury frowned with raised eyes that said, *No, we won't.*

He grinned, unable to stop the reaction.

"Who was murdered? Someone you know?" the blonde asked Drury.

"I can't discuss the details." He saw Cora coming toward them, a moderately tall, thin woman with brown hair up in a bun. "If you'll excuse us." Then with a practiced smile, "Back to work."

"Oh…all right." The two retreated, glancing back several times as Cora came to their table, excited to catch a glimpse into the real Brycen Cage at work.

"You must smile like that a lot. I've seen you smile when you mean it. That smile was for the stage."

He shot a glance at Drury before Cora stopped at

their table. In her late twenties, she looked a little older than her years with the first signs of wrinkles appearing.

"You came to see me?" Cora asked.

Brycen explained who they were. "We understand you've already been questioned about the attack that occurred roughly a year ago?"

"Yes, Trooper Nichols came by."

"Well, I read in the report that you and a friend of yours had a falling-out. You had relations with her brother and broke his heart. Something along those lines?"

"Yes. Trooper Nichols asked if I had any enemies. Since the man who came into the bar that night I was attacked proved not to be guilty, he looked at others."

"Like maybe your friend's brother came after you?"

"Yes, but he had an alibi."

She revealed nothing different than what he'd read in the report.

"Trooper Nichols asked me all these questions," Cora said, rubbing her arms and looking off into the distance.

"How well did you know Noah Decoteau?" Brycen asked.

Cora's head turned with a startled jerk. "The trooper? Not well. He just talked to me the night of my attack."

"You didn't meet him before that?"

"No. Why?"

"What about any of your friends? Family? Did anyone close to him know you?"

"No." Her alertness softened as she must see why he'd asked. "No one I know would have wanted him dead. That's a question Carter didn't ask."

"When did he last come to see you?" Drury asked.

"Carter? Why, just last week. He comes by every once in a while. Grabs a bite to eat and talks to me. He asked

if my friend had forgiven me yet. Of course, she hasn't."
She breathed a sad laugh. "You'd think I robbed her or
something. I couldn't help it if I didn't feel the same way
as her brother."

"Does she have a boyfriend? Did she at the time of
your attack?"

"Yes. Trooper Nichols asked about that when he was
here. He said he'd look into the possibility that maybe her
boyfriend did it, you know, one of those 'I love you, so
I'll go after this girl for you because you asked me to.' I
think that's a reach. My attack must have been random.
Maybe some man I didn't notice saw me working and
followed me. Who knows?"

She seemed ready to let her ordeal go. Troubled that
her attacker still ran free, but ready to move on with her
life. It had been a year. In all that time she hadn't been attacked again. If someone local had gone after her, maybe
they'd noticed Carter still worked the case and backed
off. If the man wasn't local, he'd have been long gone
since the time of the attack.

"Did Carter talk to you about anything else? Any other
leads? Issues? Suspects?" Brycen asked.

"No. He didn't have time. We were interrupted when
a man came to the table and needed to talk to him. It
seemed urgent. Duty called." She breathed another laugh,
this one less sad. "He had to leave."

"Was your friend's brother involved in any suspicious
activities?"

"No. Her brother was pretty straight. That's one of the
things that bored me about him. He didn't even drink.
And I mean, not even one. I don't like to go out and get
hammered, but I enjoy an occasional glass of wine. My
friend wasn't a drinker, either. Her whole family was that

way. Maybe that's why it's so hard for her to forgive me. She lives so simply. When I ended things so abruptly, and I admit, with not much finesse—I just told him not to call me anymore—I think that shocked her as much as it hurt him." She sighed. "Anyway, nothing I can do about it now." She looked from him to Drury and back again. "Is there anything else I can help you with?"

"I don't think so. Thanks, Cora." Brycen hadn't expected this to lead to anything.

"I hope you catch him." She left their table and went back to work. As she did so, he thought he would have to do just that. A criminal had gotten away with attempted rape. He couldn't allow that. Ever since leaving Alaska, he'd received immense satisfaction catching criminals. He had control over solving the cases. He'd had no control over what had driven him to leave.

As he drifted off into that depressing thought, he spotted a woman watching him. And she wasn't a fan.

"Let's go." He stood up.

"Hey, no," Drury protested. "I'm hungry. What's the matter?" She twisted around.

Seeing Avery Jefferson get up and walk toward him, Brycen headed for the door.

What the hell? Drury got up from the table, her stomach growling, and went after Brycen. She stopped when she saw a woman in a figure-hugging, knee-length blue dress with blond hair up in a prim bun intercept him in the entry. She was tall and slender, with frail shoulders and arms, her oval face and dark eyes bearing the stamp of indignation.

"What are you doing back here?" the woman asked.

Drury stopped before the entry, uncomfortable with spying, but also needing to know more about Brycen's past.

"I'm not breaking any laws by being here, Avery." Brycen pushed the lapels of his jacket aside as he put his hands on his hips, tall and imposing, but Drury didn't think the woman recognized the pained tightness of his jaw or the flaring wariness in his eyes. "Don't worry, I'm not back permanently."

The woman took in his posture, misreading it, Drury was sure. Disdain radiated from her. "If Dad finds out you're here, he'll have a coronary."

"Don't tell him, then." He turned and resumed his trek toward the door. "I should have known nothing would have changed by now."

The woman trotted in her heels. "I can't believe you had the gall to show your face here again."

"Good to see you, too." Brycen opened the door.

The woman planted her hand on his chest, stopping him from leaving. "Why are you here?"

Drury stepped forward. Brycen didn't see her, letting the door close again.

"You have no idea what our family has been through," the woman ranted. "You ruined our lives! Why don't you just leave and never come back? We thought you'd gone for good, but then a few years ago Harry at the real estate office told Dad you still had that cabin. Ever since then he's been plagued with the anxiety that you'd return. He never wants to see you again, Brycen. None of us do. I'm glad I'm the one who ran into you first." She had a haughty air about her, both in the tone of her high, smooth voice, and the way she used her jewel-adorned hands as she talked.

What had Brycen done to upset her and her father so much? And to harbor the feeling for so long…

With a somber, taxed face, Brycen didn't respond at first. Then he said, "I don't know how many different ways I can apologize, Avery. My apology is all I can give you. It's all I've ever had. I never meant anyone any harm."

Someone was harmed? Who? Drury stepped forward again, not wanting to eavesdrop without them knowing she was there.

"You're not sorry." Avery sneered. "You left us in ruins and went off to become a celebrity. It's bad enough we have you in our past, but to have to see you on television?" She made a sound of disgust. "It took Dad a month to recover from that news."

"You and your father are still blaming everyone else for your unhappiness, I see."

"You're the heartless one, Brycen Cage."

Brycen noticed Drury and pushed the door open, forcing Avery to drop her hand and step back.

Drury followed him, giving the woman an admonishing but incredulous look as she passed. Regardless of what Brycen had done all those years ago, her personal attack had seemed unjustified, more like a retaliation, and exactly what Brycen had said. Blame.

"I'd watch out for him if I were you," Avery said to her back.

Drury ignored her and hurried after Brycen. When she caught up to him, she had to walk fast and jog intermittently to keep up.

"I don't suppose you want to tell me what that was all about?" she asked.

"No."

"Who is Avery?"

"Nobody." His hard, long strides put an exclamation point on the end of that.

"I believe that you meant no harm. Whatever it is you did."

"Just drop it, Drury. This qualifies as something personal. I don't want to talk about it."

Off-limits. He'd conveniently laid down the law. They didn't talk about anything personal. He *wouldn't* talk. She'd have to respect that for now. What had he done to turn a family against him? It must be something serious, despite Avery's air of superiority.

Chapter 4

Carter had a helicopter waiting for them the next day. Brycen said very little to Drury on the way to Mica Island. He wished she hadn't witnessed his encounter with Avery. He'd hoped things had changed in the decade or so he'd been gone. Absolutely nothing had changed. The same stench and rot he'd left remained. The disappointment after learning that stayed with him, dragging him down and thrusting him back in time, back into memories he wished he could forget forever.

"That must be it." Drury's voice came through the headphones. She pointed through the side window in the back.

Evette and Melvin Cummings lived near Tate, Alaska, a tiny village southeast of Anchorage. No airstrips had been built in the mountainous terrain. The only way in was by boat, helicopter or air with water landing. The helicopter pilot began to descend. A ramshackle cabin came into view, completely isolated and about twenty miles from the village, which had a population of less than two hundred and had recently lost their sheriff, who'd moved to the Lower 48 last year.

The landing chopper got the attention of the inhabitants, who appeared on their front porch. As the helicopter touched down, Brycen studied Evette. Wearing a long dress and a shawl, she stood away from her husband, on one side of the porch, with a downturned mouth. Melvin, on the other hand, stood tall and imposing in front of the door with an assault rifle in his hands, also with a downturned mouth, but in a menacing way, whereas his wife seemed to live in constant fear and unhappiness.

Brycen took out his pistol and readied it to fire.

Drury looked over at him as he did so.

"Just in case." He tucked the gun back into its holster under his jacket.

Opening the door, he jumped down and turned to help Drury. She hesitated but then let him put his hands on her waist and lift her down. As she stood before him, close enough to feel her breasts against him, he stepped back. He couldn't even touch her without having a sexual reaction. It was like touching a live wire.

Walking toward the cabin, he kept her behind him in case this hillbilly decided to start shooting. He held up his hand in greeting. People who lived like this had their own method of defense.

The closer he came, the more he saw Evette. He climbed up the porch steps. Dark circles under her eyes. Chapped hands and lips. Wrenching emptiness in her eyes. And most infuriating of all, the faint signs of a healing bruise along the corner of her lower lip.

"Who the hell are you?" Melvin asked, a man hiding behind his ego.

Brycen had to work hard to stop himself from grabbing the man and giving him a memorable taste of what he inflicted on his wife.

"Brycen Cage and Drury Decoteau," he said, indicating Drury standing to his right at the top of the porch steps. "We're here to ask you some questions about Noah Decoteau's death."

"I've already answered questions. Police already came here. Been here two, three times in the last year."

"I'm not from the police," Brycen said. "I'm with a private investigation agency."

"Then I don't have to talk to you. So why don't you get back on that helicopter and be on your way?"

Brycen turned to Evette. "Mrs. Cummings, I'd like a word with you alone if I could."

"She ain't talking to you." Melvin sent a threatening look to her. "Get inside where you belong."

She started to move toward the door behind Melvin.

Brycen used his distraction to his advantage. He knocked Melvin's arm and had the rifle in his possession. Using the butt of the rifle, he gave the arrogant, worthless man a good knock on his jaw. Brycen heard Drury gasp as Melvin stumbled back and fell against the door, making Evette flinch and then gape at Brycen.

"Maybe I didn't make myself clear," Brycen said.

Melvin stared at him, still against the door, now having no illusions about the kind of man who stood before him.

"We can do this in a civil fashion." Brycen released the magazine from the rifle and tossed it to the ground behind him. "Or we can do more of this. Either way, I'm going to talk to your wife."

After wiping some blood off his jaw, Melvin straightened from the door.

"You know." Brycen pressed the bolt catch and then pulled back the charging handle, sending the round flying from the chamber. "I'm always amazed how a man as big as yourself can be so puny." He inspected the chamber to ensure that it held no more ammunition, and then admired the weapon. Rather nice for a villager. "Do you enjoy hurting your wife?"

"What?" The man shifted from one foot to the other in an attempt to look macho. "I don't hurt her. Do I, honey?"

Evette turned frightened eyes to him and shook her head.

Brycen used the butt of the rifle to hit the side of Melvin's temple, sending him back against the door again, only this time he slumped to the wood planks of the porch.

"What the…" He put a hand to his temple, at first taken aback and then angry. He climbed to his feet, staring Brycen down, or attempting to.

"I don't like liars." Brycen leaned the rifle against the railing next to the stairs. "You and I both know Evette called for help a year ago, and you and I both know why. So, since you don't want her to talk, why don't you start by telling me why she didn't press charges?"

"We had a fight." Melvin took a brave step forward. "That's what married couples do. Fight."

"They don't have one-sided fistfights. Try again. I asked you why she didn't press charges."

"She forgave me, that's why."

In the time it took the troopers to reach her? "So, you admit to hitting her."

"I admit to nothing. You ain't no cop." He made the mistake of lunging for Brycen with a fist.

Drury jumped out of the way, grabbing hold of the railing on that side of the porch as Brycen easily blocked the man. Turning, he grabbed him and rolled him over his back. Melvin fell down the porch steps.

Going down after him, Brycen leaned over. "I'm much worse than a cop, Melvin. You're going to wish you wouldn't have threatened Evette not to press charges."

"I didn't threaten her." He crawled away from Brycen and stood.

"I don't think you heard me." Brycen moved toward him.

"Brycen," Drury warned.

"Listen to your lady, mister. I got no quarrel with you. Just leave and don't come back."

While Melvin had begun to show signs of fear, Brycen worried if he left as requested, what would happen to Evette? Would Melvin take out his injured pride on her?

Melvin made the decision over whether or not to give him a warning easy. He lunged again, all bravado and ego, with fists balled.

Brycen swatted his hands away and punched Melvin's nose. His head jerked back and he stumbled.

Crowding the man, Brycen forced him to step backward with his sheer size. Melvin was a thick man but not as big as Brycen. He shoved him to change directions, around the side of the porch, away from the women.

"You have no right coming here."

With one more shove, the man came against the side of the house.

Taking a fistful of the man's uncombed hair, Brycen leaned closer, looking dead into the man's cold eyes. "If I find out you hurt her, I'll come back here and put you in the hospital. Do you understand?"

Melvin reacted in offense to the threat of serious harm. "Get off my land. You ain't welcome here."

"No," Brycen said. "I don't think you do." He pulled his head toward him and then slammed it back against the wood siding, hard enough to cause a bump.

The man grimaced.

"Do you understand now?"

"Just leave, please," Evette pleaded, beginning to cry.

Drury went to her, putting her hand on her shoulder.

Brycen let go of Melvin's head and then moved into a kick, hitting the man's sternum. As Melvin groaned and fell to his knees, Brycen grabbed him and put him back against the house, giving him two more well-placed punches in the sternum.

"Now I think you understand." Brycen let him go.

He slumped to the ground, holding his middle and lifting his bleeding face. "I didn't threaten her. She decided on her own not to press charges. Tell the man, Evette!" He rolled to his rear.

"H-he didn't threaten me," Evette said. "I forgave him. Please, mister. Leave us be. It's best that way."

"I'm afraid I can't do that, ma'am. An Alaskan State Trooper was murdered shortly after coming to your house in answer to your call for help. Now I'm visiting everyone he came into contact with before his death. I need to eliminate your husband's involvement."

"I didn't have anything to do with his murder." Still holding his middle, Melvin used the side of the house to stand. "My wife didn't press charges. Why would I kill the cop who came here?"

"That's what I need you to tell me."

"Well, I can't tell you. I don't know how or why that officer was killed."

At least he talked freer now. He understood what kind of man he'd come up against.

"Evette?" Brycen said. "What about you?"

Her gaze flew to Melvin. "No, I don't know anything about that cop. I'm sorry he's dead, but I had nothing to do with it."

"I didn't think you did, ma'am." He took in her stiff, fear-stricken stance up on the porch next to Drury and said gently, "You can come with us right now, you know. We'll fly you away from him. I have resources that can help you relocate. Get reestablished. You'll never have to see him again."

For a moment, he thought she'd contemplate doing just that. But then defeat brought her back on down. "I have children."

"Bring them with you."

"They're at school." She shook her head. "No, thank you, sir. I'll stay here with my husband."

With that, Melvin relaxed, turning to Brycen with smug triumph. "You see? She loves me. She wouldn't stay otherwise."

Drury grunted in disbelief, drawing Melvin's unappreciative look.

"Why don't you step down and come talk to me, Mrs. Cummings?" Brycen moved back from the porch, away from Melvin.

She looked at Melvin, who nodded once. Had she assured him that she'd not betray him, so he felt confident in allowing her to speak alone with Brycen?

Melvin climbed the porch steps as though each breath and step pained him. Drury reached to help him but he waved her away.

Out of hearing distance from Melvin, Brycen kept his tone low. "Mrs. Cummings, is there anything you can tell me about that day Trooper Noah Decoteau came here?"

She shook her head. "No. I'm sorry I called. I over-reacted."

He looked down at her healing bruise. "Did you?"

"Please, Mr. Cage. You have to leave. My husband does have a temper, but he's a good man. He loves me and the kids."

"A good man doesn't beat his wife, Mrs. Cummings. He has no right to hurt you. And he better not hurt your kids."

Again, she shook her head, more adamantly now. "No. He doesn't hit them." Tears sprang to her eyes.

"He only hits you, then?"

She said nothing.

He hoped she told the truth. He checked on Melvin, who stood on the porch talking to Drury. She kept a good distance from the man.

"I think you should come with us." He had a bad feeling about her reasons for staying, but most of all about Melvin.

She put her hand on his arm. "You're a good man, Mr. Cage. You don't hit those you love. But I'm fine. And I will be fine. My entire family lives in the village. I can't just up and leave."

"Yes, you can. I can help you."

"No, I can't." She shook her head. "I'll be fine." She would not change her mind, not today.

Brycen took out his card and handed it to her. "If you need me, call. I can take care of Melvin so he will never hurt you again."

She took the card and tucked it under her shawl, going back toward the porch. Brycen followed, stopping at the foot of the porch. Evette went inside without looking back.

Drury joined Brycen down on the ground. "Let's get out of here."

"Don't make me have to come back here," he said to Melvin, and then he let Drury take him toward the helicopter.

Before getting in, he checked the porch. Melvin still stood there, holding his stomach.

In the helicopter, they put their headphones on and the pilot lifted off.

"Is that how you usually solve cases?" Drury asked.

"I hope it's enough to make him leave her alone."

"It won't be."

How could she say that?

"Men like that are like angry drivers. Once they're enclosed in their own environment, they do what they want. He might take out his humiliation on her. He might not. The best we can do is try to get her to leave. In the end, it's her decision. If she chooses to stay in that violent place, there's nothing anyone can do."

"I just couldn't stand knowing he hurt her."

"Yeah. I saw the bruise, too. I also think she was too scared to press charges."

"She lied when I asked her if she knew anything. I could tell."

Drury sat straighter. "She knows something? Is her husband involved?"

Maybe, that was what his gut told him. But how? Melvin had a point about motive. Why would he kill the cop who answered his wife's call when she didn't press charges? And especially, why would he wait to gun him down? Anonymity? If he shot him on his property chances were he'd have been caught.

"Noah must have seen something." Melvin slapping his wife around? It didn't seem like enough.

"You want to help everyone," Drury said, pulling him out of his analysis. "Evette, and also Cora. You're going to catch her attacker, too, aren't you?"

Yes. He was. He couldn't stand men who felt they needed to dominate women with violence. Those had always been the most difficult cases for him.

"Why do you have such a passion for that?"

Again, Drury jarred him. The headphones sank into her thick hair, and her blue eyes pinned him.

"It's my job."

"No. It's almost…personal to you. It's like you have to… I don't know…make everything right. Like you can't leave anything alone until you do."

That began to dig into too much personal baggage. Oh yeah, he had a reason to crusade the way he did, a reason that it gave him immense satisfaction.

"It's my job," he repeated.

A half smile inched up her soft face, a knowing one. She sat back and faced forward. "I wonder if Melvin is the one who threw the rock."

And left a dead cat on her porch? "He's a long way from Anchorage." Had he recognized Brycen and Drury today? If so, he'd covered it well.

"He's got a nice boat," Drury said. "He's a commercial fisherman. Told me business was slow right now, but that's how he makes a living."

He had a nice rifle, too, but his home needed lots of repairs. Maybe he didn't care about its condition. He cared about his fishing and expensive weapons and—most of all—controlling his wife with his fists.

Yeah, Brycen wanted to put a stop to that, all right. He just needed to find a way. And a reason.

At the end of a long, winding, one-lane road, a modest two-story red cedar cabin with a wraparound porch sat nestled in a clearing. Thick forest surrounded the structure, white-framed windows dark under an overcast sky. Snowflakes had begun to fall. Drury stepped up to the front door with a shiver, Junior beside her, awkwardly carrying his small luggage. He'd put up a fuss over going and sulked all the way here. Drury wondered if he'd hoped to spend more time with Brycen and disappointment had thrown him back into withdrawal. That had been his standard protective measure since Noah's death. Withdraw into a shell, a protective shell where he didn't have to face what he had to know, at least on some level. No child should ever have to lose a parent. A boy lost his father. And Junior still struggled with accepting his father would never come home.

She'd welcome any method of bringing him out of this phase. If Brycen could do that, how much was she willing to let him get to know her son? Would the time they spent with Brycen help her son? Junior's curiosity made her think *yes*. And as for Brycen's no-marriage, no-kids policy, he was about to test his resolve.

Inside, Drury found the interior warm and welcoming, with a real cabin feel. Big fireplace with big rocks stacked to the roof. Exposed beams crossing the ceiling. Leather furniture. A bit masculine, but a tinge of hominess in the rugs and throw pillows. It smelled dusty and she ran a finger through a layer of neglect on the entry cabinet, lifting her finger to show Brycen, teasing.

He smiled back at her. "I haven't been here in years and I only pay to have it cleaned and maintained twice a year."

"Excuses, excuses." She removed her jacket and hung it on one of the hooks by the door, rubbing her arms against the chill and wishing Brycen would use his arms to warm her.

"Hey, you're the one who makes kid meals for dinner." Brycen went to the thermostat, and the furnace kicked on.

Junior dumped his bag and went into the living room in search of a remote. Brycen followed him, picking up the remote from the bookshelf and turning on the television.

"Luckily I restarted the satellite service before leaving Chicago," he said.

"Bet you didn't think to get family channels, though."

"No, but there's a good variety."

When her son took the remote from him, he withdrew his hand quickly, as though touching the boy burned him. Junior eyed him a little, still in his decision phase over whether Brycen passed certain criteria. Then he pivoted and went to the TV.

Brycen stood there a few seconds longer than necessary, watching Junior settle in and begin surfing. She wondered if fascination from lack of exposure riveted him or something else, something much darker.

Finally he turned, his brow shadowing troubled eyes. "I'll show you to your rooms." He picked up the luggage left by the door and she picked up Junior's bag.

More interested in him and his history, she followed him up wood-railed stairs that were open to the great room below. Past a small landing, a hall led to three bedrooms and a main bathroom. The heat had yet to drive the chill away.

She put Junior's bag in the first and smallest room and saw that Brycen had placed her bag in the room across from his. When he emerged back into the hall, she couldn't stop from staring. Tall and well built, he made an imposing and manly figure in the shadows.

Turning to cut off the building attraction, she went to the stairs. The panel of windows in front had no coverings. Darkness had settled.

Downstairs, she busied herself finding a cloth and began dusting. She'd rather be flying her plane or barbecuing in winter, but she needed something to do.

Brycen came in with a cooler of food and beverages. He'd already brought in the bags of groceries they'd bought before leaving Anchorage.

"You don't have to do that." He put the cooler down in the kitchen.

"Not quite camping, but it will do." She didn't want to explain her need to keep busy. He didn't need to know she could stare at him all night and savor the butterflies tickling her insides.

"You like camping?"

She wiped another shelf. No pictures of family here. "Loved it as a kid. My parents took us lots of places. Yellowstone. Yosemite. Glacier National Park. We went to Colorado, too."

"Where in Colorado?"

"Leadville." She laughed a little. "My dad thought the name sounded cool. Nobody told us how cold it gets there, though."

She turned from the shelf and walked to the kitchen, where Brycen put away dry goods into an upper cabinet. His biceps bunched and extended beneath the smooth, light gray Henley as he moved.

"No RV?"

"Heavens no. My parents liked the adventure of tent camping. Until that trip." She reached into a bag and started helping him put away food. But that brought her next to him and their arms brushed during one transfer.

She stuck to the memory of the Leadville trip. "Did you know that the temperature is at or below freezing 62 percent of the time? The warmest it gets is seventy-one degrees."

"Life at ten thousand feet." He put the last can away and looked at her, his gaze going all over her face before dropping to her chest. She wore a long-sleeved shirt like him, nothing revealing at all, but he made her feel exposed.

They finished emptying the bags and Drury leaned against the counter, hanging on to the memory to interrupt the heat building between them.

"We set up camp at Twin Lakes, but our car broke down on a day trip to Turquoise Lake. It was late in the day and getting cold. My dad said we better hike to a lodge we passed on the way up. The weather rolled in. Nobody else was out. Most people camped in RVs. The lodge was about four miles down the road. We froze. But my parents kept the mood light. My sister and I didn't know the danger we were in. By the time we made it to the lodge, it was snowing and I couldn't feel my fingers and toes. I think I was ten minutes from getting frost-bite."

"You camped in winter?"

"September. Everything was an adventure to my parents. They turned everything into fun, a celebration. That night at the lodge, my dad played the guitar in the lodge restaurant. People had nowhere to go. He entertained them and my mom danced all night. My sister and I had macaroni and cheese and stale fries and drank chocolate milk until we got stomachaches. My dad got the car fixed and we went back to camp. Froze for two more nights and then went home." She smiled and caught her son looking over at her with that same kind of wary suspicion he'd had when he first met Brycen.

"Sounds about like my childhood." Brycen took out a pan and started frying some hamburger. "My parents took us skiing a lot. Once we went on a yurt tour and got stuck in a blizzard. My dad rescued a couple who got lost. They were newly married."

He didn't go into any great detail and began chopping onions and green peppers.

"That's a nice memory," she said. "Is that when your parents still loved each other?"

Pausing in his chopping, he turned to see her. "My parents never loved each other. They both liked to ski, but I think they liked the diversion more. As a family, we were always doing something. That way they wouldn't have to spend time alone at home. Whenever they did that, they fought."

"Were you close to them?"

He put the onions and peppers in with the browned meat. "I was close to my dad. Still am. My mother wasn't a typical mother. She didn't show very much affection. She didn't hug or talk in great length about things. Unhappiness did that to her. Made her a withdrawn, go-through-the-motions kind of woman."

That seemed so sad, not only for his mother, but for him, too. He'd learned love from his father, who kept him busy all the time.

"She took a lot of trips to see her sister in California," he went on. "Maybe her sister saw her when she was happy. Those were the only times I spent at home on weekends. And the best times I had with my dad. We played chess and watched sports. Guy things."

"He was a good dad."

He nodded and stirred his meat and vegetables. "Yeah." His stirring slowed. "I just wish they both could have been happy when we were all together." He drifted off as he stirred. Then he snapped back to the present and found a package of Sloppy Joe mix. Pouring that into the mixture and adding water, he resumed stirring. "I found out later that my mom wasn't going to see her sister on all those trips. She went to see a man she had a crush on during high school but she didn't run in the popular crowd like he did. She was one of those late bloomers. Not very attractive in school but a real beauty as an adult."

Drury couldn't tell if that had bothered him. Giving him time, hoping he'd keep talking, she took out some plates and put buns on them.

"My dad wasn't even upset," he said.

She stopped and turned to him.

"They didn't even hire attorneys. They just…split up. I couldn't remember the last time I saw my mother smile.

But she did the day she said goodbye to my dad. She even thanked him."

Wow. That explained his misguided view on marriage.

"Not everyone is unhappily married," she said.

"I believe most people are." He turned the burner on low and faced her.

"Okay, fairy-tale marriages are probably rare," she conceded, "but most marriages *are* happy. Maybe everyone doesn't find mind-sweeping, soul-wrenching love, but most people find companionship that is satisfying and good. Most people are happy, Brycen. You shouldn't base your future on what you saw your parents go through."

"I don't, trust me. I won't be one of those people who marries someone they don't really like, someone they tolerate."

"Is your mother happy now?" Drury asked.

"Yes. She is. So is my dad. He remarried a few years ago. He took longer than my mother."

"Well, there you go. That's all that matters. Your mom and dad are happy."

Without responding, his crooked mouth and sardonic look told her enough. She made light of his parents' nearly three-decade marriage, which he considered a gross waste of time. The clock couldn't be turned back. All anyone could do in that situation was look forward. He should take lessons in that. From her vantage point, he spent too much time looking back.

Something banged against the side of the cabin, on the outside wall of the kitchen area. Drury jumped and Brycen pulled out his gun. What had made the noise? It was too loud to be the structure settling with nightfall. When Brycen moved toward the back door, she trailed him at a cautious distance. Peering outside, he didn't seem to see anything.

As he opened the door, Drury checked her son. He watched Brycen, but looked at her. She held up her hand to indicate for him to stay put. Then she went to the door and cautiously looked out. All appeared calm.

Brycen inched his way along the back, gun raised, head turned toward the direction of the sound. Cool air breezed in through the open double French doors. She stepped out onto the patio, waiting for something or someone to leap out of the shadows and attack. Her heart slammed. Brycen moved like a stealthy soldier, focused on the corner of the house.

Something moved then. Sliding down from the side of the cabin, a tree crashed the rest of the way to the ground. A scream lodged in her throat—until it registered what had caused the noise. A dead tree had fallen from the edge of the forest.

Brycen lowered his pistol and turned as he tucked it back into the waist holster.

He wore a wry lift to his mouth. Both on high alert, they held an outward appearance of safety, but lurking deep down, the expectance of the unexpected.

She smiled with a breathy laugh.

His wry grin changed to matching humor and he moved toward her.

"The bogeyman isn't here," he said.

Rubbing her arms against the chill, she didn't go back inside. His strong, confident strides and solid thighs held her riveted, and then his eyes when he stopped before her.

"Th-that's reassuring," she said, her voice low and revealing her reaction. "Unless you consider a tree a bogeyman."

He grinned and stepped closer. "I might have as a kid."

"Were you afraid of things like that when you were a kid?" He didn't strike her as someone who feared anything, as a kid or an adult.

"Scary movies, but they had to be real movies, not your typical horror film. Thrillers."

"A born detective." She shivered but didn't want to go back inside. Being alone with him did that to her. Made her irrational.

"You're not the first person who's said that to me." He put his hand on her arm and started to say, "Let's…" but something stopped him from finishing. Would he have said, *Let's go back inside?*

The cold faded to the background as she met his eyes and the intensity in them. She moved a step closer, until she could feel his warmth. His head came closer.

And then something hit his biceps.

She saw a remote control tumble to the stone patio and looked inside. Junior stood in the kitchen, chest heaving, lips pressed tight.

Chapter 5

Breaking apart from Brycen, Drury stared in shock at her son. Junior had just thrown something at them. No. At Brycen. He'd seemed so awed by him—a man he likely saw as a hero, a superhero, one of his characters in a game. What had caused him to change so abruptly to this? Losing his father left him struggling with how to cope, but...throwing something after seeing Brycen almost kiss her? His little body stood with feet planted apart and fists clamped at his sides, stormy eyes fiery and pursed lips nearly white.

"Noah Jr....you can't throw things at people!"

He had never behaved like this.

Junior pivoted and ran through the living room toward the stairs. Drury ran after him. At the first bedroom door, he saw his bag inside and would have slammed the door shut if she hadn't put her hand on the wood.

"This isn't our cabin and you don't throw things at people. Do you hear me? What's the matter with you?" She stepped inside the room.

Without answering, he went to the bed and plopped down with a bent head, going into his withdrawal mode. That had worked to get him by this past year, but it was time to start pulling him out. Maybe she'd allowed him to cope in his own way too long. She'd been racked with her own heartache and consumed with finding Noah's killer.

She went to the bed and sat beside him.

"What's the matter?" She rubbed his back. "Talk to me. Don't shut me out."

He bobbed his feet against the mattress.

"Junior?"

At last he lifted his head and his anger burst free. "Daddy's coming home and you're acting like he's not!"

How had seeing her with Brycen made him come to that conclusion? He'd seen her with Noah. Maybe the show of intimacy, however innocent, had reminded him of that. He thought Brycen would take his place. Her heart sank with pity and love. How could she make him understand?

Continuing to rub his back, she said, "I thought you liked Brycen."

Junior lowered his head again. "I do."

"What, then?"

He bobbed his feet harder. After thinking it over in his troubled mind, he looked up at her, still fiery with emotion. "He's not my daddy and I don't want him to be!"

"He won't be, honey. Nobody can take the place of your father."

"Daddy's coming back. He doesn't belong here!"

"You don't mean that. Brycen does belong here." Sliding her hand from his back, she touched his arm. She needed to get his attention, to calm his temper. Make him understand. She berated herself for not sitting down with him before now and having a very frank talk. She'd explained about Noah, that he wouldn't be coming back because someone had hurt him badly and he had to go to heaven. How did a mother explain to her child that someone had actually murdered his dad? Killed him dead? She didn't have the heart to then and still didn't. But she had to.

Junior knew people died, but somewhere along the way he'd let his imagination take over. Denial made it easier.

"Junior, your daddy isn't coming home. I've told you that."

"Yes, he is!" He jumped up off the bed and faced her. "He's coming back! You just don't want him to!"

Drury reached out and took each of his hands. "It's time you accept the fact that your father has passed away."

"No, he hasn't!" He jerked his hands away.

She took them again and pulled him to her. She brought him against her and held him. "You have to stop imagining he's still alive, honey." She could feel him begin to breathe heavier as anger gave way to sadness and he fought tears.

"I'm so sorry." She had to fight her own tears. Seeing him this way tore at her soul. "He was killed, Junior. He's dead." She leaned back and held his face between her hands. "Do you understand what that means? He can't come back to us. As much as we want him to, he isn't coming back. Not ever."

"Stop it! No!" He batted his tiny hands on her upper chest.

She took his hands in hers to still them.

"He's coming back!" he yelled right at her face.

Drury held on to her resolve. "Do you know what it means when someone dies?"

"Daddy's not dead." Tears streamed down his cheeks, breaking her heart even more. "Dead people are in grave-yards."

"Yes, that's true. Remember his funeral? That was at a graveyard."

Crying from deep within but not sobbing, he looked forlorn and empty. She could barely take seeing him like this. Taking him into her arms again, she simply held him. "I'm so sorry."

Maybe, after a long year of silence and confusion, of incomprehensible disbelief, he'd finally broken through. This meltdown might have released pent-up grief, grief a young boy had not understood. Otherwise, he would have told her. Junior before Noah's death had been talkative and loud and full of play. He liked lazy mornings when they'd make dinner instead of breakfast and watch mov-ies until midafternoon. When he had homework he did it with enthusiasm. At school he did well and interacted with the other kids. She missed that little boy.

"Where did he go?" he asked quietly.

She leaned back and put her hands on his small shoul-ders. "He went to heaven."

"What's heaven?"

She'd taught him about heaven before, but he must not believe anymore. As he grew up, he'd make up his own mind what to believe about the afterlife. Drury kept an open mind on religion. She believed in the existence of a divine energy that could be called God. "Heaven is what people call the place we go when we die. We go to be with God."

He sniffled. "Is it real?"

"Nobody knows exactly what it's like when we die. No one alive can experience it before it happens. But it's a good and loving place. Your father isn't in any pain. He isn't lonely or unhappy. He's just waiting to see us again, and he'll wait until it's our time to go and be with him, which will be a very long time."

Junior searched her face and eyes, an innocent child needing to find the truth. "But he didn't want to be with God instead of us, did he?"

"None of us want to die. But once we do, we're okay and we're surrounded by love."

"Did the bad man force him to go there?"

"By killing him, yes." She hated even saying that. But Junior received it better than she expected.

"Why can't we see him anymore?" he finally asked.

How could she answer that question? "Because he isn't in his human body anymore. That's what happens when we die. The life you feel inside, the thoughts you have, the awareness of who you are, all of that is what passes on to another world, one we aren't meant to have contact with. We're supposed to live here in our bodies until we go to that place."

He looked at her face for several long seconds. "Daddy's okay?"

"Yes." A couple of tears slipped free and she kissed his cheek. "Daddy's okay."

He put his arms around her neck as she hugged him, hugging her back.

"Mommy?"

"Yes."

"I'm glad Brycen is going to catch the bad man."

She couldn't hold back a sob but managed to control any that would follow. "Me, too, sweetie. That's why I hired him." She moved back and stood, taking his hand. "Now, how about you go back out there and apologize to Brycen for throwing something at him?"

"Okay," he said glumly, and walked out of the bedroom.

Downstairs, Brycen had finished the Sloppy Joe mixture, stirring with the burner on low. He saw them and put the spoon down.

"Everything all right?"

Junior came to a stop before him, head bowed. "I'm sorry for throwing something at you."

"No need for an apology. Happens to us all. You hungry? I am." He opened the oven and took out the french fries.

Drury watched Junior stare up at Brycen in wonder. He hadn't gotten upset. He understood where Junior's anger came from.

More than sexual awareness stirred her heartstrings. For a man who felt awkward around kids, he sure had a way with them. More than ever, she wanted to know the cause of that awkwardness.

He scooped Joe mixture onto a bun and then put a handful of fries on a plate. Handing it to Junior, he said, "Fries are hot."

Junior took the plate and stared up at Brycen a second or two longer before going to the table.

Drury fixed her own plate. "Thank you."

"Don't mention it." He made his Joe and put fries on

his plate. "This is the most french fries I've had since I was about ten."

He made light of what had happened. But Junior's breakdown made her realize what her quest to avenge Noah had cost her son. She'd missed important signs. She'd seen him withdraw but attributed it to the normal grieving process. What she hadn't seen had her thinking about things Brycen had said. While she would always disagree that people were meant to love more than one person in a lifetime, he did touch on a significant point. People did marry for the wrong reason, and she hated to think she was one of those people.

Ever since she met Brycen, the feeling had begun to bubble up from way down deep. Her attraction to him had triggered it. Being married to Noah, she'd thought she'd found true love. How could that be, when just a look at Brycen gave her more intense sensation than she'd ever felt with Noah?

She was falling for Brycen.

Did that mean she avenged Noah out of obligation and justice? Maybe not entirely. She'd lost her family unit when Noah was taken from her, and she had loved Noah. But now she had to admit what she'd thought was true love had only been a close match.

"You okay?" Brycen asked in her long silence.

She shook off her thoughts and picked up her plate. "Yeah."

After Junior's tentative apology last night, Brycen sensed the boy still wasn't sure about him. This morning, he kept watching him. He didn't talk much, only when he had to. Brycen could see Drury's concern. She'd been melancholy ever since, as though the talk she had with Junior had shaken loose some residual regrets. Did she fault herself for Junior's lingering grief? Or did she worry the mutual attraction she had with Brycen had done and would continue to do damage to her son's progress?

When they parked in front of the house, Junior got out and ran to the door. Brycen followed Drury to the porch steps as Drury's mother emerged, startled as Junior raced past her, on his way to toys he must only play with when he came here. A slender woman in jeans and a long-sleeved T-shirt, with graying dark hair and blue eyes resembling Drury's, she examined him with unabridged interest before hugging her daughter.

"Hi, Mom," Drury said.

"Is this the detective?"

"Yes. Mom, Brycen." Her dad appeared out onto the porch, tall and also in good shape, his native Alaskan heritage showed in his wide cheekbones, graying dark hair and dark eyes. He also wore jeans and a T-shirt.

"Handsome," her mother said.

"Mom," Drury complained, looking at Brycen with a silent apology.

He grinned. "Hello…"

"Robert and Madeline Burke," Robert said, leaning over from the top step to shake Brycen's hand. "We've heard a lot about you."

Madeline smiled with glances from him to her daughter.

"We've got to run." Drury hooked her arm with Brycen's to get him to go with her. "Thanks for watching Junior."

"Anytime," Madeline called after them. "Looking forward to seeing you again, Brycen."

He looked back with a wave.

"They seemed to want to talk more," he said at the SUV, opening the door for her.

"My mother gets ideas in her head."

"Like the two of us together?"

"Yes," she said absently, discounting what she obviously considered an issue. "Sorry about that."

"Don't be sorry." He grinned as she paused to get in. Then he winked and shut the door. As he went around to the driver's side, he wondered why he'd done that. He'd already told Drury no marriage and no kids. Why, then, did Drury's mother fancying them as a couple appeal to him?

No one had followed them to the airport. Brycen had made sure of that. He'd tried to talk Drury out of going on her scheduled early-afternoon trip. Couldn't she wait until after he closed her husband's case? No. She needed the money. He couldn't argue with that.

The couple Drury had to fly had just gotten married. They'd fly them to a remote area north of Fairbanks.

Carrying two cups of lidded coffee, he climbed into the belly of the plane, moving between the front of one passenger seat and the back of another. Drury stood from loading a small refrigerator with cheese and fruit and a bottle of champagne. Seeing her bent over like that made him falter. He stopped.

She smiled, revealing her own awkwardness. "Newlyweds. Just your thing."

He moved toward her. "Funny."

She looked down his body, an unconscious action, and unbidden desire raced forth.

Standing before her, he felt the air between them grow

hotter, steamier. The way her eyes drooped in passion stirred the animal in him. Alone as they were in the plane, nothing prevented him from reaching out and pulling her to him. He didn't think, only acted. Bringing his head down, he did what he'd wanted to do for a while now. He kissed her.

He didn't understand his need. He held her and touched her carefully, reverently, gently. Sensations floated through him, making him crave more and more and never stop.

A woman giggling along with masculine laughter came to an abrupt halt at the open plane doors.

Brycen lifted his head, looking into Drury's bewildered eyes a moment before letting her go and turning. A couple stood there, watching them in silent apology for the interruption. The woman wore a white hat over long, fine blond hair and a heavy parka with gloves and calf-high boots. The man had his arm around her, also in winter gear but not wearing a hat over his darker blond hair. The ground crew loaded their luggage.

"Mr. and Mrs. Canterbury?" Drury said.

"Yes…sorry…we're a little early," the woman said.

A ground crew member peeked his head in the doorway. "All set." He slapped the side of the plane.

"Thank you," Drury said, then turned to the couple. "We'll get an early start." With an uneasy glance at Brycen, she headed for the cockpit, partially open to the rest of the aircraft.

Brycen watched the couple take two of the four seats, the man letting his new wife have the window. The way he regarded her struck Brycen in a way he had never experienced before. He'd seen lots of couples together, but he never noticed tender exchanges. He always dismissed them as foolish disillusionment, ignorant bliss. But now he saw love. Genuine love. The woman looked at her new husband the same way he looked at her as they'd taken their seats. If Brycen could see that in this couple, maybe love wasn't so rare after all.

Disturbed by that unwanted revelation, he joined Drury in the cockpit. He sat down in the copilot chair.

"Does it bother you whenever you see couples like that?" she asked without looking at him.

"No."

"You looked bothered."

"It's not every day you see a couple like that." He sure hoped she'd stop talking.

"No, but it's a lot more often than you think." As the engine revved to readiness, she turned to him.

"I've never noticed it before."

"Before now?" Instead of cornering him and challenging his beliefs, she seemed to honestly want to know.

"No."

She contemplated him for a while. "Maybe that's been your problem all along. You turned a blind eye."

Even though he sensed her thinking the same as him, he was glad she didn't put the thought into words. Kissing her had opened his eyes. Wanting her made him see things he otherwise wouldn't have. *True love.*

He shut down any further analysis. Just because he'd noticed the young couple in love didn't mean he felt the same for Drury.

Drury landed on the dirt landing strip where a car waited to take the couple to their remote and romantic getaway. Mr. Canterbury was the son of a wealthy hotelier and a recent grad from Harvard. His new wife was a book editor. She'd learned that from their reservation information and talk from the ground crew. But Brycen's notice of the couple had her most preoccupied. She resisted the urge to believe he'd change his thinking. Seeing the couple's love had penetrated his stubbornness, but would he let down his guard?

She didn't think so.

Nor did she feel ready to let go of her husband. Well… she didn't *think* she was ready. She *chose* not to be ready. She needed to solve his murder first.

With the couple deboarded and on their way to their destination, the ground crew—which was minimal in these parts—prepared them for their return. They had about an hour.

She left the plane with Brycen and headed for the single building. The wind blew at a pretty good clip, biting through her outer layers and chilling her. "I'm going to get another cup of coffee."

"I'll meet you in the terminal. I've drunk too much coffee."

Inside the building, he headed for the bathroom and she went to the only kiosk selling items travelers might need. Food. Snacks. Drinks. Books. Not much in the way of quantity but an impressive variety for somewhere this remote.

She paid for a coffee and turned to head back to the plane.

A man fell into step beside her. "Drury Decoteau?"

Startled, she nearly dropped her coffee and took a few steps back from the tall dark-haired man with glowing blue eyes. Fit and well built, he had a menacing air about him despite his good looks.

"Who are you?" She glanced around for Brycen and didn't see him.

The stranger held up his hands. "I didn't come here to hurt you."

"Who are you?" she repeated.

He lowered his hands. "I came here to warn you."

"I've had plenty of those." She started walking for the exit. There weren't many people here but enough to make it difficult for him to try anything.

He walked with her. "You have no idea what you're getting yourself into. Send that cop home and forget about your husband's murder. You can't do this without a lot more help."

Do what? She started to push through the door, but the man stopped her with his hand on her arm.

"If you want to live, forget about investigating his murder, Mrs. Decoteau. Leave it to the police. I'm sorry for your loss, but I'd sure hate to see something happen to you if you keep digging where you shouldn't."

"I'll ask you again, mister. Who are you?"

He let go of her arm and stepped back. "Let's just say, I know the people you're crossing, and they aren't the kind who give second chances. Back off and you'll be all right."

He didn't talk like a man out to kill her, or use violence to stop her.

"Why are you warning me?"

He hesitated and glanced around, probably searching for Brycen. "I met your husband. He was a good man. I don't like it that he was killed."

"If you know something, you should talk to Brycen. The police."

"I wish I could, ma'am. Unfortunately I made my

bed long ago. I'm stuck in dirty sheets." He began to back away.

"Wait. Please. You can help us."

He shook his head. "Back off, Mrs. Decoteau. Stop investigating your husband's murder, at least until you can get a bigger team, like the FBI." He turned and walked away.

The FBI? What did the man know? She would have tried to get him to tell her, but knew he would not.

"I can't," she said to his back.

The man saw Brycen coming out of the restroom and hurried in the opposite direction.

Drury pointed, jabbing the air. "That man!"

Brycen looked in that direction, but the man had vanished.

She took Brycen's hand and tugged him that way. "He just stopped me and warned me. After I got coffee. He must have been waiting for me. Except he didn't seem threatening. I mean he warned me to stop investigating Noah's murder, but it was more to protect me. He said he met Noah, but he wouldn't say how or where."

"Do you recognize him?"

At the corner, she stopped and searched the corridor. A few people walked this way and that, not very busy, but no sign of the stranger. Where had he gone? Side doors and restrooms could have given him a way out. She stopped and looked back. They'd passed another men's restroom, a different one from the one Brycen had used.

"No," she said.

Brycen backtracked their steps and went into the men's restroom. When he reemerged, he said, "He's gone."

"Of course he is. He knew you'd be here. He didn't try to approach me until he saw you go into the restroom."

She went to the front entrance to the small airport terminal, opposite the entrance she'd used from the tarmac. She didn't go outside. No cars moved. A couple approached the entrance. The stranger had planned to get in and out fast. He'd planned carefully, and he'd taken a risk in coming here to warn her. A friendly face on the inside of a dangerous crowd. Whatever Noah had begun to uncover, it was more than a domestic violence call or a robbery or an attempted sexual assault. One of those calls, or another he'd responded to, had led him into something much, much darker.

Brycen didn't like how easily a stranger had penetrated his watch over Drury. But it told him a lot about his adversary. He didn't work alone, and Noah had threatened him with more than an arrest in relation to responses for calls for help. Talking to Noah's partner wouldn't help. Carter didn't appear to know much.

Through the SUV windows, he spotted Drury tugging Junior toward the vehicle. The boy pouted and resisted, clearly not wanting to go with her.

Her parents came out onto the porch and waved at Brycen. He waved back, watching Madeline wrap her long sweater tighter.

Junior broke free from her grasp and would have run back to his grandparents if Drury hadn't snagged him by his arm. She pulled him to face her and crouched before him, talking to him sternly until the boy's head lowered and he finally nodded. Whatever talk she'd had with him hadn't worked. Taking his hand, she stood and took him down the sidewalk, turning to wave to her parents. They waved back and continued to watch.

Drury opened the back door and Junior climbed in, head low, giving in to a good pout.

"What's the matter, Junior?" Drury asked in the open doorway.

Junior's gaze lifted and he glowered at Brycen. His guess would be he now understood his father was dead but had difficulty accepting another man in his mother's life. His curiosity had taken a backseat to the threat of having to give up on his father ever coming home.

"Nothing," Junior said.

"I thought we had a nice talk last night. Is something bothering you about that?"

"No." His curt response said the opposite.

With a sigh, Drury started to move out of the doorway.

"Why don't you give me a minute alone with him?" Brycen suggested.

She looked at him a moment and then nodded. Closing the door.

Junior slouched in the back, mouth tight, smooth skin creased above his nose. Getting out, Brycen went to sit in the back. Junior ignored him.

"I was an only child," Brycen said.

The boy still ignored him and didn't look at him, but began kicking the back of the front seat as he swung his foot.

"I can't say I know what it's like to lose my dad. I had a pretty good relationship with him. But my parents didn't love each other and ended up divorcing. Do you know what that means?"

Junior nodded, still without looking up.

"I was older than you when they did so it didn't really

affect me much." After he felt an inner feeling disagree, he decided honesty would work best with a kid like Junior. "Well, I mean, I didn't think it did. But it did bother me. I didn't understand why they stayed married so long. I still don't. But they're both happier now." Drury had made him see that. "I was mad at them for not splitting up sooner, maybe I was mad at them for getting married in the first place." He grunted derisively. "Which is kind of self-defeating. If they hadn't been together, I'd never have been born."

The boy stopped swinging his foot and finally looked up at him.

"Your situation is a lot different than mine," Brycen went on. "I'm not trying to make it seem like we have anything in common there. I guess my point is things happen with your parents that you don't always understand. It's tough to work through, but eventually you will."

"I miss my daddy." He sounded defiant, mad. Probably that was a good sign.

"Yeah. If I lost my dad, I'd miss him, too."

"I want him to come home, but Mommy says he can't." Again, angry defiance gave bite to his words.

Junior understood his father would never come home but didn't want to accept it. Acceptance would take some time. He needed relief, sympathy or for someone to tell him everything was going to be okay.

"I wish I could bring him back home for you," Brycen said. "But all I can do is catch the man who took him from you."

The boy lowered his head again. Several seconds passed before he asked, "Is that really why you're here?"

Junior wanted the bad guy caught but struggled with

another man getting close to his mother. "Yes." Brycen had to reassure him in a way that wouldn't end up being a lie if he couldn't control his desire for Drury. "Your mom's a pretty special woman, Junior. You probably feel like you need to step up for her now that your dad is gone."

Junior shrugged without looking at him.

"I like her," Brycen said. "But I think you need to know that no matter what happens between me and her, I would never try to take your dad's place."

The boy looked up at him again, no longer antagonistic. Now he listened. Really listened.

"I'm not your dad. I won't try to be. I'll just be your friend…if you let me."

Junior took some time mulling over that. Then he asked, "Are you going to leave after you catch the bad guy?"

Why did he ask such a question? Did he rebel out of fear of abandonment or did he feel threatened over the possibility another man could end up with his mother? Brycen suspected it was a little of both, but probably more of an abandonment issue.

"Is that what you want me to do?" Brycen finally asked. "Leave?"

With the boy's hesitation, he took heart. Then he shrugged.

"Not sure?" Brycen asked.

With a quick glance up at Brycen, Junior nodded.

"You want me to catch your dad's killer, but you're not sure if you want me to leave once I do."

"Yeah."

"Well, after I solve your dad's case, I'll have to go back to Chicago where I live."

When Junior started kicking the back of the seat again and didn't respond in any other way, Brycen knew the boy suffered from abandonment issues. He may have imagined the cool detective staying. They'd play games together and do boy stuff. Likely Junior had not imagined such things since before his father passed. But he did not want his mother with another man.

"How do you feel about that?"

Junior shrugged.

"Tell you what," Brycen said. "How about we be friends like I suggested earlier? We'll start with that. How does that sound?"

Junior looked up at him. "Will you be my mommy's friend, too?"

"I'm already her friend. And no matter what happens between me and your mother, she'll always be here for you and I'll always be your friend."

He didn't respond, only continued to look at him.

"But if I do something you don't like, let me know and we'll work through it, okay? If I have boogers in my nose or I start drooling, you'll let me know, right?"

Junior smiled with a laugh and nodded.

"Everything's going to be all right, kiddo. You're going to be all right." Brycen messed up the top of his head. "Okay?"

"Okay." He was still smiling.

Brycen had started to get out of the backseat when Junior said, "Mr. Cage?"

He looked back. "If we're going to be friends, you have to call me Brycen."

"Why did my mommy want you to come here?"

He kept asking that. "Because it's my job to catch bad guys and I'm told I'm pretty good at what I do."

"Is she in trouble?"

Trouble? Why would he think such a thing? "No. Why do you ask?"

The boy tentatively looked over at him a few times. "She wanted you because you're the best?"

"Yes." He must have already been told that but needed reassurance. And Brycen began to suspect why. "Nothing or no one can take your mother away from you."

"But…someone took my daddy from me. What if the same thing happens to her?"

The poor kid dealt with a serious burden. Had he revealed this fear to anyone else? Brycen crouched in the open door and reached over to put his hand on Junior's where it rested on the seat. "I won't let anyone hurt her the way your dad was hurt. No one is going to take your mother away from you."

"But what about when you leave?"

"I won't leave until I'm sure no one will hurt her."

Junior scrutinized him some more.

"I'm the best, remember?"

At last Junior smiled again. "Yes."

Brycen would give him time for all that to sink in. Maybe he'd made headway, maybe not. He hadn't felt pressured to catch a killer in a long time, but this time the importance hitched up a few notches. All for a boy. Drury's son. An alien feeling for a man ordinarily hardened to the horrors of violent crimes, a piece of his steel barrier chipped away. Try as he might to put it back in place, he figured he'd lost it for good.

Chapter 6

Two days later, a snowstorm descended on Anchorage. Drury loved to watch the big, heavy flakes propelled to the ground by a driving wind, but she didn't look forward to getting out of Brycen's SUV. By the time she adjusted the hood of her jacket and slipped on gloves, Brycen appeared outside the passenger-side door, braving the weather in a jacket and nothing else. His eyes squinted against pelting snow.

Drury climbed out when he opened the door. Putting her foot on the runner, she slipped and might have fallen out of the SUV if not for Brycen wrapping his arm around her and setting her firmly down.

"Oh." With her hands on his sturdy chest, she stared up at his handsome face and decided to make light of the instant heat the close contact caused. "Well, I couldn't have staged that better."

He grinned. "Do you always fall into your men?"

"Are you my man?"

His grin dimmed a bit, but at the same time, a biting gust of wind whooshed snow in their faces and pushed the door open wider.

Keeping his arm around her, he manhandled the door shut and shielded her from the wind as they walked toward the state troopers' Bureau of Investigations unit. Carter had been out of the office until today, so they'd had to wait to speak with him.

Opening the terminal building door for her, he ushered her inside and made sure the door closed with the next gust. Out of the noise and fray, he heard an officer behind the reception counter finish saying something to a woman standing on the other side.

Drury stomped her feet and pushed her hood back before stepping farther into the building.

"I demand to talk to someone who can help me!" The fortyish chubby woman with short, curly dark hair and busy, multicolored long shirt over leggings slapped her hand on the reception desk. "My friend is missing. Don't you care about that?"

Drury slowed, something about the woman's urgency and her mention of a missing woman compelling her.

Brycen slowed with her. "What's the matter?"

"We have the report, ma'am. We're looking into her disappearance."

He followed her look just as the woman slapped her hand again. "You aren't listening to me. I want to talk to the person in charge of her case."

"He isn't here right now, as I've told you. I'll pass along your number."

"I want to talk to someone *now*. Every day Evette is

missing is another day she could wind up dead, if that monster of a husband hasn't killed her already."

"Evette Cummings?" Drury asked.

The woman turned, green eyes bright and surrounded by healthy white and a layer of mascara. "Yes." She approached them. "Are you in charge of her case?"

"Not exactly." Drury glanced at Brycen, waiting for him to answer. Some details should be withheld until they learned what this woman knew.

"You're that detective." The woman pointed at Brycen, her gold loop earrings swaying. "The one who came to solve that trooper's murder case."

"Brycen Cage. This is Drury Decoteau," he said. "You are…?"

"Juanita Swanson."

"Are you sure Evette is missing?" Drury asked.

"Oh, I'm sure. I've called her, and I've gone to her house and Melvin keeps telling me she isn't home and he doesn't know where she is. I reported her missing yesterday and nobody is doing anything." She sighed her frustration, glancing back at the desk officer in annoyance.

"When's the last time you saw her?" Drury asked.

"Two nights ago. She called me in a panic. Melvin smacked her around real good. He's a regular at that."

"Why did he beat her?" Brycen asked, even though he probably already knew.

She humphed. "Melvin needs no excuse or reason to beat Evette. It all depends on his mood or the amount of booze he's had. But it so happens, this time he had a reason. It goes way back to when that state trooper was killed. He beat her bad then, too. Told her if she ever called the cops again, he'd kill her. I went to see her two days after. She said he was mad because the state trooper came when he had a meeting with someone. She should have gone to the hospital after that beating."

A man had arrived between the time of Evette's call and the state troopers' arrival? They couldn't reach people who needed help in a matter of minutes when they lived in remote areas as Evette and Melvin did.

"What meeting?" Drury asked.

"Don't know what it was about. Neither did Evette. She spent most of her time trying to stay out of the way of Melvin's fists."

"Who was the man?" Brycen asked.

"Don't know that, either. Evette didn't know him and Melvin didn't tell her his name. He never talked business with her. He only threatened her with her life if she told police he was there."

For a fisherman, he had secretive business meetings. Something didn't add up. "But...you said the troopers arrived when the meeting was scheduled."

The police report said Evette showed no sign of abuse when Noah and Carter had answered her call for help. Melvin had beaten her after Noah and Carter left. But Noah and Carter hadn't seen the stranger. Or had they?

"That's why I reported her missing. After that trooper was killed and I went to see her again. I asked her why Melvin beat her. She brushed it off into something insignificant. I asked her if it had anything to do with that trooper's death and she said no, even though he was the same trooper who answered her call for help. She told me she was mistaken that the man had been there when the trooper arrived. She said he left before that because Melvin told him to."

She kept saying trooper and not troopers.

"There were two troopers who answered that call," Brycen said.

"She only mentioned the one." Juanita didn't seen troubled by the discrepancy, but her loop earrings wiggled as she looked from Brycen to Drury.

Why would she only refer to one of the troopers? That also didn't add up. Carter had been there, or so he'd claimed. Why hadn't he been killed if Noah's murder had anything to do with that call? Had only Noah seen the stranger? Why would he not tell Carter? Had he gone off onto his own investigation? Kept it secret?

If so, why hadn't he told Drury anything about it? They'd had a good marriage. They talked about everything. Or so she'd thought. Maybe their communication hadn't been as spot-on as she'd believed.

"Do you think Evette lied about the man not being there when the troopers arrived?" Brycen asked.

"Not lied. Beaten and battered, she was too scared to say. I forgot all about it until now. She came to see me the day before yesterday. Scared to death again, because of *him*. Saying Melvin was paranoid over a detective who'd taken over that trooper's murder case." She inspected Brycen. "You."

Drury could tell Brycen had to hold back his temper knowing Melvin hadn't heeded his warning—that he'd been unsuccessful in protecting Evette. "And are you certain Evette only referenced one trooper?"

"Yes. She said a trooper came to the door, not troopers."

Brycen glanced over at Drury, who grappled with all that implied. Had Noah gone on that call alone, and not told Carter? Why?

"Thank you, Juanita." Brycen took out a card and

handed it to her. "If you have anything else for us or have questions, just call."

She took the card and removed a pen from her big leather purse. She wrote a number on the back of the card and handed his card back to him. "Why don't *you* call *me* when you find my friend?" She met his eyes dead-on.

He smiled slightly as he took his card back. "That will be my pleasure, Ms. Swanson."

When the woman turned to go, heading through the doors, Drury said, low enough for only him to hear, "Is it possible Noah discovered something about Melvin and went alone because he suspected Carter's involvement?"

"Quite possible." He turned to meet her look and she didn't like the certainty she saw in his eyes.

"Why would Carter lie about being there?"

"So he could say no other man was present when they made the call."

"He didn't write the report. Noah did." Noah hadn't included a stranger present at the Cummingses' residence in the report.

In a blue state trooper uniform, Carter smiled when he saw them approach down the well-lit hall. Brycen noticed no insincerity, but he'd learned long ago not to trust a man who might have secrets to protect. He shook the man's hand.

"Drury." Carter opened his arms.

She leaned in for a guarded hug, something Brycen hadn't seen in previous exchanges. While she hadn't yet accepted the possibility that Carter knew more than he let on, she didn't discount it, either.

"Let's go in here." Carter gestured toward an open

conference room. "What brings you by? Did anything come out of the Cummingses' visit?"

Brycen entered the room ahead of Drury, not missing how Carter always sequestered them when they came for visits. He went halfway inside the room and stopped alongside a rectangular table. He turned and faced Carter, Drury doing the same on the other side of the table.

"Evette said she overreacted when she called for help the night you and Noah went to her house," Brycen said, laying out where he intended this conversation to go.

"The scared ones always have some excuse." Carter put his hands on his hips above a duty belt packed with handcuff case, gun, cross-draw TASER, magazine pouches, portable radio and collapsible baton.

"Did you talk to Juanita Swanson after Noah's murder?"

"Who?" He shook his head, hands still on his hips. "Name doesn't ring a bell. Who is she?"

Brycen kept his face steady while he thought the oversight anything but. What good cop would miss talking to one of Evette's closest friends after his partner's murder? He could see not talking to her after the domestic violence call, but not the murder. Family and friends of those last in contact with a victim could reveal things important to a case.

"A close friend of Evette's," he finally said. "Juanita went to talk to Evette after Noah's murder, but Evette downplayed the connection to the domestic violence call, and Juanita forgot about it until now."

"She reported her missing," Drury added with a subtle edge to her tone, maybe even a challenge.

Carter looked from Brycen to Drury, his pause indicating he'd noticed. "What connection?"

Brycen didn't know why he asked.

In his pause, Carter said, "You said Evette down-played Melvin's connection to Noah's murder."

Either Carter had just made himself appear guilty or semantics had. "I didn't say Melvin. I said the domestic violence call."

Carter laughed slightly, nervously. "I meant the same thing. Evette called because of his abuse. What connection? I don't see one."

Or was he trying to find out what they'd discovered?

"Did you know Evette has been reported missing?" Drury asked.

He turned to her. "Yes. I was going to tell you."

Was he?

"Evette told Juanita a man was at her and Melvin's house when Noah arrived in answer to her call for help," Brycen said.

Carter frowned, lips curving down and eyes clueless, or appearing so, as he shook his head. "I didn't see anyone. Who was the man?"

"Were you there?" Brycen asked, all in a calm, even tone, unfaltering.

"Of course I was."

"Evette told Juanita only one trooper answered the call," Drury said accusatorily.

Carter's face softened. "Drury, I was there. Evette and Juanita must have miscommunicated. It's all in Noah's report."

Yes. Noah's report. Brycen didn't like the smell of this.

"Did Juanita say who the man was? Did Evette tell her?" Carter asked.

"She didn't know and Evette didn't tell her." Brycen

hoped Drury wouldn't give away that Evette had claimed to be mistaken.

"Is it possible that Noah saw someone there?" she asked.

Carter took a few seconds to think on that. "I don't know how. He was with me the whole time. But I suppose anything is possible. Could Evette's friend describe the man?"

"No. Evette didn't tell her much about him," Brycen said. "Did Noah investigate Melvin after you left the Cummingses' residence?"

"Not that I'm aware. What reason would he have had?"

"Depends on what he discovered about the stranger," Brycen said.

Carter took several seconds before he responded, "I didn't notice anything unusual."

"About Noah?"

"About Noah, about the Cummingses. It was a domestic violence call and the wife was too scared to press charges." He sounded certain, which convinced Brycen he told the truth.

"Noah didn't go off on his own at all?" Drury asked. "He didn't seem preoccupied with something he wasn't telling you?"

Carter shook his head. "No." He lowered his hands. "He never mentioned anything to me."

Drury looked down and off to the side, her disappointment showing. Did she believe him? Brycen didn't. Carter might not have noticed anything unusual about Noah or the Cummingses at first, but if Noah had unearthed something that might implicate him in illegal activities, he'd sure notice then. But Brycen didn't think he'd caught on until after he discovered Noah had gone on the domestic violence call alone.

"If you want, I can check his last movements again," Carter said. "Maybe I missed something."

"That won't be necessary." Brycen walked around the table to Drury's side, putting his hand on her back. She looked up at him and he heard her soft intake of breath as the chemistry between them heated. Just like that, out of nowhere, intense magnetism sparked.

He had to shake off the building heat and desire and turn to Carter. "I'll take it from here."

As he guided Drury toward the door, he couldn't be sure if Carter's hardening eyes were from insult or menace.

After a few steps to cool off from his hand on her lower back, Brycen noticed she had done the same.

"I can't believe he'd have anything to do with Noah's murder," she said as they made their way to the reception area.

"Maybe he didn't."

"He and Noah were close. He came to our house for dinners and football games."

Most people don't suspect friends and relatives capable of the crimes that get them arrested. Most criminals play nice to avoid detection, and they're good at deception.

"He comforted me after Noah was murdered," Drury said.

Before letting her go out into the storm, Brycen stopped her, taking her hand and drawing her to face him. "First of all, don't go there."

She averted her head and he sensed her overanalyzing the whole situation.

"Have you stayed in touch with him?"

"Carter? Only regarding the case."

"He was your late husband's friend. You trusted him. He spent personal time with you. That's the tough part, but if it turns out he's crooked, we know Noah conducted his own investigation and kept it from him. Our focus becomes what Carter knows. And more important, what Noah knew."

And hadn't had time to tell anyone.

Her disgust over Carter faded and their previous, snow-melting encounter chased away darkness. "For a guy with secrets and a depressing career, you sure can be a softie."

Transfixed by her megawatt smile, Brycen remained speechless for a moment. He hadn't seen her smile like that. Losing her husband to murder had doused her sense of humor. But for some mystical reason, it had popped out right now.

What she'd said wasn't so funny, though.

"Put your hood up. It's stormy out there."

Her gaze roamed all over his face, smile waning. "And in here, apparently."

They created a storm all right, and he suspected it would only intensify. What would he do when it did?

Chapter 7

The benefits of belonging to Dark Alley Investigations became obvious to Drury when a sleek helicopter landed on the helipad of the private airstrip where she flew her plane. Tinted windows, shiny black paint—she imagined concealed weaponry and surveillance equipment strategically installed on and in the bird. Brycen would no longer use the resources of the state troopers' unit. While the cost went up, so did their defenses.

They had to wait for the storm to pass, and now on this chilly morning, they reached the high-tech helicopter.

Brycen jumped into the back, giving her a hand up after him. His strength brought her bumping against him, and another zing sparked. But he let go to tell the pilot they were ready and then sat across from her. He lifted some vests from the seat beside him and handed her one.

"Put it on under your jacket," he said. She saw the

set of earphones next to her and put them on. He did the same with his pair.

"Buckle up," the pilot said into the earphones.

Drury fastened her seat belt and Brycen fastened his before digging into a duffel bag, also on the seat beside him. Out came a mean-looking pistol. Next came magazines and holders, then an ankle strap for another gun.

"What's that? Backup?"

"Kadin never skimps."

She watched him remove his jacket and put on the bulletproof vest that came equipped with a gun holster. As he put his jacket back on, she slipped into her vest, wondering if she'd really need this and if so, if she should even be going along.

Brycen didn't seem bothered by any harm that might come their way. No, his confidence came through loud and clear. Besides, he wouldn't want her alone for Noah's killer to come after her.

Right now he lifted another gun from the bag and handed it to her. It was smaller than his.

"Ever shoot a gun before?" he asked as she took the gun.

"Yes. Married to an Alaska State Trooper...?"

He smiled slightly. "How good a shot are you?"

"Good enough." Probably not his caliber, but she could aim well enough. She tucked her gun into one of the holders on the vest. "But your question should be, *have you ever shot someone?* The answer to that is no. And I hope I never have to." She didn't think she could kill another person even if her own life depended on it. She didn't know. She'd never been in that situation before. She only could imagine how terrible it would be to take a human life.

"Don't worry. I'm a good shot." His smile changed to a sexy grin.

She didn't ask if he'd killed anyone. Odds were he had. "That's why I hired you, Detective."

"You hired Dark Alley."

"Same thing. Stop being bashful." She slipped back into her jacket, realizing yet again that he brought out her sense of humor.

The helicopter lifted off and flew over the outskirts of Anchorage, flying along the coast toward the remote village. A clear day after the storm had passed; the beautiful scenery below and Brycen's relaxed mood offered an opportunity to broach a sensitive topic. They had some time before reaching Tate anyway.

"Who is Avery?" she asked.

He instantly tensed and his face lost its pleasant expression. "I told you. Nobody."

"She must have been somebody at some point."

He turned back to the window, no longer appearing to enjoy the view.

"Is she the reason you left? Was she your girlfriend?"

"No."

"Someone who knew your girlfriend?"

He said nothing.

"Did you cheat on her or something?" She really knew nothing about this man, other than his profession and his skewed view on marriage, which had prompted the question. A man who spurned marriage might not have much respect for the sanctity of relationships when he decided they'd run their course and the time had come to move on to the next one.

Slowly he turned back to her and she saw his offense. "No."

So this did have something to do with a woman, a woman who must either be related to Avery or be one of her good friends.

"What happened?"

"Something personal."

Giving up, Drury sat back against the seat, her gaze drifting to the front of the chopper and the pilot. Then she remembered the headphones. He'd heard everything.

A few minutes later, they circled the Cummingses' place. It looked deserted. No vehicles. No movement.

The helicopter landed near the same area as the last time they'd come here.

"I'll go see if Evette is inside." Brycen hopped down to the ground.

Since it didn't appear anyone was here, Drury hopped down with him. He gave her a wry look before heading to the house. He knocked on the door. When no one answered, he turned the knob. The door had been left unlocked. A remote area such as this didn't require locks, or so some thought.

Inside, trash littered kitchen countertops and a beat-up round wood coffee table. The smell of old food stung her senses. Or was that ketchup that had been left sitting out too long? She followed Brycen over old, shaggy brown carpet that would surely show more stains were it a bit lighter.

Was Evette a clean housekeeper or did the state of the cabin indicate she hadn't been here in a while?

Brycen searched the kitchen and living room area, lifting a woman's sweater from a chair and checking the pockets. Finding those empty, he looked over the family pictures set out haphazardly on the traditional fireplace mantel. A pair of women's shoes sat by the chair, as though Evette had taken them off in trade for a cozy pair of slippers.

Down a short hall with only three doors, one a bathroom, Drury switched on the bathroom light. Hair spray and a container of blush and mascara lay on the counter. Brycen entered the room the kids shared and then the master bedroom—just a slightly larger room than the other. Clothes lay everywhere, on the unmade bed, on the floor, draped over the only dresser and spilling out of the tiny closet.

Drury was accustomed to bigger closet space.

While Brycen opened dresser drawers, Drury went into the closet. Full of clothes. It didn't appear that Evette had packed anything. Drury dragged out a suitcase and saw a matching one tucked against the wall in the corner.

"Have you found a purse yet?" Brycen asked.

"No."

That may be a good sign. No purse could mean Evette had taken that with her when she went.

Brycen began lifting clothes and sifting through piles. On a chair in the corner by the only window in the room, he went through the clothes there, digging down to a throw blanket. Under that he found a purse.

Drury's heart and hope sank.

He opened the purse and lifted car keys and a wallet. As he opened that, his face gave away the confirmation that it belonged to Evette. He put the purse back in place and took out his cell phone, taking photos. He took photos of the closet and anything else that indicated Evette had left with only the clothes on her back.

"What now?" she asked as they left the cabin and headed for the helicopter, the pilot still inside, wearing sunglasses and watching them approach.

"I want to talk to people in the village."

They got into the helicopter and he didn't have to tell the pilot where he needed to go. The pilot took them a short distance over the forest. She began wondering if Brycen had prepared ahead of time for this.

She saw the town over the tops of trees, disappearing as the pilot landed in a nearby clearing. When it was safe to open the door and jump out, Brycen did so, turning to offer Drury a helping lift down. She leaned on his shoulders, not because she needed the help, rather because the temptation to touch him urged her.

She stayed close and he didn't move for a few seconds, feeling the energy between them, seductively pleasing.

Then his lawman mode kicked back in and he stepped back. "This way."

She walked with him toward the trees, then into them, finding a path that the locals must use to either exercise or reach other destinations. If there were any. She hadn't seen much from the air. What few houses dotted the landscape were spread apart.

"Did you know this path was here?" she asked.

"I saw it on aerial photos."

He'd planned ahead.

"Where are we going?"

"To see Evette's mother. Her sister lives here, too."

"You don't talk much, do you?" And not only about personal things. He volunteered almost nothing. They reached the other side of the forest and the town came into view.

"I had a teleconference with Kadin while you were in the shower. He emailed me the photos."

Why hadn't he gotten them before they'd gone to Evette and Melvin Cummingses' house? Maybe he hadn't anticipated needing to know the town, as well. She stepped from path to the dirt road, the main road through town. "And you didn't think I'd be interested in knowing where we were going?"

They passed a diner that also functioned as a convenience store and coffee shop. A few people sat inside, watching them go by with interest. Not many strangers came to this village.

"You knew where we were going."

"To look for Evette."

"We are looking for her." He guided her down a side street. Ahead, four houses lined each side, each with stairs going up to porches and painted different colors. White, yellow, blue and gray. The gray house needed a fresh coat and repairs to the stairs.

Brycen guided her to the yellow house. Up white stairs, they stood before the door and rang the bell.

A round woman, maybe five-three in height, stuck her face between the drape and edge of the narrow window on the door. In rectangular glasses, she had her medium brown hair up in a hair clip.

Brycen showed his business card from Dark Alley Investigations. The woman read the card and then unlocked the door.

"Yes?"

"Mrs. Patterson?"

"Yes." She looked from him to Drury.

"We're here to ask you some questions about your daughter, Evette."

Her face lit up. "Have you found her? Juanita reported her missing for us. She moved to Anchorage a few years back. She told us some disturbing things about Melvin. I always thought he was bad news for her. I've asked him to his face what he's done with my girl and he says he doesn't know where she went, that she just up and left one night while he was asleep."

She talked fast.

"You don't believe him?" Drury asked,

"Oh, hell no. Evette's been trying to get away from him for more than a year now. Her kids keep her there, though."

That corroborated what Evette had told them the first time they came here.

"Where are her kids now?" Brycen asked.

"They're in school. They've been staying here while Melvin works."

Drury heard and saw part of a television in a clean, neat living room with a floral couch that had to be twenty years old.

"He's working now?" Brycen asked.

"Yes. Went on a fishing trip the morning after Evette went missing. Didn't even care to stick around to find out what happened to her."

"Where did he go?" Brycen asked.

She swatted her hand in dismissal. "Who knows? He never says."

Melvin revealed very little about his fishing business.

"What do you think happened to Evette?" Drury asked.

Her face sagged with worry, lips pressing together and eyes going distant. When she recovered, she looked at each of them. "I dare not imagine what he might have done with her. Dragged her off into the woods and killed her. That's my worst nightmare."

"Did Evette ever tell you anything about Melvin, anything suspicious? Was he doing anything unusual, meeting anyone unusual?"

"No. She didn't mention anything like that. Just that things were getting bad between them, that he hits her now."

"Is that something new? He's never hit her before?"

She waved a hand in disgust. "Oh, he's always been a mean soul, talking nasty to her. Emotional abuse. But like I said about a year or more ago, things started changing. She called the police on him the first time."

"Yes, that's in our report," Brycen said. "Evette never mentioned anything that stands out?"

"Believe me, I wish she had. My girl would do anything for her kids, to hang on to them, and to be around for them. Live, if you know what I mean. She started out thinking she could handle Melvin and stay in the marriage for them. But I'm afraid she may have discovered she couldn't."

She might not have survived her desperate husband. Drury wished they could comb the island for her. See through trees. And if she didn't turn up here, then they'd expand the search.

She waited until they left to tell Brycen the idea that came from those thoughts.

"Maybe you should go on television and broadcast that Evette has gone missing," she said as they walked back toward the field.

"Already alerted the local news stations."

She angled her head as they neared their ride. "When?"

"When you were getting ready this morning. Kadin said he'd handle it."

"Very good. Teamwork."

He chuckled, low and breathy and a little flirtatious. "I'll start telling you about my teleconferences."

She wished he would share more than that. He put his hand on her lower back as they made their way along the street. She didn't think he'd done it to guide her, he did it as an intimate touch. That inexplicable heat came alive again. Where did it come from? Why him? And did he feel the same? That almost frightened her. If he did feel the same and she tumbled into a relationship with him, what would become of her? Would she have her heart broken again, this time not by the hands of a killer, but a man who didn't believe marriage lasted?

Just then a rally of bullets pelted the ground not three inches from Drury's feet. She stopped a scream and searched for the source of the gunfire. What few people moved along the street ran. A woman screamed. Where was the shooter?

Brycen grabbed Drury's hand and pulled her into an all-out run toward the helicopter. Of course, they'd be safest there. Bulletproof glass...

If they could make it there.

Running past a stop sign, Drury heard the ping of a bullet on the metal.

"Go ahead of me. Run to the trees!" Brycen turned with his gun drawn and shot toward the buildings where the shooter had taken cover.

With a glance back over her shoulder, she saw the gunman had taken shelter in an alley.

Brycen's gunfire kept him back and out of sight.

She reached the trees and stopped behind one, drawing her own gun and aiming for the alley, hoping she wouldn't have to fire.

Brycen took care of that, pausing in his run to once

again fire toward the alley. He reached the trees. Taking her hand, he ran with her along the path, frequently looking back.

In the opening, the pilot must have heard the gunshots. He had the rear door open and the blades rotating for liftoff.

More gunfire made Drury duck. She nearly tripped. Brycen lifted her and swung her into the back of the chopper, jumping in after her with bullets hitting the side of the chopper. He closed the side door and the pilot lifted them into the air.

The gunman continued to fire from the trees, ducking back as the pilot fired back with a bigger-caliber gun attached to the helicopter. Chunks of bark flew where the gunman hid.

The gunman peered out from his cover, wearing a heavy jacket and a hat, firing at the helicopter. The bullets didn't penetrate and as the helicopter rose higher, the gunman stopped and watched them fly away.

Holding pages from Noah's crime report, Brycen paced to the other side of his cabin and stopped. Drury watched him from the kitchen, her son at the table drawing one of his favorite superheroes. He hadn't put up much of a fuss this time in going with Brycen, but he'd also not said much. He withdrew a lot, going off into his own little world.

She stirred spaghetti sauce as Brycen moved toward her, focused on a page. He turned that page over and then paused, going back to the previous page. His brow creased deeper and he stopped again. Studying the page, he stepped to the table where Junior was drawing and put the pages down, running his forefinger down the edge and flipping through more pages. He came to the last page and then raised his head, not seeing anything, immersed in thought.

"What is it?" Drury stopped stirring.

Junior looked up at her and then him.

Without answering, he bent for his briefcase and set it on the table. Opening the case, he searched through the documents inside. He took out one of them and put it on the table next to Junior's drawing.

Junior looked down at the document, his interest and curiosity captured. Drury wondered if Brycen had done that on purpose, included the boy in what he'd been studying. He waited for her as she left the stove and went to the table between Junior and Brycen. He'd taken out the copy of Noah's report on the domestic violence call.

"What did you find?" Drury asked.

"Did somebody make a mistake?" Junior asked.

Drury messed up his hair at the cuteness. Maybe only a mother would find that cute, his innocent question, as though another kid had made a mistake on his homework or something.

"Somebody made a mistake all right." Brycen put down a copy of another report, the one of the rape attempt, and pointed to the side of the document. "See this copy? There are no marks on it. It's clean."

"Nobody drew on it?" Junior asked, confusion crowding his brow.

"Now look at this document." Brycen moved the attempted rape report over to reveal the domestic violence report and pointed to the edge of both with his forefingers. "This one looks like a copy of a scanned document."

Drury leaned closer. "Why is that significant?" So

what if someone had made a copy of a scanned document? Anyone could have printed it and then Carter could have copied the scanned printout.

But why scan the report in the first place? To preserve Noah's signature.

She saw him reading the report, running his finger down the lines and then stopping at the point where Noah had typed about meeting Evette and Melvin. His finger moved to the line boxing in the text, then down lower, to the blank space above Noah's signature.

"Someone covered up the rest of this text and modified what was originally typed here. With the right Portable Document Format, the text could have been edited."

Some text had been edited and some had been completely covered, then the page copied and scanned to replace the original. "Where is the original signed report?" she asked. Would Carter have risked saving it? Maybe he had done so as leverage against whoever had been at the Cummingses' house, in case things didn't go as planned and he found himself facing charges.

Brycen looked up and didn't have to say anything. Now more than ever, he thought Carter had something to do with Noah's death.

Chapter 8

Brycen made Drury wait for him while he broke into Carter's house and searched for the original file. He'd struck out. The file hadn't been on his computer or anywhere in the house. He hadn't found anything suspicious, either. Carter—if he was involved in Noah's death somehow—would know what to hide as a state trooper familiar with the case. If he'd kept a copy of the original, either in paper or electronic form, he'd put it somewhere other than his residence.

Now Brycen waited with Drury for Carter to meet them once again in a conference room. Drury stood before one of the photos hanging on the wall. A water-landing plane flew over the smooth surface of a lake, the low angle of the sun casting colorful reflections, and light disappearing in the thick forest.

He went to admire the photo with her.

She glanced over and up at him before continuing to absorb the picture. "This reminds me of a time my dad took us on a day trip near Fairbanks. He flew to a cabin on the shore of a remote lake. We had to land on the water. It was my first water landing. The water was smooth as glass, like this picture. He came in for the landing, flying just above the surface, and then touched down. Soft tap and gliding. He was a good pilot. Still is. Good at landing, especially on the water. I think that's the day I decided I would be a pilot when I grew up."

"That's a nice memory." He put his hand on her lower back, as he seemed inclined to do more often now.

She looked up at him and an instant later, their fire roared to life.

"Did the rest of the trip match the landing?" he asked.

"Not quite." She smiled. "I thought of the landing the whole weekend."

Dreaming had magical charm in childhood. He had dreamed of becoming something of a Sherlock Holmes, or one of the characters who solved the multiple mysteries he had read.

He looked down at her as her eyes lifted. A warm, sweet moment of connection passed between them. Each still floating with fond memories that had influenced their paths, a bond strengthened with the common thread they shared. Inspiration.

He drew his head closer to hers.

"You're back."

Brycen jerked his head back and turned with Drury at the sound of Carter's voice. He lowered his hand from her, seeing Carter's gaze move from there to Brycen's face in barely masked disapproval. Why did he disapprove? Was he threatened?

Turning from the photo, Brycen dropped the falsified file onto the conference room table.

"What's that?" Carter moved toward the table.

"Things will go a lot easier for you if you confess," Brycen said.

Carter's brow lowered and he looked from Brycen to the file, which he opened. A few second later, he recognized the report. "It's Noah's report."

"Why did you tamper with it?" Brycen asked.

Drury stayed by the wall, leaning back and watching Carter, disappointment clear in the way she did so.

"What are you talking about? I didn't tamper with anything." He picked up the report and leafed through the pages.

"What was in Noah's original report?" Brycen asked. "What did he have to say about the stranger at Evette and Melvin's home?"

"You're taking this to the extreme."

Brycen ignored his attempts to evade the truth. "He noticed something, didn't he?" he said. "And then he began to look into things himself. In fact, he started doing that before the domestic violence call, didn't he? He noticed something about you. Maybe places you went. People you met. He was onto you."

"Onto me." Carter laughed as he spoke. "I have done nothing. You're making this all up. Is that how you got your zero-unsolved case record? Accusing the innocent of crimes they didn't commit?"

"What crime am I accusing you of?"

"I didn't kill Noah."

"Maybe not, but you know who did, don't you?"

Carter's entire face hardened. "I think it's time you

left. I can have you shut out of this investigation, you know."

Brycen stepped forward, putting his face close to Carter's, looking down from his greater height. "You can't stop me from finding Noah's killer. And you can't stop me from exposing your involvement. If you don't come clean now, you'll face a much worse sentence."

Carter didn't back down, only continued to meet Brycen's stare.

Drury moved away from the wall and came to stand at Carter's side. "Noah was your friend."

At last Carter faced her. "Drury…"

"He was your friend and you betrayed him. Why?"

"I didn't betray him.'

"Why did you lie about being at the Cummingses' house?" she demanded.

Instead of denying his presence, he didn't answer this time.

That served as enough of a confession for Brycen. He didn't know yet what role Carter played in Noah's death, but he had played a role. And he knew something critical to the investigation, something he wouldn't reveal.

After leaving the station, Drury went with Brycen to the coffee shop where Noah had been shot. She still felt the aftereffects of Brycen nearly kissing her when Carter had interrupted them. Looking at the picture had stirred up things that held deeper meaning and entwined them together in that moment. She had to tell herself to stay focused on Noah's investigation, which also came with shame for straying, even for a bit.

Noah had gone to this coffee shop often, but had his

visits been strategic? Did it mean something that he'd been shot leaving that particular coffee shop?

She couldn't grasp how Carter could betray his friend and partner. More than what he'd done to betray him, the apathy for Noah. How could he have not cared what happened to Noah as a result of whatever action he'd taken, or whatever, or whoever, he'd gotten himself entangled in?

Stepping inside the quaint store, she took in the jazzy music and rustic decor along with a giant gas fireplace in the middle. Early on a weekday, several patrons sat at tables or stood in line for their prework coffee. Nothing sinister popped out at her. In fact, this place had a popular reputation, competing with a chain store three blocks down. Noah had liked it for its originality and its ambience.

"Want to get some coffee and sit down for a while?" she asked.

Brycen finished searching the shop for suspicious faces or something else—as though he feared running into Avery again. "Sure."

His reluctance to go anywhere public made her wonder why.

He bought her coffee and she chose a table at the window, a good vantage point to see the entire shop and also outside in the front.

Brycen sipped his coffee and looked outside, going still when he saw something.

"What is it?" She put her cup down.

Without answering, he followed the movement of someone entering the shop. She twisted to see an older man dressed in a suit and tie beneath a long overcoat get in line. Very sophisticated.

"Who is that?" she asked.

Brycen turned away from the man and didn't answer her.

"Why are you so secretive about your past here?"

"It's no big secret." He drank some coffee and put his cup down, looking at her unapologetically.

"Maybe not the part about you being a detective, but there's something you haven't told me."

"Something personal," he said with an icy note.

She sat back and sipped her coffee, seeing the older man pay for his coffee. As he waited for the barista to prepare his order, he glanced around the shop and saw her watching him. Next his gaze shifted to Brycen, who had his back at an angle to him.

The man's everyday expression, someone just stopping for a hot cup of joe, changed, going hard with dislike.

"He saw you. Who is he?"

"A retired army colonel," he said without looking back.

The man retrieved his coffee and headed toward them.

"Here he comes."

Brycen muttered a curse just loud enough for her to hear.

"You," the man said as he reached their table, brown eyes beady with dark circles beneath, wrinkled skin beginning to sag. He kept his gray hair neatly combed and clipped short.

"Mr. Jefferson."

Although this encounter clearly didn't settle well with Brycen, he still managed to maintain politeness. He'd been that way with Avery, as well.

"Avery told me she ran into you." The man held his

coffee without drinking. "I see you didn't do the right thing and leave."

"I'm here on business that doesn't concern you, Mr. Jefferson."

"Yeah? Well, that business has already taken too long. I'd have gone the rest of my life happy to never lay eyes on you again."

Drury doubted he felt happiness often with his attitude.

"I'm not here to cause you any grief, Mr. Jefferson."

"I heard why you came." Mr. Jefferson looked at Drury. "I'm sorry for your loss, miss, but you don't need this man to solve your husband's murder. Nobody here wants Brycen back. We were all glad to see him go."

"You talk as though everyone in the city wanted me gone," Brycen said.

"Everyone I know did." He sounded rather pompous.

"I'm at a loss, Mr. Jefferson," Drury said. "I don't know who you are."

Brycen shot a look her way. What did he expect? If he wasn't going to tell her, she had to find out from someone other than him.

Mr. Jefferson chuckled low and full of cynicism. "So he hasn't told you."

Brycen moved his eyes back to the other man, not volunteering any information or defenses.

"I'm Kayla's father. Has he told you about her? Avery is her sister. You've met her."

"Yes."

"Kayla was my girlfriend," Brycen said, unwillingly, but at least he'd told her. "She died in a car accident."

"Accident," Mr. Jefferson sneered. "That was no accident. You knew what was going to happen and you took her with you anyway. You took her to spite all of us. And she was so smitten with you that she'd do anything you asked."

"What happened?"

Reluctantly Brycen lifted his gaze to her, with naked regret. She felt bad for making him reveal something he'd rather not.

"A drug addict came after me when he was released on bail," he said. "It's true, I knew this, but I didn't know he'd come after me while I drove in the car with Kayla. When the addict started shooting at us, I shot back. Unfortunately my attention wasn't on my driving. At a turn in the road, I ran into a tree. Kayla died."

He lowered his head and then looked up at Mr. Jefferson. "Her family has never forgiven me. Mr. Jefferson is right. I should have been more careful."

He spoke matter-of-factly. She didn't think he realized that. He was so consumed with remorse that he missed how readily he accepted responsibility. It couldn't have been easy with Kayla's family against him, full of animosity and blame.

Mr. Jefferson's dislike didn't waver; he only became more empowered. A man like him fed off weakness, which he perceived in Brycen. The oddity of that struck Drury. Brycen? Weak? Someone needed to let these people know who Brycen Cage really was.

"Your problem is you think too much of yourself, of your abilities," Mr. Jefferson said. "You thought you could take her anywhere and keep her safe. Well, we all know that isn't true, don't we? You and that show have everyone fooled." He turned to Drury. "You should have hired somebody else."

"Brycen is the best for Noah's case," she said simply.

"And frankly, for a retired army colonel, you have a terrible attitude."

"Excuse me?"

Brycen looked at her with brief surprise before he covered it.

"Do you honestly believe Brycen meant to kill your daughter?" she asked the incorrigible man.

"Drury, don't," Brycen interjected. "It won't make a difference."

"He may as well have pointed a gun at her head and fired." Mr. Jefferson's retort supported Brycen's conclusion. Nothing Brycen said would change his opinion. But Brycen wasn't saying much. He certainly wasn't defending himself, not as much as he could. Was he afraid of appearing too arrogant? No. He agreed with this man. He was at fault for Kayla's death.

Mr. Jefferson believed taking Kayla with him when he knew a mad drug addict was after him had been a gross miscalculation, a deliberate risk to Kayla's life. Careless and self-centered. Brycen had a reputation as a rock-star detective. Yes, he was good at what he did. Yes, he had a popular crime show on TV. But Brycen was not a conceited man. She saw him as someone who'd rather avoid all those women who fawned for autographs and a fanciful date, but who treated them with respect and kindness.

"That's an awfully strong statement, Mr. Jefferson," Drury said.

"He didn't have to take her with him that day. But he did. And now Kayla is dead and he's living the good life, without a care in the world for my daughter."

He did have a negative view on marriage. But did that flow into his view on women to the point he didn't care what happened to them? Drury disagreed.

"He has a lot of gall showing his face around here again," Mr. Jefferson said. "You have no idea what kind of man he is."

His other daughter, Avery, had warned her about Brycen's dark side. Drury didn't see a dark side in Brycen. She only saw a secretive side. His ex-girlfriend's family not liking him because of her death didn't seem like enough to warrant keeping a secret. There had to be more to his relationship with her. And his relationship with her family. What had happened? For Kayla's family to harbor this much resentment—and for so long—there had to be a good reason. Not that Kayla dying wouldn't be enough of a reason. Dying in a car accident wasn't enough. Blame for taking Kayla with him when he shouldn't have. Blame for his arrogance. Had they known his view on marriage? Kayla had likely told them, which might be enough to bolster resentment. Still, ten years was a long time. Why couldn't Mr. Jefferson move on?

"Brycen is doing a valiant thing, coming here to help me solve my husband's murder," she said.

Jefferson smirked. "Valiant. Valiant only as long as it suits his needs. He refused to marry my Kayla. She loved him and he threw that love aside. She all but drowned in his selfishness. Until his recklessness killed her in the accident." He turned to Brycen, who didn't meet the man's angry gaze. "Every day I wish she'd never have met him. She'd still be alive if she hadn't."

The last of what he said didn't need to be so harsh, but Brycen did have a terrible outlook on marriage. Had Kayla experienced firsthand what it was like to fall in love with a man who would never fully commit to her? How sad.

But Mr. Jefferson was off base in judging Brycen.

Brycen hadn't intended to kill Kayla, and although he may never have married her or any woman for that matter, he didn't deserve a life sentence of blame.

"Kayla told me about how hard you were on her," Brycen finally said. "I didn't bring it up back when I lived here, after the accident. But she resented you for trying to mold her into your perfect idea of her. All she wanted was your approval for the things she did accomplish. She didn't want to go to college. She wanted to work for the Forest Service."

Drury inwardly cheered that he fought back.

"She couldn't make a living doing that. I tried to guide her to a better life, that's all. She knew I loved her." Mr. Jefferson's beady eyes grew fiercer with anger.

"She knew you would love her more if she went to college."

Now Mr. Jefferson visibly flinched. His relationship with Kayla must have been strained, and Brycen dug where it hurt most.

"You're still looking for someone else to blame for the things you regret in your relationship with her," Brycen said. "If that has to be me, then go ahead. Blame me."

Mr. Jefferson swallowed and Drury could feel his inner turmoil, the anguish over his regrets and his intense loss.

"I supported my daughter," he finally said, sounding choked. "I only wanted the best for her."

Brycen said nothing. The best hadn't been him.

"If she hadn't been with you, she'd still be alive," Mr. Jefferson said again, pain drawing down his eyes.

Still, Brycen said nothing, only met the other man's agony with stoic resolve.

Drury didn't approve of Mr. Jefferson's method of attack, but she sympathized with him. Maybe all he needed was a show of kindness. She reached out and took his hand, giving him a squeeze.

He turned to her in surprise, some of his suffering easing. With his defensiveness, few likely did offer a comforting hand.

"You be careful with this one." He slipped free of her gentle grasp and turned to Brycen. "We managed to move on with our lives after you left. Do the right thing. Go away and don't come back. Just…leave us in peace."

She watched him leave. What would it take for the man to overcome his bitterness?

Maybe Brycen was a little selfish, but not when it came to Kayla's death. He shunned marriage and kids and that might make him selfish. Had he led Kayla into a relationship he never intended to commit to? And then something else came to her. She could see why no marriage, but why no kids?

She watched Mr. Jefferson walk outside and cross the street, wiping his eyes. The father of a lost daughter still in mourning, a wound reopened with Brycen's return to Anchorage. She understood that agony all too well. But Mr. Jefferson and his daughter Avery seemed extreme in their reaction.

Drury faced Brycen again, who looked at her during her thoughts. She met his eyes a while, resisting the pull of attraction.

"What happened the night of the accident?" she asked.

Brycen's face never altered. He continued to meet her eyes. And when she thought he would refuse to answer, he finally said, "We were coming back from a trip to Colorado. We drove. It was a road trip. Late summer. Early fall. I introduced her to my parents and then we drove back. We stopped at all the touristy places. Yellow-stone. Jackson Hole. We took a ferry to Victoria Island and then from there to Anchorage. It had been snowing awhile, a cold spell moved in. Driving was treacherous."

He folded his hands on the table, his cup of coffee encircled by his arms. He lowered his head slightly, and then met her eyes again. "I wanted to drive her to my cabin. I had just bought it." His eyes drifted, memory taking him back into time. "We didn't make it. I noticed someone following us. He rammed into the back of me before I had a chance to lose him. When he couldn't drive us off the road, he started firing. I swerved to avoid either of us being hit and crashed into a tree. I saw Kayla unconscious, but the shooter approached the car. The drug addict. I got out and shot him. Then I pulled Kayla from the wreckage." He lowered his head again, this time lower than before. "But she was already gone."

He pinched the bridge of his nose.

They had more in common than she'd realized. Except she still felt there was more he wasn't saying. "And Kayla's family has blamed you ever since."

He nodded. "Her father tried to get the police to arrest me for murder. It was all very dramatic. He's a prominent figure here, at least in his corner of the city. He used media and his connections to try and destroy me."

But he hadn't been able to, because Brycen had his own reputation. Drury remembered hearing about the scandal in the news. She hadn't paid much attention back then. Around that time, she'd met Noah and they'd fallen in love. They married and then she had gotten pregnant with Junior.

"I didn't fight him. I didn't even have to defend my-self. Clearly I didn't murder Kayla. But he was overwrought with grief. Her mother and sister, too. I tried to understand why. That grew more difficult as time went on. After a year, I left."

And the incident had haunted him ever since.

"You think her father is so emotional just because he blames you for her death and his rocky relationship with her?" She couldn't get past the amount of time that had gone by.

"He blames himself. He hasn't found a way to come to terms with that. Maybe he never will. I pity him."

Which explained why Brycen apologized and didn't argue back when Kayla's family verbally attacked him. He felt sorry for them and, certainly, terrible for his involvement in causing so much pain. And most of all, his part in Kayla's death.

"You left because of Kayla's family?" she asked.

"No. Not completely. I left for me, mostly."

"Because you loved her? Kayla?"

"I did love her. Alaska as a whole became the source of bad memories. I left to start fresh."

He'd definitely started fresh, successfully so.

"Let's go." Brycen stood. "We'll come back later. I don't want to look too suspicious."

Nothing deterred this man from his job. Even a run-in with his dead ex-girlfriend's father. Or maybe he'd just gotten good at shutting out things that upset him.

"What are we going to do now?" she asked as they left the coffee shop.

"Send our own report to the deputy director who oversees Carter's unit. Maybe he'll order a search warrant of Carter's house and finances. Then I'd like to go back to Melvin's to look for anything we missed. There must be something."

"You're sure the deputy will get a warrant?"

"I can be persuasive."

"You haven't been persuasive with me." She couldn't resist the barb. Teasing though she might seem, she hadn't missed how controlled he'd been with her. They had hot chemistry at times, but he kept his cool. She needed to know if he felt as much as her.

He put his hand on her lower back, guiding her toward the vehicle. "Why do you need persuasion?"

At the passenger door she stopped and faced him. What she'd learned about him softened her, touched a deep place in her. She acted now on impulse, on instinct…on what her heart led her to do.

She slipped her hand along the back of his neck. "I'll show you." Going up on her toes, she kissed him.

Chapter 9

Still rattled from the kiss Drury stole from him, Brycen gladly alighted from DAI's helicopter. It had started to snow, falling lightly now, but the forecast said it would pick up by noon. The helicopter pilot had warned them they'd have to get back before then.

Drury kept smiling at him all the way here. This morning. In the helicopter. Her sparkling blue eyes held a knowing, intimate light. She haunted him. He wondered if he overreacted to a kiss. Ridiculous that he should feel threatened by Drury, her mouth, her softness. But she did do that to him. Her lifestyle and her beliefs didn't match his. She had a son. And she lived in Alaska. He swore he'd never come back here, that he'd move forward and live a life of abundance away from bad memories and people who despised him. And yet here he was, back in Alaska, reminded of bad memories, facing people who despised him. He wished he could resolve the latter, but Kayla's family would never let him. Part of Kayla's death would stay with him always, but he had succeeded in moving forward—up until now.

He felt in danger of being drawn back to Alaska, through a beautiful woman who fit him more than he'd like to accept right now.

Her mouth touching his, her hands gliding up his chest and around his neck, breasts pressing to him, thighs against him, replayed for his pleasure as he walked toward the Cummingses' home. She had tasted him in sultry urgency. He'd wanted to lift her and put her on the passenger seat and take her right there. He'd imagined it. He imagined it now, removing her pants and opening her just for him.

He didn't think she'd been prepared for the Kelvin scale heat they generated. She'd taken hold of his jacket as though to remove it and looked up at him in a daze. Both of them had lost their breath. He met her passionate face and barely managed to heed their location—in public. He could take her to the back of the SUV…

He imagined what that would have been like. The windows were tinted. He could start the engine to keep it warm inside—not that they'd have needed heat. They could have gotten completely naked. He could only imagine what she looked like without clothes. Stunning. Soft. Wet for him…

"You going in or what?"

He snapped out of that hot dream and realized he'd come to a stop at the door. Drury had knocked and rung the bell. No one was home. He turned the doorknob. It was unlocked. No one locked their doors here. And Melvin must not fear anything if he still left it unlocked. He went inside. Much of the place was similar to the last time they'd been here. He did a quick search, finding Evette's purse in the same place as before.

She hadn't been home at all. Ignoring that bad sign, he left the bedroom and looked for anything they might have missed. In the spare bedroom, he found a door in the wall that led to a crawl space. He'd seen it last time, but this time he opened the door and found a light switch, a chain hanging from a bare bulb. He turned that on and went still. To the right, a hole had been dug and stairs constructed. Crouching, he made his way to the stairs, seeing a horizontal door laying open with a padlock looped through a metal latch. The door could be locked from above. Going down the stairs, he found himself standing in an underground bunker of sorts that had been roughly constructed.

Drury stood beside him, wiping her hands on her pants. The stairs didn't have railings, only the dirt wall for support.

Not directly beneath the house, the bunker had been dug along the side. Shelves contained canned and dried food, several cases of water and other supplies someone might need in an emergency. A generator would power a refrigerator and stove, and three mattresses lining the far wall would provide a place to sleep.

"Melvin is a survivalist," Drury said.

"So it would appear." He looked for signs that Evette had been kept here and found none. Why hide a bunker? Or had Melvin hidden it? He couldn't dig through the concrete foundation of the house, so maybe he'd dug it here.

Drury used her phone to take pictures, a precautionary step in case the bunker had importance they had yet to realize.

Brycen's radio crackled before their pilot said, "Cage. Over."

He pressed the push-to-talk button on the wire connected to the radio clipped to his belt. "Cage here. Over."

"Weather is moving in fast. It's heavier in Anchorage and moving this way. I'm going to have to head back in fifteen or I'll be stuck here. Over."

Brycen climbed the stairs after Drury and looked out the window. The snow had picked up since they'd come inside but still had yet to accumulate on the ground. He didn't want to waste time and leave so soon. He needed to do a thorough search, and they couldn't see the ground through snow.

"We'll stay in town for the night. Come back for us when it clears."

Drury stopped and turned to him in surprise. It would be a bit of a hike into town, unless he found a vehicle to steal.

"Roger that. Over and out."

"Over and out." Brycen lowered his hand and said to Drury, "Weather is getting bad in Anchorage. The pilot needs to head back."

"Where are we going to stay? What about Junior?"

"Junior will be safe with your parents. I saw an inn the last time we were here." Hopefully one night wouldn't bother Junior too much.

"You mean the one where someone shot at us?"

"That would be the one." Grinning at her sarcasm, he guided her toward the door and was glad she didn't put up any fuss. Being raised by her adventurous parents had conditioned her to be flexible. He liked that.

Outside, they began to search the surrounding land, looking for any disturbed earth to indicate Melvin had dug a grave. Another reason why leaving wasn't an option.

"Let's search in a grid." He looked up at the gray sky, clouds sinking lower than when they'd arrived. "You take that side." He pointed to the other side of the house.

"Okay." Drury hiked that way and he started a grid pattern on this side.

By the time he met Drury in the middle, the snow had picked up in intensity. "Let's search the woods."

She headed for the trees and he spaced himself far enough from her to cover more ground.

"There's a path." Drury pointed ahead.

Brycen saw the bare dirt exposed between patches of snow and went there. They followed the winding path down a slope. Only a few snowflakes filtered down through the canopy. Logs had been placed to make stairs, shoring the dirt to the next level below. At the base of the slope, the forest ended at a clearing along the shore. A boathouse and dock looked empty.

"Does Melvin go on his fishing trips from here?" Drury asked.

"It's small for a commercial fishing vessel, but maybe he doesn't fish with a large boat." It was feasible that he docked here between fishing trips.

"There's a port on this island, isn't there?" she asked.

"Yes. I saw it when we went to town last time."

"Convenient access here, though," she said.

"Yeah. Convenient." He stepped onto the dock. The boathouse was open on the dock side. There were no boats inside, but it was big enough to fit two, with docking running along the outer sides except, of course, where the boats could float inside from the ocean. There was nothing here that triggered any suspicion, only tools and supplies necessary for maintaining a fishing operation.

"If Melvin has two boats, maybe Evette took one of them to escape," Drury said.

"They only have one vehicle. We'll check the town port to see if she went there."

"Most likely she would not stay on this island."

If she was still alive. "Probably not." Her family didn't even know where she was. If she'd taken a boat, she might have had what she needed on board or stopped on another island, assuming she was still alive and had cash. She'd left all her things at the house. Brycen didn't want to think about Evette being dead.

Drury took more pictures and heard the sound of a boat out on the water. She looked there with Brycen.

A man stood on deck of a moderately sized vessel, holding binoculars and looking at them. It wasn't Melvin. He lowered his binoculars and watched them as the boat passed; then, just before he disappeared behind some trees, Brycen saw him take out a cell phone.

"Come on." He turned. "Let's get out of here."

"Do you think that was someone who knows Melvin?"

"Hard to say." He didn't want her here if something went wrong like the last time they'd been here.

"How long before we reach town?"

"An hour." He looked up at the falling snow. In the trees they would be better protected. He wasn't worried about making it to town safely. He was, however, wondering who the man on the boat had called.

Drury hiked next to him into the woods. "I have a bad feeling about this."

So did he, but he wouldn't alarm her.

"Everything looks normal, but it feels abnormal," she said. "Dangerous."

He squinted up at the sliver of cloudy sky he could see through the canopy and then all around them.

"Do you feel it?" she asked.

Just then the sound of approaching motorcycles or ATVs grew louder. Brycen stopped with Drury. He exchanged a single look with her before taking her hand and running through the trees.

He looked back in time to see two ATVs pass along the path. The rider of the second saw them and stopped, veering into the trees. The trunks were too close, so he had to stop and get off.

Brycen ran with Drury deeper into the woods. He'd studied the map of this area before coming here, so he had a pretty good idea of where to go. Dense forest would prevent the ATV riders from following. They'd have to chase on foot.

As he ran, he spotted movement to their left. He tugged Drury behind a tree trunk just as a gunshot vibrated off the mountainside. He took out his pistol and aimed, seeing the man pop out his head from the cover of a tree. He fired and the man dropped.

Searching for other movement and seeing none, he took Drury's hand again. "Come on."

He ran with her through the woods, veering around trunks and glancing back. When Drury's breathing alerted him to her exhaustion, he stopped. Turning in a circle, scanning the trees while she bent over with her hands on her knees, he saw someone duck behind a trunk.

"Wait here. Stay behind a tree." When she lifted her

head and nodded, mouth open and drawing in deep breaths, he began his approach toward the man.

Keeping to the left and watching for any other movement, he made his way closer to the tree where the man had taken cover. The man looked out around the trunk and then started forward, toward Drury.

That would not do. Brycen began stalking the man, coming up behind him, quiet and ever watchful for anyone else in the area. Rushing up behind him, he hooked his arm around his neck and put his pistol to his temple. "Drop it."

The man dropped his gun.

"Who do you work for?"

"I'll nail my own coffin if I tell you that," the man said.

"I'll nail it for you if you don't. Just like your friend." He shoved the man, giving his shoulder a push so he faced him. With one kick, he sent the man smashing against a trunk.

The man gaped at him, stunned with the knowledge his friend had been killed.

"Start talking," Brycen said.

"Man, you might as well pull that trigger. I'm dead anyway if I tell you anything."

Brycen waited, unflinching.

"What they said about you is true," the man said. "But you can't win this."

Brycen saw and heard his fear. The man wouldn't talk. Whoever paid him must be far more dangerous than he or anyone realized. This wasn't just a one-man operation. Whatever the stranger from the Cummingses' house the day of the domestic violence call had to hide, it was big.

Brycen stepped closer, a head taller than the other man, who watched warily. "I'm going to let you go."

The man blinked a few times.

"But if you try to come after us again, I'll kill you."

The man stared at him awhile. "I believe you."

Stepping aside, Brycen said, "Tell whoever sent you I'm coming for them next."

The man walked away from the tree and then looked over his shoulder as he started to run.

Reaching a clearing, snow pelted Drury's face. They were probably five miles from town. By the time they reached it, they'd be frozen and caked in snow. She hadn't dressed for a long hike in this kind of weather. Her feet were cold and she felt the chill seeping into her core.

"We should have left with the pilot," she said, loud enough for him to hear over the wind, which had picked up considerably since he'd scared off the ATV rider. She still didn't like recalling how he'd capped the other one. He had no choice, of course. The man shot at them and would have killed them if he had the chance.

"We'll take shelter just ahead. I saw a place on the aerial photo."

"What place?"

He didn't answer, instead stopped at the top of the hill they'd been climbing. She came up beside him. Through the blowing, thick-falling snow, she saw a cabin. It had a propane tank and it didn't look like anyone was there.

She followed him down the hill and up the wood stairs to the front door. He tried the handle. It was locked. He looked around and found a rock after kicking through some deepening snow. Removing his jacket, he wrapped his hand in the sleeve and used the rock to smash one of the two front windows. Then he climbed inside and opened the door.

Drury entered the small cabin and shut the door, which didn't do anything to warm her. Though they were out of the wind, the chill had invaded the place and came through the broken window. She curled her fingers in front of her mouth and blew warm air on them while Brycen went to a three-sided fireplace in front of the door and between a small kitchen area and living room. A low rock base that bordered the fireplace ran all the way down the living room wall, wood stacked to the ceiling there.

She wandered into essentially a single room, on the left a rustic living room with an elk-patterned couch and recliner around a deep blue area rug and a bulky rectangular coffee table. No TV or any electronics. A painting of Mount McKinley, now renamed Denali, hung above the couch. Two kerosene lamps made charming light sources for the side tables, and some battery-operated lanterns on a shelf with several books. Beside the shelf, a back door had a window on top. Through that, snow fell at an angle with increasing wind.

Her boots tapped the rough wood floor until she stepped onto the area rug on her way to the bookshelf. She found many prominent titles. Hemingway, Charles Dickens, Faulkner and even Machiavelli. More modern titles from popular mystery and suspense authors took up the bulk of the space, however.

"Whoever owns this cabin must not be friends with Melvin," she said. "They're intellectual aliens compared to his Neanderthal ways."

He chuckled without pausing on the fire, which he

stoked to a pretty good roar. Standing, he went to the front door as the warm fire drew her.

"I'm going to the shed to see if I can find something to board up that window," he said.

"There's a shed?" She held her cold hands toward the flames. The fireplace opened to the kitchen, as well.

"Yes. I saw it from the top of the hill."

She hadn't. She'd been too preoccupied with her cold body. She warmed herself by the fire until he returned with a board, hammer and nails. She saw him on the other side of the broken window, concentrating on his task.

"It's a work shed," he said through the broken window.

People had to be self-sufficient here, so Drury wasn't surprised he'd found building material.

He put the board over the hole in the window and began nailing it in place. It covered the entire window and would be more than enough to keep the chill and the weather out until the owners returned. When he finished, he came back inside, pausing before closing the door to inspect the surroundings—what he could see in the building storm.

Seeing the snow billowing and drifting, she worried if they'd be able to get out of here tomorrow. Would they be sitting ducks for the next gunmen to come after them?

Closing the door, Brycen set the lock and stomped snow off his boots on the thick front entry rug.

Already the fire had chased away the chill.

"Those ATVs arrived fast," she said. They must have been watching the Cummingses' house, in particular the boathouse.

"Yes. They were prepared."

"Expecting us?"

"Expecting someone to come looking, yes."

She removed her jacket and draped it over one of two kitchen table chairs. A cabin made for two? The table had a clunky sort of shabby chic going, with fading paint revealing previous colors it had been painted. She doubted the style had been created intentionally. This had to be the real deal.

The kitchen itself didn't offer much in the way of conveniences, only a gas stove and a small countertop and a few cabinets in the narrow space. This cabin must be a getaway from noise and electronics. She imagined a middle-aged couple with no kids as the owners.

Brycen came to stand beside her. "No one is going to come after us here. Tonight or after the storm clears."

She looked up and over at him, amazed he'd noticed her nervousness, however subdued. "How can you be so sure?"

He only met her look awhile before going back to the fire to add more wood.

He'd killed one and nearly the other. Surely that one would not attempt to kill Brycen a second time. He'd fled, as he should.

She went back into the living room. There were no interior doors. The cabin consisted of this and the kitchen area. She went to the couch and felt for a handle down low and center. Sure enough, she found one. The couch extended into a bed, and it was the only one.

"There's dry food in here," Brycen said from the kitchen. "Crackers and sardines or tuna. Some chili, too. Ah. Noodles. Not much else. Cereal."

Dry without milk. They'd be fine for the night.

"Bottled drinking water," he said. "Some for cooking, too. Five-gallon jugs."

"Fantastic." With the light beginning to fade, she slid open a drawer in one of the side tables. Finding only some magazines, she went to the other and found a few lighters. Removing the glass cover from the first, she turned up the wick just a bit and lit the lamp. Replacing the cover, she lit the other kerosene lamp. The cabin had a soft glow now, together with the fire.

Hearing Brycen clanking things in the kitchen, she went to the bookshelf and chose one of the modern mysteries. Then she went to a trunk under the second window in front and opened it to find pillows and blankets.

She took out a light blanket and went to the couch, where she curled up in a warm cocoon and opened the book. With the crackle of the fire and Brycen whipping something up for dinner, she relaxed. Might as well make the best of this.

Alone with a man like Brycen…

That part gave her a pleasurable tickle.

Read.

She tried to follow the story, but the romantic setting kept interfering, especially when he appeared with a steaming cup of tea, the string and tag hanging out.

"It's hot," he said.

She carefully took it from him, putting the book open and faceup on her lap, and set the cup on the side table.

Catching sight of Brycen at the gas stove, only seeing his rear through the fireplace, she forgot the book and contented herself with the smell of ink, the warmth of the fire, and the man cooking dinner—something that had begun to smell rather good. He'd lit the kerosene lamp on the table, as well. While he'd done it so he could see, he'd also put plastic forks and bowls there.

The fire began to lose its robust flame, so she left the

book and blanket and fed it with more wood. Then the activity in the kitchen tempted more than the blanket and book. She brought her tea to the table and sat. He'd only used one pan to boil noodles and had washed and dried it in the removable bowls that served as a sink. Wind slapped snow against the kitchen window, a small square at the far end, all but one corner frosted.

Brycen opened the off-the-grid oven and removed a medium-sized tin pan full of a hot casserole. More delicious aroma wafted into the cabin.

"The homicide detective from Dark Alley can cook?" she asked.

Lips smiling, he spooned some of the mixture into her bowl and then his.

"Wow. The things you can do with canned food." He'd made a tuna casserole with tuna, peas, mushrooms, noodles and an Alfredo sauce. And was that a cracker crust on top?

She took a spoonful and blew to cool it off and then took a bite. "Delicious."

"Not bad." He ate with her awhile.

"We'll have to leave a thank-you note." She laughed at her quip.

"Actually I'll leave a business card. DAI reimburses for damage done to innocent people's property."

"Really? That could get very expensive."

"We get donations from wealthy families and organizations for abused or missing children. Kadin works hard promoting the cause. Not for noteworthiness, to keep the business thriving."

The agency was truly all about avenging the innocent. Impressive. She covertly admired him for more than his heroism while she ate. And then Junior popped into her thoughts.

She almost regretted enjoying this evening so much, when her son might be expecting at least a call from her. "Junior is going to think I left him."

He put his spoon down, having finished his meal. Now he looked at her as her revelation dawned. "I'm sorry. We should have gotten on the chopper. I should have thought more of Junior, that he might feel abandoned."

He'd noticed that about him? That he had abandonment issues?

"Finding Evette is important," she said. "What if she learned something about Melvin and the same people are now after her? She could be in hiding."

"Or she could be dead."

More likely she'd been killed. Drury's spirit and her hope in finding the woman alive dimmed. Whoever had been at the Cummingses' house during the domestic violence call must be very dangerous indeed and have many resources to carry out his hidden agenda. A woman like Evette would be no match against someone like that.

With her tea cooled, she rose and found that Brycen had kept a kettle of water warm on the stove. She put a new tea bag in the cup and poured water. Then she bobbed the tea bag, still plagued with worry over Evette's fate.

Brycen stood, taking their plates and dumping them into a trash bag he'd set out on the floor. Then he washed his hands, glancing at her. Drying his hands, he dropped the cloth and moved closer.

He brushed her hair back from where it fell over her shoulder. "Let's not think about that tonight."

His touch sent sparks shooting all the way to her toes.

"It's either that or Junior," she said, more to douse the passion stirring.

"As soon as the storm clears, the pilot will come get us. When he lands at the Cummingses' place, he'll be within radio range."

He sure thought of everything. "That's a relief." She turned with her cup in both hands, leaning against the counter beside the stove.

He put his hand on the counter, facing her.

"For someone who doesn't like kids, you sure seem conscientious of them," she said.

"It's not that I don't like them. You've accused me of that before."

He sounded genuinely put off.

"Well, you never explained why you distance yourself from them. Not lately, I don't mean that. You've been really great with Junior, but I sense something in you, something that pushes you away, or puts a wall up."

Looking at her face, his steely gaze going from her mouth to her eyes, she thought he'd brush her off the way he had done before.

But he did the unexpected and said, "The reason I quit the CPD is my last case was the murder of a child."

She felt her mouth drop open. "Oh, Brycen..."

"This murder was brutal, the child about Junior's age. I just couldn't do it anymore." His head lowered and turned aside with what must be a wave of sorrow. When he lifted his head and met her eyes again, she saw the depth of his anguish. "I've never told anyone this."

She put her palm on his cheek, wondering how he could be so profoundly affected by the death of a child he never knew. The murder of a child was horrific, but surely that one hadn't been his first.

"Did something like that happen in Alaska, too?" she asked.

He put his hand over hers, burdens of the past haunting him.

"You don't have to tell me."

"The accident did play a role. Kayla and I were returning from getting married when it happened."

He dropped another bomb with that statement.

"You married her?" She moved so he stood directly in front of her, resting her hands on his chest.

He put both hands on the counter on each side of her. "She understood how I felt. She agreed to separate if we grew apart."

Did he feel guilty about that?

"She must have hoped you never would." She needed to keep calm, to keep from responding to his nearness and the closeness that came from his revelations.

"We had a good relationship."

Only because she'd gone along with his philosophy on marriage. Did he realize that?

"She must have loved you," she said.

"I loved her."

In his own way, but Drury suspected he hadn't loved her as much as he could love a woman. If he had, he would see how wrong he was about marriage and what it could mean to a man and a woman. It made her reflect on her own marriage with Noah. She had loved him, but could she love another man more?

"Why didn't you tell anyone?" she asked.

He straightened from the counter, giving her more space. She took a deeper breath.

"Her family was already devastated. Hell, I was devastated. And given that her father didn't want her to be with me, I didn't see any point."

Drury didn't know what she'd have done. She could agree, what would be the point in telling Kayla's family that she'd married Brycen that day? She died.

The tragedy tugged at Drury. No wonder he'd left Alaska. And no wonder he'd started his show. He'd left painful memories, and the murder of a child explained so much.

"The accident wasn't your fault," she said.

"My line of work led to it," he admitted with brutal honesty.

Drury didn't agree. "So you think you shouldn't have gone into homicide?"

His look stayed locked with hers, but his harsh self-criticism softened and his eyes passed down over her mouth and back into her eyes. "No."

He sounded as though he hadn't thought of it that way before, that he hadn't been wrong to choose to fight crime. Everything that led him to become a detective rang true. He stood on the right side of the law and shouldn't allow choices criminals made to doubt his integrity.

"It doesn't mean you should move back to Alaska, although you should face what happened."

"That's a little impossible when Kayla's family is so against me. I did harbor some hope they'd moved on, but I can see that was useless."

"They're against you for the wrong reason. And personally I think they need to face what happened even more than you. Your leaving only enabled them to keep blaming you."

He put on a wry grin, a sure sign he'd rather not talk

about this anymore. "Yeah, but if I hadn't left I wouldn't have my show."

She smiled back, unable to resist. "With all that charm, the show would have found you anyway."

A low, deep and slow, sexy chuckle touched her most intimate senses. She felt the release of tension in him.

"You're not just smart, Drury. You see things in their natural light. You make everything seem so simple. Maybe it has been...all this time."

"Yeah..." She sank into his incredible eyes, and his mouth as he spoke. "Maybe."

Moving closer, he slid his hand into her hair at the base of her neck, bringing his mouth a breath from hers. "Why was it so easy to tell you that? I feel like weight has been lifted off me."

"Maybe it came naturally." She didn't think he'd come full circle in dealing with the way Kayla had died, but he'd just crossed a critical milestone on his path to letting go.

"Yes... Naturally." He pressed his lips to hers.

"Oh," she breathed against him, the sensation sweeping her away. She kissed him back.

Just when they both were about to lose control, he stepped back. "The fire."

Looking there, she saw the flames had dwindled and only the embers glowed red. Of course, they had to stay warm.

She put her hand over her still-tingling lips as he went to stoke the fire.

"If you have to go to the bathroom, I'll take you to the outhouse," he said as though needing to redirect urges. "It's behind the shed."

More than gunmen could lurk out there. Wildlife

posed a danger, too, except not in this storm. If she had to go, she'd hold it until morning.

"Yeah. Sure." She went back into the living room and moved the coffee table out of the way so she could make the bed.

Brycen finished with the fire and reached for the sofa handle, pulling out the mattress before she did. She went to the trunk and retrieved the pillows, and he lifted out more blankets. There were sheets at the bottom, as well. Drury started with those.

Brycen stood on the other side of the mattress and tucked in the first sheet. Drury kept looking up at him, watching his manly hands smooth out the top sheet. He looked up at her and the connection zinged. Try as she might to minimize the symbolism of the bed between them, it loomed with the night.

She tossed the pillows at the head while he shook out a blanket over the mattress. She helped him straighten that and two more, all the while unable to calm her warm awareness of him. They finished with the bed, now a cozy nest ready for the night.

He stood across from her. Neither moved. She felt awkward and he must, too.

Picking up her book, she removed her boots and climbed into the bed, making a valiant attempt to read.

He went to the fire and poked the burning wood, even though it didn't need stoking. He put another log on, bringing the fire to a rumble. When he could no longer use the fire as a distraction, he went to the bookshelf. Finding something, he sat on the recliner.

Outside, the wind whipped in a gust, almost shaking the cabin. But they were warm and safe and dry in this blessing of a cabin. In Brycen's note to the owners, she really would have to add a thank-you. They might not have made it to the village in this storm, which had arrived much sooner than forecasted.

The gust died and a steady wind persisted. She heard snow hitting the windows. Drury managed to read a little, and that made her tired enough to drift off to sleep.

When she next woke, darkness engulfed the cabin. The fire had dwindled to glowing embers. Brycen must have put her book on the side table for her.

Turning her head, she saw him lying beside her. The covers came to his chest, his muscle-sculpted arms on top. His face angled toward her, lashes fanned under his eyes, chiseled cheeks sloping to jawline, lips resting closed and beckoning her for another kiss.

She told herself the chill made her snuggle deeper into the covers and move closer to him.

His eyes opened a sliver and without hesitation, his arm opened for her. She didn't analyze why she positioned herself against him and put her head on his shoulder. The wind had eased. In fact, she didn't hear any blowing or snow hitting the windows.

"Are you warm enough?" he asked in a sleepy, deep voice.

"I am now." She lifted her head and met his equally sleepy eyes.

They stayed that way awhile, in the quiet, warmed by the chemistry they generated. Then Brycen lifted his hand and brushed her cheek. She closed her eyes briefly, overwhelmed with sensation and incredulous she could feel so much with just a touch. He moved and kissed her, softly, lightly. And then with growing ardor.

She slid her fingers into his thick black hair. This kiss could go on forever. She melted into the movement of his lips, meeting his leashed passion, savoring the promise of what would come. He didn't rush. Like fine wine, he sipped, tasted and enjoyed each second.

Gliding her hand down from his hair, she reveled in the muscular contours of his shoulder and chest, resting there as he took the kiss to the next level, deeper, more urgent. He'd removed his shirt before coming to bed last night. He rolled farther onto his side and she lay on her back. Rising up a bit, lingering over her mouth, he looked into her eyes while they caught their breath amidst the wonder of such a light, loving sensation.

Then slowly he touched her mouth again. Airy tingles spread with just that. She had never felt so connected to anyone, not intimately. So intangible, so incredible, she flew away, out of her body and into a realm of awe-inspiring buoyancy.

Again he took her gradually to the edge of control before ending the kiss. Reaching for the hem of her maroon, body-hugging cotton, polyester and spandex top, he pulled it up and over her head. She raised her arms and he tossed the garment aside. Pausing to admire her black bra embellished with lace, he got up onto his knees and unbuttoned his jeans.

"You do all the work," she said. "I'll watch."

He grinned his approval and pushed down his jeans, sitting to slide them the rest of the way off.

The chill in the cabin didn't bother her with the racing beat of her heart and the excitement of anticipation as he pulled the covers off her and unbuttoned her jeans. He knelt between her legs and looked up at her as he unzipped the jeans, his face close. He revealed her matching black lace cheeky panties and paused again.

"You're full of surprises," he murmured.

"Why? Because I wear sexy underwear?"

"Did you wear them for me?" His hot, light gray eyes lasered her.

She did on occasion wear sexy underwear, sometimes just for the heck of it, because it made her feel good. But lately she'd been wearing them every day. "Yes."

He pulled her jeans down. Drury lifted her butt to accommodate him. He left her panties in place. Tossing the jeans aside, he removed her thermal socks to reveal her dark pink toenail polish.

"I didn't think you were into such girly things," he said, kissing the top of her foot and moving up her leg.

"I look like a boy?"

He chuckled low and deep as he kissed his way up her calf. "No. You're a hot, sexy woman. I just didn't think you painted your toenails and wore lingerie." He stopped to look up at her. "I'm glad you do."

She smiled as he resumed kissing his way up her leg.

"What surprises do you have for me?" she asked. He still had on his underwear.

"You're going to have to wait and see." He kissed her inner thigh and toyed with the hem of the panties. Moving up more, he kissed the lacy material, warm breath penetrating.

"As much as I like these, they have to go." He slid the panties down, kissing her flesh before taking them off and dropping them onto the jeans.

He came down on his hands, looking at her. She shaved her hair there, leaving only a thin, close-cropped strip.

"Nice and tidy," he said.

"It's your turn." She pointed with her index finger and gave it a playful twirl. "Off with them." Never had intimacy been so easy. Natural. Playful as much as intense with passion.

He removed his underwear and now she had her chance to admire him. Clean-shaven and ache-worthy.

"All the ladies must love you," she said.

Without returning her humor, he lowered himself down and kissed her. "You're the only lady I want right now."

Right now.

She wouldn't let the thought take root. Right now was enough for her.

He unfastened her bra and it went the way of the other pieces. As he kissed her again and his hands ran over her breasts, she forgot any reason why she shouldn't allow this. How could she stop something so beautiful? Brycen had to feel it, too.

She gave in to yearning and felt his statuesque body from his shoulders to the tops of his thighs. She reveled in his weight on her and the first penetration. He moved slowly, touching her body as she touched his, looking into her eyes. Each treasured moment passed with care, not a second wasted. She felt, as he must, too, every sensation to its fullest.

When she could restrain no more, he finally took up a smooth rhythm, building force as sensation mounted, burning to the inevitable eruption.

It took Drury several seconds to float back down to the bed, the cabin, Brycen on top of her breathing beside her head. The real world.

The sound of a helicopter spared them any reflection, any thought on consequences.

Brycen climbed off the bed and dressed.

"How did he find us?" Drury asked, dressing on the other side of the bed.

He went to find his radio, digging it out of his jacket pocket. As he disconnected the wire, the sound of the pilot's voice filled the cabin.

"Cage. You there? Over."

"This is Cage. We're in the cabin."

"It's about time you answered my damn calls. I've been looking for you for two hours now."

He looked at Drury. "Sorry. I meant to radio you earlier."

Luckily the pilot couldn't see them or know what had transpired over the last two hours.

"There's enough room for me to land."

"Give us a few minutes."

"Roger that."

They'd dispensed of the formality of saying "Over."

He helped Drury fold the blankets and left the sheets in a pile on the floor so the owners would know they'd been used. Brycen folded the mattress back in the sofa and replaced the cushions. When Drury had the living room tidied, and books back on the shelf, she met Brycen in the kitchen, where he'd put away the pan and tied a trash bag and put it by the door. He took out a business card and used a pen from a kitchen drawer. After he wrote an explanation on how to get reimbursed for the window, Drury wrote a thank-you note.

Leaving the card on the table, she left the cabin ahead of Brycen, who carried the trash bag to the waiting helicopter. Once inside, Drury found she couldn't meet his eyes. What had just transpired between them? She no longer felt a connection to Noah. And she didn't feel safe with the feelings she had for Brycen.

Chapter 10

Back in Anchorage, Brycen drove Drury to pick up Junior. Sitting across from her on the long flight back had twisted him into knots. Last night had felt so great. He clicked with her so…mmm. No words could convey the passion in his mind. Looking at her, with her hair draped down over her breasts, long thighs in jeans and those stunning blue eyes looking at him with such intimacy, made his head swim. At first he'd responded in kind. How could he not? It had taken a while for the fantasy to wear off. But it had.

Then he'd started picturing the future.

He pulled to a stop in front of her parents' house. "I think we should leave Junior here."

She turned a surprised look toward him, her hand on the door handle. "No. He won't like that. Besides, he isn't any safer here than with us. If the people after us want to go after my family, too, they'll find my parents and Junior."

He couldn't argue with her. And maybe he'd feel better taking on the responsibility of protecting them both. The three of them together just gave him a case of dread. A bad feeling in the pit of his stomach. Making love with Drury had changed the dynamics for him. He could actually see himself hooking up with her. Practically that made no sense. What about his life in Chicago? Did he really want to leave that behind? Did he want to move back to Alaska? Drury had already said she wouldn't leave. Her home was in Alaska. Both of Junior's grandparents were there.

He didn't want to move back to Alaska. Even if he did, he wouldn't torment Kayla's family any more than he had to.

Pulling up to Drury's parents' house, he followed her to the door.

Drury knocked and opened the door. "Weird. They usually see me drive up."

Brycen heard Drury's mother say, "Your mother is here, Junior. Let go of me!"

"Oh." Drury rushed through the Victorian-style house, furnished with collectibles that revealed a long marriage and family in the same house for decades. No central color theme, just lots of memories made.

His parents had always kept up with the times. They never saved mementos. Only his school pictures were framed and set out on the bookshelf.

He waited in the living room, not comfortable with interfering in the drama unfolding down the hall.

"I don't *want* to go anywhere with you!" Junior shouted.

"Junior…" Drury's shocked tone drifted off.

"He kept asking where you were last night," her mother said.

He'd felt they'd abandoned him. His reactions were getting worse, not better. During a time when he needed stability the most, when he'd begun to overcome a terrible tragedy, his mother kept leaving him. Now he feared she'd leave for good—just like his father.

"We were trapped in a snowstorm," Drury said. "Now come on, you have to come with me."

"No, I don't!"

"Go with your mother, Junior. Your grandpa and I need to run some errands this afternoon."

"I can go, too."

He saw them as stable. His grandparents didn't leave him.

"No. You have to go with your mother," Madeline said.

"I don't want to go with her!"

Now instead of pushing just Brycen away, he pushed his own mother, lashing out. But that lashing was really a cry for help.

"You're only saying that because you're mad at me for not coming to get you yesterday," Drury said. "I'm sorry. If I could have come to get you, I would have. Now come on. Let's go." Her tone grew sterner with the last.

After a long silence, Drury appeared with Junior in tow. The boy's angry eyes zeroed in on him.

"Hey, Junior." Brycen tried for the light approach. "How about we swing by your Mom's house and pick up your PlayStation? We can go up to my cabin and play a few."

Drury gaped at him. He didn't really know what he

was doing. He just knew the child felt abandoned and lived in fear of being left by another parent. How terrible for him. He must never feel safe.

"Everything was okay until you showed up!" Junior yelled.

Everything had not been okay, not for the boy, but Junior didn't see that.

"You're not going to find whoever took my daddy." With that, Junior stomped toward the door, one of his superheroes in his hand.

Drury stopped him as he wrestled the door handle.

She crouched. "I would never leave you anywhere. I swear."

"Daddy didn't want to go, either. Someone made him!"

"No, he didn't, and someone did make him go, but Mommy isn't Daddy and no one is going to take me away, not even Brycen."

Junior looked up at him.

"That's true," he said. "Your mother won't leave you. Even if she's late or can't call, she'll come and get you. You have to trust me on that."

Junior contemplated him and what he'd said awhile. "You promise?"

"I promise." He stepped forward and ran his hand over the boy's head. "Sorry for not bringing her home last night, kiddo. It won't happen again."

The boy's anger eased. He stared up at him, some of the curiosity returning. Brycen felt a tug in his heart that reached all the way to his soul. He wanted to help Junior. He and Drury could tell him his mother wouldn't leave the way his father did but the boy didn't believe it. He had to start believing it.

Drury took his face with her fingers and moved his head to her. "Baby, nothing can ever take me away from you. I love you. I'll make sure nothing happens to me, okay?"

After a bit, Junior nodded, although with uncertainty.

Brycen's cell phone chimed and he saw it was the deputy director of the Alaska State Troopers he'd contacted about Carter.

"Cage."

Drury said goodbye to her parents, giving them hugs. Brycen held up his hand in farewell.

Robert did the same and Madeline waved.

"Mr. Cage. Deputy Director Chandler," the deputy said. "I received your report and found it very interesting, if not far-fetched. However, I did some digging and was able to corroborate some of your claims."

Brycen left ahead of Drury. "Have you arrested Carter?"

Drury closed the door and followed him down the sidewalk.

"Well, now, there's the rub. Carter's gone missing."

Brycen stopped walking. "Missing?"

Holding Junior's hand, Drury stopped next to him, searching his face and listening to his side of the conversation. Junior stared up at Brycen, absorbing other details. Brycen winked at him as the deputy continued.

"We searched his home and bank accounts. He did have some suspicious deposits and we've confirmed the report on the Cummingses' domestic violence call was forged. Additionally our IT records prove he worked on the report, even though he tried to delete any evidence of doing so."

Carter had something significant to do with Noah's

murder. Brycen stopped walking down the driveway, seeing Drury put her son in his SUV.

"I need the original report," Brycen said, walking toward the driver's side of the SUV.

"So do I. And I'm counting on you to find it. When one of our own goes rogue, I don't take it lightly. I'm not sure who I can trust around here anymore. I need you to expose what's going on and make sure it stops with Carter."

Brycen sat behind the wheel, feeling Drury watching him and now listening.

"Where was Carter last seen?" he asked.

"Here at the office. We think he left the building after you talked to him the last time. He knows you've got him. Good work, son."

Brycen appreciated the vote of confidence, but he didn't dwell on it. "You can say that when the case is closed."

"I will. I've got a file here for you," the deputy said. "It's everything Carter recorded doing after Noah's murder."

"We're on our way."

"One more thing," the deputy said. "Juanita Swanson came by asking for you. She said she won't talk to anyone else."

"I'll give her a call. Thank you."

He disconnected and started driving, his hands-free system switching to the speakers.

"Hello?" Juanita said.

"This is Detective Cage. I received a message you were trying to contact me. What can I help you with?" He looked in the rearview mirror and wondered if Junior should listen to this. Drury should, but her son?

"I have something for you. I can't tell you how I got it. But it's important."

"What is it?" Why couldn't she say how she obtained whatever she had in her possession?

"Not over the phone. Let's meet somewhere safe."

"Okay. The State Trooper Building in thirty minutes."

"I'll be there."

The deputy took them into his office and handed Brycen the promised file. He opened it. Junior sat in one of the chairs before the deputy's desk, arching his neck to look up at Brycen standing behind him and to his right. Drury leaned from where she stood on the other side of Junior's back to see what was in there, and he angled the file to accommodate.

"There isn't much," the deputy said. "He responded to a few calls. Phone record is in there. I found it peculiar that he contacted that coffee shop several times. I'd expect him to do so right after the murder, but the calls are regular."

Brycen looked up at the deputy and then searched for the phone records. He spotted the ones the deputy had highlighted. "Yes, that is peculiar." Not wanting to share his thoughts on the coffee shop, he leaned over and shook the man's hand. "Thank you for giving me a copy."

"This isn't a go-ahead to exclude this office from your investigation."

"Of course not. I'll brief you as we uncover things," Brycen said.

"Weekly, if you can."

"Weekly. I'll call you. Do you have a card?"

The deputy handed him one. Junior took the card and gave it to Brycen so he didn't have to lean farther.

"Thanks."

Junior looked proud to be of help.

"If I'm not available here, call my mobile," the deputy said. "I've got your contact information. I'll know it's you."

Brycen nodded once. "All right, then." Down to Junior, he said, "Time to go."

Junior got up from the chair and walked behind his mother for the door. They were late meeting Juanita.

"Mr. Cage."

He stopped and so did Drury and Junior, turning back to the deputy.

"I meant it when I said I don't know who to trust here. Whatever Carter's involved in, it's got to be way over his head. Noah must have been onto something, and I suspect the coffee shop is somehow linked. Noah didn't go there because he liked the ambience. He went there to investigate a lead. I'm sickened to think his partner may have been responsible for his death—or at least known something that could have spared it." He glanced down at Junior as though regretting speaking so frankly.

Brycen put his hand on the boy's shoulder as a show of support and nodded again. "My thinking exactly. This conversation stays among us." To Junior, he said, "Agreed?"

Junior nodded as though his participation mattered greatly. If this made him feel important, what harm could come to them? Even if Junior bragged with other kids at school, chances were nothing adverse would come of it.

Now the deputy nodded, once to Brycen and then to Drury. "I'm sorry, ma'am." And then to Junior. "Son."

"It's not your fault," Drury said.

"I consider myself partially to blame for not seeing Carter Nichols for what he was a whole lot sooner."

She gave him an appreciative smile and then steered Junior through the door.

Down in the main lobby, Brycen didn't see Juanita. It had been forty-five minutes since he'd spoken with her.

Drury went to the woman behind the counter. "Has a woman been here asking for Brycen Cage?"

The woman shook her head. "No one's come in since you arrived."

Drury looked at Brycen and he sensed the same alarm. He went through the doors to the parking lot, searching. Juanita wasn't there. She hadn't made it to the State Trooper Building.

"Something must have happened," Drury said.

"I know where she lives."

"Did that bad man hurt her?" Junior asked.

"We should take him back to my parents' house."

"No!" Junior wailed from the back.

She glanced back. "This is an—"

"It's okay," Brycen interrupted. "I won't let anything happen to him. I don't want to leave him anywhere. We'll just go and make sure Juanita is all right. You can wait in the car with him. If anything happens, drive away to safety."

Drury waited with Junior in Brycen's SUV. In the backseat, Junior made rocket sounds, blowing air through softly closed lips to create what must be an awesome rumble, flying his superhero high up into the sky. She loved seeing him like that, lost in a magical world where no one died.

Looking toward the house again, she began to get concerned. Several minutes had passed and still no sign of Brycen or Juanita. Just as she put her hand on the door handle to go check on him, he appeared with his cell phone to his ear, talking. Juanita didn't come out with him. She hadn't answered the door, either.

Lowering his phone after finishing the call, he walked toward the driver's side and got in. When he turned to her and shook his head, she understood. Juanita was dead. Someone had murdered her.

"Whatever she had for us is gone," he said.

That was what had taken him so long. He'd searched the house.

His cell rang and he answered. "Deputy. Thanks for calling back so soon. I've just been in Juanita Swanson's house." He looked into the rearview mirror at Junior.

He watched Brycen with intent curiosity.

"You'll need a crime scene team," Brycen said into the phone. "Get a ballistics expert." After a few seconds where the deputy must have questioned him he said, "Yes, I'm afraid so. I also found footprints in the snow in the back, so be careful when you arrive. Someone broke in through the bathroom window. The shape of the heel and curve at the toe look like what the troopers wear. Might want to get a mold of a clear print." He fell silent as the deputy spoke. "Let me know when the print analysis comes back."

He disconnected the call and put his phone down.

"You can tell that from looking at a shoeprint?" she asked.

"I made mental note of everything Carter wore the last time we saw him."

"Down to his shoes."

"Down to his shoes," he confirmed.

"You liked his shoes?" Junior asked.

Brycen grinned into the rearview mirror and drove into the street. "Yeah, I sure did."

Brycen wanted to stakeout the coffee shop but didn't think Junior would react well to being left again so soon, so he took him and his mother back to his cabin. Junior sat on the floor playing a video game.

"Has he always played so many video games?" he asked Drury. He probably shouldn't take too much of an interest in the boy. The raw memories meeting Junior exposed had somehow morphed into curiosity. Brycen realized he'd become fascinated by the mind of this young boy, and cared that he grow out of his difficult time.

Drury looked over at her son, her hands busy whipping together one of her kid dinners, early since they'd skipped lunch. "He played before, but...yeah, maybe he has spent more time doing that."

"It might be a crutch. A way of withdrawing from the world." A big, bad world a little boy might find too scary to cope with.

"Why don't you go play with him?" Drury asked. "Do you like video games?"

"I've played a few. I'm no *gamer*, though."

"Go play with him." She stirred the hamburger and turned the heat down. "It might help him."

Brycen helping Junior by spending time with him? Something tugged at his heart and soul, something that told him to do it.

"Okay." He went over to Junior.

"Have you played in dual screens yet?" he asked.

Junior looked up. "What's dual screens?"

"It's when two players play at the same time. Want me to show you?"

"Yeah."

Taking up a controller, Brycen sat on the ottoman in front of the couch. He navigated to show two screens and picked out a Disney Infinity character.

"Mr. Incredible?" Junior laughed a little.

Junior played Randy.

They flew and ran and crashed things until Mr. Incredible fell off the platform and Randy jumped off his.

"Good playing, kid," Brycen said.

"Let's play different characters."

"Okay."

Brycen went to the sofa. Seeing him do so, Junior got up and sat next to him. Junior leaned back against the sofa cushion, looking over at him. He probably missed times like this with his father. Brycen wasn't altogether comfortable filling *that* role, and aside from an inexplicable curiosity, he needed Junior to be strong enough to be left with Drury's parents when they needed to do potentially dangerous things. Staking out the coffee shop qualified as potentially dangerous enough.

He also didn't want to lead Junior to believe he'd stay. Because when he left—and he'd have to leave when he solved the case—Junior would be heartbroken and his abandonment issues might get worse. Brycen did not need that on his conscience.

He caught Drury's fond smile as she watched them play while she stirred the Sloppy Joe mixture. Ever since they'd arrived, there had been a real family kind of aura passing around. He let himself enjoy it, but too much might be hard on all of them.

"How come you don't have any kids?" Junior asked.

"How do you know I don't have any?"

"You didn't bring any with you."

Ah, the simplicity of a young mind. "I can't bring kids with me while I work. It's too dangerous."

Junior mulled over that awhile. "So, how come you don't have any?"

"I guess I haven't had the chance to."

Would he ever have kids? Or welcome a child not his own into his life? Try as he might not to, he couldn't stop wondering what would happen if he and Drury ended up together.

"I think you'd make a good dad," Junior said.

Stunned, Brycen could only search Junior's face for verification. How did a boy so young know such a thing? Had just a man's attention, doing father-son-related fun, given him that impression?

The innocence portrayed in his upturned face, smooth skin, slightly parted lips and healthy whites of his eyes surrounding blue, arrested Brycen. The sweetness.

Then those lips smiled big and his eyes rounded with happy excitement. "Do you wanna go play catch?"

Unexpectedness punched his chest. Junior both dredged up unpleasant memories and showed him what a wonder being a father could be. The latter held warm meaning for him. But concerned him for the boy's welfare.

He turned away briefly, and landed on the sight of Drury wiping a tear from her cheek.

Do something. He had to act. Despite the firestorm going on inside, he had to consider Junior's development. While his defenses told him to back away, his heart ruled.

"Yeah," he said, forcing a smile.

Chapter 11

Drury still couldn't believe her son had asked Brycen to play catch. She stood at the front window watching them, Brycen talking, instructing, while Junior occasionally caught the ball and mostly dropped it or completely missed the mark. The sun had slipped low in the sky and a chill moved in. That wasn't why Drury stayed inside. She didn't want to ruin this pinnacle moment for Junior.

Brycen had made leaping headway with the boy in such a short period of time. As a detective, he must seem like somewhat of a superhero to Junior. That and Brycen's sensitivity to the boy's abandonment issue must be the missing ingredients. While she had to push off some tinges of hurt that she—his mother—hadn't been able to provide this, the signs of improvement had to be celebrated.

Hearing the Sloppy Joe mixture in need of a stir, she

returned to the stove. The french fries smelled done, too. She took the fries out and prepared plates for all of them. Then she went to the door and called out, "Dinner's ready!"

"Aw!" Junior answered.

Brycen started toward the cabin. "Come on. We can play again tomorrow."

Never mind winter had set in. But of course, Junior had not been raised to pay heed to the weather. As a family they'd had barbecues in February.

She brought the plates to the table.

"Hang on a second." Brycen stopped Junior from sitting.

Her son faced him, all ears and eager to listen to anything his new idol would say.

"Can I talk to you about my investigation?"

"You mean my daddy?"

"Yes."

Junior nodded, three jerky ones.

"A lot has to be done to catch bad guys. They have to be found first, and then we have to catch them." He waited a beat. "That means I have to go places that aren't good for kids."

Now Junior lowered his head and Drury feared Brycen had lost him.

"Your mother, too, because it involves your dad."

Brycen's eyes lifted.

"People would probably take me off the case if I brought you with us. Besides that, I don't want you anywhere near danger. That's why we had to leave you the last time."

"But I can fight the bad guy, too."

"I'm sure you could, Junior. But right now I'm only

trying to *find* the bad guy. Once I find him, then that's when the fight begins."

Junior lowered his eyes.

"Junior?" Brycen was going to make him pay attention.

Her son looked up at Brycen with his sweet, innocent face, and, yes, with growing trust for the man who'd come along in his life.

"Your mother and I have to go to another one of those places tomorrow. A place where kids can't go. So we need to drop you off at your grandparents' house again."

Junior's face angled and his forehead crinkled into disagreement. "No. I don't want to go back there."

"It'll just be for the day," Brycen said. "Then we'll be back to pick you up. We'll play catch just like today."

When Junior continued to frown, Brycen said, "You can be my partner. My partners help me in my investigations."

Junior's scowl smoothed and unbridled enthusiasm burst all over his face. "I can go with you?"

"No. This is a different kind of partnership. You watch my back by staying with your grandparents. As long as I know you're safe, I can do my job. You'd be a big help if you do that for me."

Junior's enthusiasm crashed the way it had appeared.

Brycen pulled out a pin from his jean pocket. It was a sheriff's star, a trinket he must have gotten somewhere. Drury had no idea where. Maybe he'd had it here. Maybe he'd ordered it online and had gotten it in the mail today. However he'd done it, Junior's face lit up again.

Brycen pinned the star to Junior's flannel shirt. "You're officially my partner now. And as my partner, you have to do your share of the work. Are you ready to do that? Can I count on you?"

Junior looked up from the star, his tiny fingers rubbing the grooves and points. "Yes."

Giving the boy's head a rub, he smiled and said, "Thanks."

When Junior bounded off into the living room and picked up one of his superheroes—Andy from the cartoon *Toys*—Brycen stood and faced Drury.

"I hope you don't mind," he said almost bashfully, or maybe she saw hesitation.

"Mind?" She laughed wryly. "Why would I mind a man helping my child? I haven't seen this much change in him in a year."

"Well…I won't be here indefinitely." He scratched the top of his cheek, more of an uncomfortable reaction. He had reservations over how much he connected with the boy. Brycen out of sorts didn't jibe with the tough detective who stirred her passion so easily.

"A little attention will go a long way. As long as he doesn't start expecting you to stay, your attention will only do good." She didn't say she wished she could have been the one to bring her son out of his grief—or on his way to doing so.

His soft smile faded as he turned to Junior, still lost in a glorious, joy-filled imaginary world, buoyed by a few hours of one-on-one time with a heroic male figure. Drury could feel his thoughts. The worry over how leaving Junior would set the boy back. The worry—possibly his biggest—that he'd grow too attached.

She wasn't fooled. His inner programming convinced him to leave. Alaska held too many bad memories. Made him feel dragged down. Backward. His show made him feel lifted and moving forward. Progress in a positive direction. Who wouldn't make the same decision? No one intended to take a step backward in life. But would staying really be a step backward?

He'd accomplished a lot in Chicago. She couldn't call that a mistake—much less his successful TV show—but that didn't mean returning to Alaska would be negative. Maybe he needed to face the tragedy that had driven him away. Maybe enough time had passed. The timing could be right for him to grow.

Drury with her long, sleek leg up with her foot on the dash provided an alluring distraction during the boring wait for something to happen at the coffee shop. When they'd gone in for coffee, he'd planted a bug. Pretending to use the bathroom, he'd sneaked in the back and stuck it above the doorway to the office. They'd drunk coffee and observed awhile, then come out here, parked on the street around the corner. The deputy had taken care of a phone tap.

The skinny jeans Drury wore showcased her legs and butt. Her long, silky hair swooped down and back over her shoulder as she played a game on her smartphone. Her petite nose sloped in perfect harmony from her brow to her mouth. Long, dark lashes shaded her stunning blue eyes. She moistened her full lips and the movement transported him back to the snowstorm and the different kind of fire they'd ignited into flames.

"Aw," she said when her phone made a few dinging sounds. Then she turned her beautiful face to him. "I failed to feed my monster candy."

Her smile faded as she noticed the way he must have looked.

Then his phone chimed and broke the fleeting moment. He wasn't sure if he was glad or disappointed.

"Detective Cage,"

"Detective. Deputy Chandler."

Brycen pressed the speaker button so Drury could hear this.

"I've got some news on the shoeprints you found," the deputy said. "The lab made a mold and we've compared it to Carter Nichols's shoes. We obtained a search warrant of his home. He had two state trooper–issue shoes in his closet. One of them is a match for type and size. Even more, the pattern of wear is also a match."

Not enough to slam-dunk a charge, but a piece of evidence toward that end nonetheless.

"He must have gone home after killing Juanita," Brycen said.

"He did. There are things missing from his house. His undergarment drawer was open and empty except for one torn pair. We found no other undergarments in the house. He had a luggage set but the midsize suitcase is missing. No car keys. No wallet. I just received a report from his bank. He withdrew his money this morning. Three hours ago."

Carter had run.

"We know he didn't board any flights. I've got every available trooper looking for him and put out a statewide alert and notified the Canadian Border Patrol."

"Good." But if Carter had withdrawn his money three hours ago, he had time to make it across the border before law enforcement caught up to him. That was assuming he even went to Canada. He could have traveled to Washington State.

"Have you alerted the ferry services?"

"In Washington, yes."

"Good." Carter could have arranged for false identification, though. Their chances of catching him weren't promising, not today anyway.

The sound of a phone ringing over the receiver of Brycen's surveillance equipment made him cut the call short with the deputy.

"Gotta go," Brycen said. "Coffee shop owner is on a call. Do a background on him."

"Will do. Report when you can," the deputy said.

Brycen disconnected.

"What are you doing calling me on this line?" a man's voice said through the receiver. "You put me and my store in danger."

"I had to. The cops are closing in, man," the caller said. "You have to lie low until you hear from *el jefe*."

"Is that Carter?" Drury whispered, typing into her phone.

It did sound like him.

"I've got to go to the Tennessee House today," the coffee shop owner said.

"I wouldn't go anywhere near there for a while," the man on the other line said. "I mean it. Lie low. I'll be in contact when I can."

"Carter?" the coffee shop owner said. And then, "Damn."

The call ended and Brycen heard only the sound of the man moving around in the office along with the moderate flow of customers buying coffee and talking in the background.

"John Pulman," Drury said, reading from her phone. "Came to Alaska twenty-four years ago with his wife and two sons. They're grown now and he and the wife divorced three years ago. He opened the coffee shop soon after moving here. Seems to have been successful."

"Let's see what the background reveals."

The sound of a door opening and closing preceded a car starting in the back of the shop.

"Get down," Brycen said, slouching low in his seat.

Drury slouched, too, and a moment later, a car passed them. Straightening, Brycen pulled out into the traffic after John Pulman. Clouds had set in again. The forecast called for another several inches later today.

John made a left at a light. The light turned red as Brycen made the turn. He saw John go right a few blocks down. He sped up and made the turn.

"Where did he go?" Drury searched along with him.

They'd reached a below-average neighborhood with some commercial businesses mixed in. Brycen spotted John's car parked in a circle driveway of the Tennessee House. The large white Colonial house with black trim had been converted to a hotel. A small parking lot in the back wasn't very full.

Brycen parked and he and Drury walked to the front entrance. Inside, mosaic red carpet and dim lights gave a different impression than from outside. A chandelier hung from a high ceiling in the lobby. A curving staircase might once have been grand, but now a dirty path ran up the center of carpet and the chipped wood railing had lost some spindles. The smell of stale beer wafted from a lounge filled with dated wood tables and chairs and more mosaic red carpeting. The bar looked equally used and poorly maintained, running all the way along the far wall.

"Can I help you?" A woman appeared from the lounge

and took what must have been her place behind a short counter angled in the lobby, the staircase behind her.

"We're here to talk to John Pulman," Brycen said.

"Oh…he isn't here right now."

"Yes, he is. We saw him drive up." He brushed the side of his jacket to reveal his pistol as he retrieved his wallet and showed her his business card. "I'm Detective Cage. Why don't you ask him to meet us in the lounge?" He gestured toward the lounge.

The woman looked from there back to him. "He's already in there."

Brycen nodded once. "Thank you."

Drury followed him and he spotted two men and a scantily clad woman sitting at a corner booth. Brycen recognized the man across from the other two from the coffee shop. John Pulman.

The woman with the other man moved her chest, brushing breasts barely covered by sheer material against the man's arm. She ran her hand down his torso.

An Asian woman in a short skirt appeared through a double swinging door and went behind the bar. "Can I get you something?" Her tight black top dipped seriously low and her nipples were clearly discernible. Another look at her face and he could tell the woman had applied heavy makeup to hide a bruise under her left eye.

"Ah… Brycen?" Drury said.

"Stay close." While he'd like nothing more than to rescue the woman behind the bar, he had to take first steps.

He stopped a few feet from the table, watching the two men for signs of either one going for a weapon.

"John Pulman?" he said to the one he knew was that man.

He was lean and dressed business casual in tan slacks

and a white shirt that sported a coffee stain, his buglike hazel eyes all but popping out from beneath a high forehead and stringy, thinning hair.

"Who are you?"

"Brycen Cage. This here is Drury Decoteau."

The man slowly looked to her, a brief stillness overtaking him a moment. He understood now.

"You a cop?" he asked Brycen.

Drury hooked her arm with his, moving closer. This was no place for a woman like her. He could feel her distaste and discomfort.

"I'm a private investigator." He handed him a card. "Dark Alley Investigations."

A stillness came over John as he took the card. Without looking at it, he put it down. From the entrance to the lounge, two more women appeared, one a slender black woman, the other another Asian woman, both dressed in skimpy clothes designed to entice a man. The bartender pretended to be busy wiping the surface, but she kept looking over at Brycen as he spoke.

"You know," Brycen said, "when I found out Noah Decoteau was shot outside a coffee shop, it didn't occur to me that the owner might be involved."

"I wasn't involved."

"Maybe not in the actual killing of a respected Alaska State Trooper, but you're definitely involved." He put a deliberate amount of certainty in his tone.

"Oh yeah? And what, exactly, do you think I'm involved in?"

Brycen moved his gaze over the lounge and then back to the table, seeing the bartender wearing a slight but smug smile. The two who'd appeared at the entrance must have just peeked in out of curiosity. "What is this place? A brothel?"

John grunted a laugh. The other man laughed with him as though it were a joke and the woman beside him smiled as though she felt forced to. She didn't seem to be here out of choice. That alerted Brycen to consider possible reasons why. A beautiful Mexican woman about twenty years old, she didn't strike him as the type who would need to resort to this line of work.

"This is a hotel," the man next to her said. "Nothin' going on here that concerns you."

"A coffee shop and brothel make an interesting combination. What I'm wondering is how you thought you could hide behind the facade of a hotel."

"If you're not a cop, you have no jurisdiction," John said. "So unless I need a lawyer, I'll kindly ask you to leave."

"What's your relationship with Carter Nichols?"

"Who? Never heard of him."

"He's the one who warned you not to come here today." He injected more deliberate certainty into his voice.

The man's gaze narrowed. "You spying on me? Is that legal?"

"Probably not for a cop."

Drury dug her fingers into his arm.

The Mexican woman sat up, moving away from the man beside her.

John's gaze grew less narrow. Brycen didn't have to follow any rules. He made his message very clear. These two had better not mess with him, and if they were forcing these women against their will to perform as prostitutes, he'd come down on them with everything he had.

"Carter Nichols?" he repeated.

John just stared at him.

"Why would he warn you not to come here today? To make sure your illegal prostitution activities weren't exposed? Or something else? Something…say…" He acted as though he were pulling it straight from the air. "Something to do with Melvin Cummings?"

Drury's fingers dug harder.

John's single blink and slight flinch confirmed what Brycen suspected. The man across the table turned now-apprehensive eyes to John.

John put his hand up. "Look. I own this building. Pete here pays the rent and runs a perfectly legitimate hotel business. Maybe you'd like to stay here sometime?"

"I'll pass. But I will be back." With that, Brycen steered Drury toward the exit. Without turning, he said, "Whatever you're doing, I'm going to find out, John Pulman."

Outside, he and Drury got into the SUV.

"That was scary."

Brycen didn't answer. He saw the Mexican woman run out a back door. She glanced back as though she'd sneaked away. At the SUV, she got into the backseat.

"I don't have much time. If you are who I think you are, you have to get us all out of there. It is not a hotel. You were right. It is a brothel. We were all brought here with lies. We were promised jobs in America and instead we were forced to come here. There are guards all the time. I got out now because John is in there freaking out and talking to them all." Her chest heaved.

"You're coming with us." Drury looked at Brycen. "We can't let her go back in there."

"No," the woman said. "I will be all right as long as I

know you are going to stop them and we will all be free. If I leave, they will be warned. They will know I talked and you will never catch them. They will take the others away from here and how long will it be before you find them again?" She shook her head. "I will go back in."

"It's a human trafficking operation?" Brycen said, incredulous.

The woman nodded. "They're going to miss me if I'm gone much longer."

"Who is behind the operation?" Brycen asked.

"I do not know. They keep us locked up in there. John is not the one running it. He only runs this house. They bring women in by boat and then take them to wherever they are going to force them to *work*."

She opened the door. "That is all I know. Please. Help us." She put her hand on Brycen's shoulder. "You are a miracle."

"I'll get you out of there as soon as I can. Be ready. It may be as early as tonight."

"Okay." The woman smiled big and bright. "Tonight." She closed the door and ran back to the building.

"What if someone noticed her out here?" Drury asked.

Brycen scanned the windows and the back door, seeing the woman go inside and then peek out with a thumbs-up.

"She made it." Drury sagged back against the chair. "You have to get them out of there tonight."

He'd already taken out his phone.

Back at the troopers' building, Brycen paced from one end of the conference room to the other. A top-ranking agent from the Alaska FBI field office sat in one chair. They had several others on the phone, including Kadin

Tandy. He'd been instrumental in ramping this up the chain of command and getting the attention Brycen needed. As an ex–New York homicide detective and the father of a murdered daughter who had inspired him to fight for the innocent, the man had people in high places who listened. He ran the politics at Dark Alley, for sure.

Brycen had just finished briefing everyone on the case and all he'd uncovered.

"This is incredible," the man attending in person said. "We have to move in now."

"I was hoping you'd say that," Brycen said. "We have to get those women out of there tonight. Before they move them."

"Someone might know who's behind this."

"John Pulman knows. Carter Nichols knows. The man renting the hotel, too."

"Get a wanted bulletin out on Nichols," an agent on the phone said. "He should be easy enough to track down. Start with Pulman's phone records. Nichols made a call to the coffee shop today. Trace it."

"I'm on it," another agent on the phone said.

"And get a team together. Olsen. Can you manage that on your end?"

"Yes, sir," Agent Olsen said, jotting a note down.

As a non-law-enforcement person, Drury hadn't been allowed to attend this meeting. The lead FBI agent had decided she should wait this one out. That had been all right with her, though. She and Junior would meet him at the cabin. He'd catch a ride from someone.

The meeting ended and now Agent Olsen would assemble a team to rescue the women at Tennessee House. All in all, Brycen would call this a pretty good day.

Chapter 12

Drury listened with Brycen as the raid commenced at the Tennessee House. He'd arranged for her to accompany him in the central command room the FBI had set up. An IT team had the comms and surveillance online with rapid expertise. No ordinary police unit could have done this. Without Brycen and his connection to Dark Alley, the raid would have taken a lot longer.

An agent from New York had arrived late in the afternoon, and after Brycen's briefing he'd organized local teams and instructed them on the sequence of the operation. He'd obviously done this sort of thing many times before. Now he leaned against a wall next to a large whiteboard that still showed his drawings, listening with the rest of them as the team of agents and a few select troopers approached the hotel.

"Elvis is in position," a voice came over the radio. From the whiteboard, Elvis had the front entrance.

"Graceland is ready. On your mark, Elvis." That team had the back entrance. There were no side entrances, only windows.

"Mockingbird one and two are standing by." Those were the agents inside vans on the side and slightly down the street in the front.

"Roger. Beale Street is in position." Those were the snipers.

"Elvis is going in."

A bang followed by an explosion of a smoke bomb crackled over the radio.

"Graceland is in! FBI! FBI! FBI! Nobody move!"

Shouts erupted, men startled to be caught by armed black-clad men. Cries of women joined in. Bluesy music playing in the lounge eerily fit the theme of the team call names.

"On the floor! Spread your arms and legs!"

The cries eased into fast-speaking women. Some spoke English. Some Spanish and dialects from Asia that Drury couldn't decipher.

"You. On the floor. Now!"

A crying woman must have run to one of the lead agents. "Are we free? Are we free?" she sobbed.

"You're free," the agent said. "You never have to live with these animals again."

She cried harder and kissing noises could be heard. "Thank you. Thank you."

"You're safe now," another agent said. "All of you, please leave through the front door. There's a van waiting for you."

Happy cries and talking voices faded as the women left the house.

"Grand Ole Opry, we've got the Pigeons."

Cheers erupted in the room. Drury's eyes stung. Women imprisoned and forced to do awful things against their will were prisoners no more. She looked over at Brycen. All because of him. She found it difficult not to succumb to hero worship.

He caught her look and smiled a little, glad like her that the raid had gone smoothly.

A trooper appeared in the doorway. "Sir," he said to Brycen. "John Pulman has been arrested. He's in interview room one."

Brycen held out his hand to Drury, indicating she should go with him. She took his hand and he helped her up. Then she followed him out of the room, smiling at the lead FBI agent and noticing he wore a wedding ring. Lucky lady.

He smiled back with a nod and a salute.

Down the hall to the windowless interview room with pale green walls, Drury went into the side room that still had the one-way mirror even though the interview room had been upgraded with cameras and recording capability.

John sat at the table facing the door. When Brycen entered, his eyes did a half roll and he shook his head.

Brycen took the chair across from him. "Do you need anything? Water? Candy? I'd offer you a cigarette, but there's no smoking allowed in the building."

"I don't smoke."

Leaning comfortably back, Brycen took his time going forward. His big frame dwarfed John's, and his presence filled the room. Drury couldn't tell if John noticed. He did a fine job of concealing any thoughts or fears, which he had to have, being arrested for serious crimes like prostitution and human trafficking.

"Did you bring those girls in by boat, John?" Brycen finally asked.

"No."

"Who did?" Smooth, how he swooped in and planted that question. John had asked for a lawyer, but he'd answered Brycen's first question.

"I want a lawyer."

"I might be able to work a deal for you if you tell us who brought those girls here against their will."

John smirked. "I'm a dead man if I tell you that. In fact, you're already dead. I don't care how much of a hotshot you think you are. You're a dead man. Me? I want a lawyer. I ain't telling you nothin'."

"So you do know... You know who brought those girls in."

"Lawyer."

Brycen leaned forward with his elbows on the table. "I don't think I'm a hotshot, John. All I know is I'm going to find whoever forced those women to work for your tenant. Just like I found you. That's what happens when people break the law. They end up with a distinct disadvantage against people like me. You're disadvantaged. Your boss is disadvantaged. Me? I'm not disadvantaged. I'm not going to jail. You are. You could make your sentence better if you cooperate."

"I'm nothing compared to what you're up against. You're a fool. And you're only one man. There's nowhere you can hide now. You've screwed yourself. You should never have gone to Tennessee House."

If the man who'd delivered the women to Tennessee House was that dangerous, wouldn't he already be on the FBI's radar?

"Who is he?" Brycen asked. "Give me a name."

"Lawyer. I ain't talking."

He wouldn't. Drury could see that. He feared the human trafficker more than the law.

Brycen stood. "All right. Have it your way." He went to the door and knocked. "I'll do what I can to get you the stiffest sentence the law can allow." He glanced back as the door clicked opened.

John didn't budge. He'd made a decision to align himself with someone dangerous. Now he had to remain aligned.

Brycen left the room and Drury joined him in the hall.

"How many human trafficking organizations have operations in this area?" she asked.

"That's hard to know. Human trafficking is a tens-of-billions criminal industry."

"Yeah, but certain criminals must stand out."

"Yes. But does ours?" He stopped at the exit. "Let's go get Junior."

"Maybe we should leave him at my parents'. If this guy is as dangerous as John indicated, I don't want him near us."

"All right. We'll talk to him, though, so he understands."

She smiled. "Of course." He sounded like a father figure. She wondered if he realized what her son had done to him.

She'd rather not think about what Brycen had done to *her*.

Early the next morning, Brycen and Drury left the hotel to go talk to Junior. Media vans waited out front. Normally he'd welcome them. Press time made for good, free advertising, but now they'd only draw unwanted attention. The human trafficker could track them.

"How did they know to be here?" Drury asked.

"Someone talked." They'd finished with the raid so late last night that going to the cabin would be a waste of time. "I saw a woman leaving the bar recognize me. I thought she might have had too much to drink, but apparently not." The raid had gone straight to the news after it happened.

Reporters rushed from the vans and questions fired at him.

"Any comment on the raid, Detective Cage?"

"Is it true you tipped the FBI on a human trafficking ring here in Anchorage?"

"How is the human trafficking bust related to Trooper Decoteau's murder?"

"Mrs. Decoteau, how satisfied are you with Dark Alley Investigations?"

"Very."

Brycen put his hand on the small of her back and ushered her through the crowd.

"Will this story be featured on his show?"

Drury turned away from that reporter.

"Is John Pulman behind the trafficking ring or is the man who rents from him?"

"We can't comment yet," Brycen said, opening the passenger door for Drury.

She looked out the window as cameras flashed and recorded. Brycen drove off.

"I'm not sure which is worse to deal with, the press or homicide cases," she said, letting a big breath go.

"When this is all over, you'll have quite a story to tell," he said, the words feeling automatic. Before coming here and meeting her, he'd have jumped at the chance to get her on his show. Dropping subtle hints like the one he'd just spoken would have felt productive. Now it felt… empty. He couldn't figure out why.

She didn't respond right away.

"I don't understand the appeal, Brycen. Why do you like the publicity? You don't really seem the type…the celebrity type. You wouldn't even talk to the press back there."

Now he had to take some time to respond. "Working active cases is a lot different than showcasing solved cases." Obviously he had to keep certain facts of an active investigation closed to the public. But she'd noticed what he had—a change in him. For the first time in a decade, he questioned whether Chicago was still good for him. Was he still running away from what had happened here in Alaska and was he ready to face it head-on now?

Kadin was right. Brycen was born to be a detective. He had run from the daily grind of homicide. He needed a break. Working Noah's case had reawakened what had driven him to become a detective in the first place.

But was he ready to give up his show? However he'd gotten there, he did enjoy it and he was successful. That counted for something.

Drury counted for something. And Junior…

Butterflies of apprehension tumbled in his stomach as he pulled up to Drury's parents' house. Even more so when Junior came charging through the front door with a giant smile, running toward the SUV.

Brycen got out and heard him talking excitedly to Drury.

"You were on the news, Mom!"

She crouched for a hug. "Easy there, Tonto. It wasn't so great."

"Yeah, it was!" Junior went to Brycen, who'd come around the front of the SUV.

He froze when Junior wrapped his arms around him, hugging as he had his mother.

"Can I go on the news with you?"

"Maybe after we catch the bad guy." He kept his demeanor light, not giving away his inner trepidation. Maybe this was where he needed to draw the line. Junior had begun to come around. He shouldn't start letting the boy hope they'd be a family unit for good.

"Speaking of bad guys." Brycen crouched to be more on his level. "Your mom and I stopped by to talk to you."

Junior looked back at his mom. "You're leaving again."

Drury moved closer, putting her hand on his shoulder. "Only because Brycen is very close to catching the bad guy and it's too dangerous for you to be near him."

"But you're near him and the bad guy was caught. It was on the news."

"The one I'm after is still out there," Brycen said. "Your mother will come back for you when it's over."

Junior faced him with downturned mouth. "What about you?"

"I can come with her. But when the case is closed, I have to go back to Chicago."

"But... I don't want you to go."

Brycen didn't know what to say. He couldn't make promises. He couldn't say he'd call. He couldn't say he'd come to visit. What good would that do?

"He'll always be your friend, sweetie," Drury said.

Junior didn't seem to understand what that meant.

"You'll always be my partner," Brycen said. "I couldn't have done what I did without your help. Now I need you to keep up that good work, okay?"

Junior thought it over a while and then reluctantly nodded.

Brycen had to smile. The kid was sure cute. More than cute. He tugged at his heartstrings too much. Leaving wouldn't be easy.

In the parking lot of the trooper building, Brycen received a call from the deputy.

"Where are you?" the deputy asked.

"In the parking lot on the way inside."

"Well, don't come in. I thought you'd like to know Cora Parker was taken to the hospital the night after Juanita Swanson was killed."

Brycen stopped walking. "What?"

Her case had nothing to do with the trafficking ring.

"She was shot. Preliminary analysis suggests the same gun was used in the Swanson case."

Brycen cursed. "What the hell…?"

"What is it?" Drury asked.

"Cora was shot. She's alive. In the hospital."

"She's unconscious and in critical condition," the deputy said, expanding his explanation.

Brycen leaned his head back and shut his eyes. What could the waitress have possibly known that would threaten Carter?

Then something dawned on him, sharp and sudden. He straightened his head and fixed his gaze on Drury. Her eyes searched his in question.

"She said someone interrupted Carter the last time he

went to see her," he said. "She said the man seemed to have something urgent to say."

"So?" Drury said as though he was only talking to her. He was only talking to her.

"That doesn't mean—"

"Carter left the restaurant." Brycen cut off the deputy, still talking to Drury. "He wouldn't talk to him there, in front of anyone." That suggested a secret conversation. What secret conversation would Carter have had that was urgent and with a strange man?

"Cora saw him," Drury breathed. "She might be able to identify him."

"It's got to be our guy," Brycen said.

If Cora could identify him…

If she didn't die before doing so…

Chapter 13

The deputy called to inform them that Cora had awakened at the hospital. Drury reached the room door after Brycen. The deputy waited outside.

"Have you talked to her?" Brycen asked.

The deputy shook his hand and said to Drury, "Mrs. Decoteau."

"Hello." She found him very personable and polite and a real dot-the-I-cross-the-T kind of man.

He turned back to Brycen. "Not yet. I introduced myself and told her you were on the way."

Drury presumed the deputy preferred Brycen do the questioning. He'd largely left Brycen unofficially in charge of the investigation ever since Carter had been exposed.

When the deputy entered the room and stood aside, Drury approached Cora's bed with Brycen. He went to the far side of the bed and Drury stopped at Cora's mid-section.

The woman's eyes were closed, but when she heard them they opened tiredly, their brown vibrancy dimmed by red. Her long brown hair was up in a ponytail and draped over the white pillow.

"Who's there," she asked in a raw voice. And then she recognized Brycen. "You're that detective. Deputy Chandler told me you'd be here." Even her injured state didn't hide her delight.

"Hello, Cora. We came as soon as we heard you were awake. Do you feel okay to talk a little?"

"Hell yes." She took a few breaths. "Is that dirty cop in jail yet?"

"Who is a dirty cop?" Drury asked, hoping she'd give the name for confirmation. She suspected where this was going.

"Carter Nichols. I told my doctor that's who shot me. Trooper Nichols came to see me at my home. At first I thought he was going to tell me he found my attacker. I let him in and he drew a gun. I couldn't believe it. I was frozen with shock." She had to pause to catch her breath again. "I asked him why and he said he had no choice. Then he shot me. "

He must have thought he'd killed her and rushed to leave, anxious over how close authorities were to catch him.

"We're looking for him now, Cora. There's something else I need to ask you. Do you remember when you told me Carter came to see you at your work and someone interrupted him?"

Cora rolled her head to the side as she thought. Then

she looked back at Brycen. "Yeah. A man interrupted him and he said he had to go."

Deputy Chandler stepped forward, standing beside Drury closest to Cora's head. "Who was the man?"

Neither she nor Brycen had a chance to fill him in.

With her eyes closed, Cora said, "I didn't know him. I had never seen him before."

"You said it seemed urgent, what this man needed to say to Carter," Brycen said.

"Yes." Cora opened her eyes and looked off as she recalled the incident. "He kept looking around all nervous and kept saying, 'Let's go outside.' Trooper Nichols had to pay his bill and the man kept saying, 'Let's go outside.' The man didn't really look afraid. He seemed not to want to be seen there—or heard. I thought whatever he had to say to Trooper Nichols embarrassed him or something."

"What did he look like?" Drury asked. "Can you describe him?"

"Yeah. He was a white man, maybe in his mid-forties, dark hair cut short." She paused to breathe. "Average in height. He had dark circles under his eyes."

"What color were his eyes?" Brycen asked.

Her eyes lifted as though searching the files in her mind. Then she blinked them closed. "Dark, I think."

"Carter didn't use his name?" Drury asked.

With her eyes still closed, Cora thought a moment and then said, "When the man first approached, he said, 'Dexter,' as though he was surprised to see him."

No last name. Drury met Deputy Chandler's glance with the significance of that. Brycen didn't seem moved one way or the other. No last name meant it would be harder for them to find the man.

"Why is the man important?" Cora asked. "Does he have something to do with why Trooper Nichols shot me?"

More than Cora had seen the man go up to Carter. There had to be another reason.

"Did Carter mention anything to you about the domestic violence call my husband went on before he was murdered?" Drury asked. "Did he ever talk about his murder at all?"

Cora nodded slowly and slightly, growing tired. "He did talk about that. He said my attack happened around the same time and…" She thought some more. "I asked him if there were any other calls and he said a few, one his partner—the man murdered—your husband—went on by himself."

"He said that? Noah went on the call alone?"

As the deputy put his hand on her shoulder as though in comfort, Cora said, "Yes. And he seemed to regret telling me. I thought he wasn't supposed to talk about the investigation with me so I didn't make a fuss over it."

Drury checked Brycen for a reaction but he just continued to watch and listen.

"Noah did go alone, Cora," she said, "but that's not what Carter put in his report. He falsified the report."

"Well." Cora blinked tiredly. "That explains why he shot me, I suppose. Why wait, though? Why didn't he shoot me before?" She looked at Brycen for an answer.

"I wasn't onto him back then," he said. "Now he's a desperate man trying to erase evidence or anyone who can testify against him."

Cora nodded slowly. "So, he'll come after me again."

"No," Brycen said, no doubt in his tone. "I won't allow him to get another chance. You're safe now, and I'll make sure Carter knows you've already told me all you know.

He'll have no reason to come after you. He'll be more concerned with escaping me."

Cora smiled as much as her energy would allow. "I knew you were different. As soon as I met you at the restaurant, I felt it. You were different than Carter."

"I'll take that as a compliment." He grinned.

"It was meant as one." She didn't open her eyes.

"We should let you get some rest," Deputy Chandler said. "We're all glad to hear you're going to fully recover."

"You can add me to that list." She laughed slightly and winced in pain.

"Thank you, Cora," Drury said.

Brycen moved around the bed and she preceded him out the door. The deputy said his farewell and followed.

Outside the room, the deputy faced them. "I'll contact the FBI and see what they have on any wanted men named Dexter."

"Thanks," Brycen said. "We'll be in touch."

"Appreciate that."

Drury gave a wave and started down the hall. But she stopped short when she recognized Mr. Jefferson and his daughter, Avery, walking down the hall. Kayla's father and her sister.

"Mr. Jefferson. Avery," she said.

Mr. Jefferson stopped walking and stared at Brycen in surprise and then disgust. "What the devil are you doing here?"

"Cora Parker is part of my investigation."

"Do you know Cora?" Drury asked.

"What's it to you?" Mr. Jefferson snapped.

"Excuse me?" She stepped right up to him and his

daughter. "I suggest you speak respectfully to me rather than passing judgment when you don't even know me."

He blinked as though realizing how far he'd allowed his control to slip.

"How do you know Cora?" Drury asked.

The deputy moved closer, more of a presence to ensure no one lost their cool.

"She's my friend," Avery said. "We went to the same school."

"Well. Anchorage is a big enough city, but small enough it would appear."

"We'd appreciate it if you'd take him and go," Mr. Jefferson glanced at the deputy. "We don't want to cause any trouble."

"Why?" Drury asked. "I find it hard to believe you didn't know Brycen would want to talk to Cora. She was attacked close to the time my husband was murdered."

"Yes, we were aware of that. But why would Cora's assault be related to his murder?" Mr. Jefferson stopped and looked at Brycen. "You always did exaggerate everything. Looking under rocks that have nothing under them. Now look at you. You're back and we could lose another person we care about."

The man's ire stirred anew and Drury wondered if he'd rant some more when the deputy stepped between the two, putting his hand on Mr. Jefferson's chest.

"Take a step back, please," Deputy Chandler said.

He did, glowering at Brycen.

"Kayla never told me about Cora and Avery being friends," Brycen said.

"Cora is like a second daughter to us. Kayla never told you because all you were interested in is your*self*!" Mr. Jefferson moved around Deputy Chandler.

"Mr. Jefferson?" Brycen called.

He stopped in the hospital room doorway, hand on the doorframe.

"Cora is going to recover."

With a dismissing grunt, Mr. Jefferson dropped his hand and went into the room, Avery having already gone there.

"What kind of trouble does he think you're causing?" Deputy Chandler asked.

Drury predicted Brycen's response before he started to turn away.

"We'll be in touch, Deputy," Brycen said.

Drury caught the deputy's perplexed look. "It's a touchy subject for him." She held up her hand in farewell and followed Brycen toward the elevators.

Waiting for the doors to open, she changed her mind about leaving with him just yet. "I have to use the restroom. I'll meet you downstairs."

He pressed the down button and before he could say anything, she headed back down the hall.

Rounding a corner, she saw Deputy Chandler leaning against the opposite wall from Cora's room.

"You're back," he said with a smile.

"You're staying?" she asked.

"Until one of my troopers shows up. I've been keeping Cora under guard given someone tried to kill her."

Of course, she should have thought of that. "That's good of you." She glanced back toward the hospital room. "Excuse me."

She peeked her head in and saw Avery talking to Cora, who both looked and sounded exhausted.

Mr. Jefferson put his hand on Cora's shoulder. "You get some rest. We'll be back."

Ducking back out of the room, she waited for him and Avery to leave, facing the door and ignoring the deputy's curious observation. A trooper walked up to him and they started talking, the deputy looking her way once before Mr. Jefferson appeared in the hall.

"Mrs. Decoteau?" he queried, looking even more perplexed than the deputy had.

"I had to come back and ask you why you both still blame Brycen for Kayla's death when it was a car accident," she said. "Why do you?"

Mr. Jefferson shared a reluctant glance with his daughter, who offered no input. "The accident happened because someone started chasing him. Danger follows him everywhere he goes."

"He's a homicide detective. Are you suggesting he not do that?"

His mouth crimped in a disagreeing frown before he said, "He takes what he does too far."

"That's what makes him good at what he does." She searched his eyes and then Avery's for indications that they realized how unrealistic their hatred was. All she found was anger in Mr. Jefferson. Avery averted her eyes.

"Kayla would be alive if not for him." Mr. Jefferson's bad attitude came out again.

"You've said that. And she might still be alive if she never met him, but she did. She *loved* him. Maybe the problem here is your regret for not supporting her more."

He blinked, slow and full of cynicism.

"You had your idea of what she should be doing with her life, and she had something different in mind. What you're missing, though, is Kayla was happy. I think you both know she loved him," Drury said. "But did you

know he also married her and that's where they had just
come from when the criminal started chasing them?"

Avery perked up with that. "What?"

Her father paled some and seemed shocked.

"Oh, I guess not. Because Brycen never told anyone.
You didn't give him a chance. You were too quick to pass
judgment. Or should I say, too quick to pass blame onto
him for your own guilt?"

"How dare you." Mr. Jefferson stepped toward her.

Drury held up her hand at Deputy Chandler, who took
a step toward them, his trooper watching the confronta-
tion with him. The deputy stopped.

She said to Mr. Jefferson in an even, honest tone,
"Brycen Cage is a decent man. He's smart and honest
and doesn't deserve the garbage you throw at him. He'll
find the man who shot Cora. But he'll get no thanks from
you. I wish I could tell him you weren't worth a single
thought or speck of regret and he'd listen. He actually
cares about what you think. You, Mr. Jefferson, a man
who drove him out of Alaska because you can't forgive
yourself for the way you treated Kayla before she died.
I don't even have to know what transpired between you.
I just know it wasn't Brycen's fault. He cared for Kayla.
Loved her. He didn't mean for her to die. Nor did he
want her to."

"Now, you wait just a—"

Drury turned to Avery and cut Mr. Jefferson off.
"That goes for you, too, Avery." Avery's mouth opened
as though she considered responding and Mr. Jefferson
ramrod stiff with insult.

Drury checked the deputy, who listened without moving to interfere, and faced the two again. "Have either of
you stopped to think what losing Kayla did to Brycen?

Did you ever think he grieved along with you? No. You didn't. What do you think it did to him to know a criminal he'd been after caused her death? When you blamed him, he let you because he felt responsible. He agreed with you. Feeling as though he killed Kayla tore him apart. Don't you see?"

Avery closed her mouth and Mr. Jefferson's defensive stance softened a fraction. They had never considered how Brycen felt losing Kayla. Maybe they'd thought it to themselves a time or two, but they had never allowed the possibility to take shape. They'd clung to hatred and blame.

"Kayla's death affects him to this day," she said. "He's only just now coming to terms with it. And if he hadn't come back to Alaska, I'm convinced he never would have overcome the blame." She searched each of their eyes, trying to find answers. "Why didn't you ever consider his side of such a tragedy? You both should be ashamed of yourselves."

Avery glanced at her father. She must have followed his lead. Mr. Jefferson didn't respond.

"Do me a favor," Drury said. "Stay away from Brycen. And if you see him again like today, keep your mouths shut and your unfair judgments to yourselves." They'd told him to stay away plenty of times. It was time somebody told them to do the same.

With a wave to the deputy, Drury started down the hall. Heading for the elevator, she spotted Brycen still standing there, hands in his pant pockets, waiting for her with wry scrutiny and taking her breath away.

"You passed the bathroom," he said.

He seemed to know what she had done. "I lied. I went to give Avery and her father a piece of my mind."

"I figured as much. Drury, I wish you wouldn't have done that." They stepped onto the elevator and Brycen pressed the ground floor button. "It does no good."

"It did do some good. You've never told them you loved Kayla and grieved when she died. You let them wallow in their judgments of you until it festered into what it is now, just as bitter and hateful—maybe more so—as back then."

"I let them?"

The elevator doors opened and she walked with him to the exit. "Enabled."

"I did try to tell them that. They wouldn't listen."

"You should have tried again."

"By the time I left Alaska, it was too late. Nothing I said would have changed their minds."

Maybe they'd change them now, with a stranger telling them the truth. If they looked inside their hearts, they'd feel it jabbing. But they'd have to let it go, to let it outside their own private thoughts, in order to move past their loss.

"You should try talking to them again," she said as he held the door for her, drawing her attention to his muscular arm.

"I'm not going to talk to them. They'll just attack me again."

She walked beside him, catching how his gaze ran down to her legs. "I don't mean for them. For you. So you can finally put it all behind you."

Almost to the SUV, he stopped. "It will never be behind me."

Because he did blame himself. Drury felt terrible for him, and angrier than ever with Avery and her father.

She raised her hand and touched the side of his face,

just long enough to show how much she cared and how much she'd like him to hear this. Hear it, and believe it. "Kayla's death wasn't your fault, Brycen."

"Just let it go, Drury."

She caressed his face, running her finger over his lips, letting him know how much she truly did care, and it had nothing to do with Avery and her father.

He took her hand in his and kissed her fingers.

Then her cell phone rang. Thinking the caller could be Junior, she took it from her pocket. Not Junior. She didn't recognize the number.

"Hello?"

Brycen must have noticed her guarded curiosity. He waited while the caller spoke.

"I warned you."

"Who is this?"

"The person you're after is Dexter Watts," the man said. His voice sounded familiar.

"You're the man who intercepted me at the airport," she said as it dawned on her. "Why are you helping us?"

"He's got a shipment coming in tonight. The boat dock at Melvin Cummingses' place. Be there, and don't go alone. Bring your friends from the FBI. I told you that you can't do this alone. If you don't listen to anything else I say, listen to that."

"Wait a minute, how do you know all of this? Why do you keep talking to me and not Brycen? Who—"

The man disconnected.

She looked at Brycen. "That man who talked to me at the airport just said there's a shipment arriving at the Cummingses' boat dock tonight. He gave me the trafficker's name, too. Dexter Watts. He knew we were in touch with the FBI."

"Dexter Watts?" Brycen said incredulously.

"You know him?"

An abrupt explosion pushed her backward and Brycen toward her. Knocked off her feet, she landed on her rear and Brycen broke his fall on top of her. He rolled off her and sat beside her, staring with her at his SUV engulfed in a ball of flames.

Brycen got up from where he'd fallen and came to her. "Are you all right?"

"Yes." A little scratched from the fall but all right. She took his offered hand and he helped her stand.

Catching sight of a moving pickup truck with a man in the passenger seat aiming a gun, she yelled, "Gun!" just as gunfire erupted and the windshield of the car next to them shattered.

Brycen tackled Drury, rolling her between the car that had been struck and the one next to it. She crouched with her back against the door while Brycen took out his pistol and peered over the hood. He had to duck as another gunshot rang out.

The truck's engine revved and grew louder. They were driving toward them!

Drury remained crouched with Brycen as they ran in the other direction, weaving between parked vehicles. At a parked pickup truck, Brycen paused to aim. He fired once.

Drury saw the passenger of the truck slump. Sickened, she ran again with him with the parked cars their cover.

Pausing once again, Brycen searched for the truck. Drury didn't hear it chasing them anymore. Had the driver given up?

Then Brycen turned to her, his eyes sharp, hard and focused. "I need you to stay here."

"Wha—"

"They've stopped and two of them are coming for us. I'll stop them. You wait here."

She nodded. She wasn't armed and she couldn't fight three grown men. But could Brycen? Apprehension churned as he ran toward the men.

Crawling to the edge of the truck, she saw him stay out of sight as the first man approached. The three had spread out, one going wide to presumably flank them while his partners came straight in and from the other flanking side.

Brycen intercepted the man coming straight for them. Hiding behind an Escalade, he moved out just as the man crept forward. One dance-like kick of his leg along with an upward chop of his arm both tripped the man and knocked his gun up. Brycen jabbed the man in the throat and that sent him down.

Checking all around her, not seeing any of the other men, she popped her head up and saw the downed man wasn't moving. She lowered herself behind the protection of the vehicle, listening.

A gunshot cracked and she flinched. Brycen. Was he all right?" She slowly rose enough to look, seeing nothing through the parked cars.

The sound of footsteps to her left made her stifle a quick, frightened breath. She ran low around the front of the parked car to the other side, then moved slow and silent to the rear of the next vehicle.

She heard someone stepping along the far side of the car she'd just left. Squeezing her eyes shut, she debated over whether she should keep moving. Someone ran past her. She opened her eyes and saw Brycen rush the man she'd heard. He swung his gun toward him just as Brycen fired. The man jerked backward and fell.

Drury moved so she could see what was going on.

The man lay on his back and moved his gun toward Brycen. He must be wearing a bulletproof vest.

Brycen fired again, this time marking the man's head.

Drury turned around and sat against the tire of the parked car, sickened even more. She covered her mouth and breathed deep. Brycen had methodically taken out three armed men. She wished she hadn't seen him in action and yet understood if he hadn't done what he had, they'd have been killed.

"Drury."

Lowering her hand, she looked up.

Tucking his gun into its holster, he bent and slid his arm around her, lifting easily and bringing her against him.

She put her hand on his chest and hoped she wouldn't throw up. His strong arms around her helped prevent that.

"It's safe now, unless more are coming, which I expect will happen. We have to get out of here."

Sirens pierced the cold. Someone had called for help.

"Who would attack in such a public place and in daylight?" she asked.

"Someone who's not afraid to."

She spotted Deputy Chandler rushing out of the hospital, seeing them, he slowed to a stop with a relieved blink.

Brycen kept his arm around her as they walked toward him.

"You're okay," the deputy said. "The staff told me gunshots were heard in the parking lot."

Police cars raced in and parked in front of the hospital. As they began to assess the situation, the deputy started toward them.

"I'll take care of this," he said.

Brycen took out his cell phone. "It's Brycen. We need some reinforcements. My SUV is barbeque and three men just tried to kill us in a hospital parking lot."

Without hearing the other person on the line, Drury knew he spoke with Kadin. He explained what happened.

"Roger that. Ten minutes." He disconnected with a wry smile and half-laugh. "He's had people here the whole time."

"Why am I not surprised?" She smiled up at him.

He looked down and over at her, still smiling. "You're feeling better. I'm sorry you had to see that."

He warmed her heart even when the subject was violent. He calmed her. Soothed her. And made her want to get warmer with him.

A car sped into the parking lot.

"Come on. We have to talk to the FBI. Dexter Watts is one of their most wanted." Brycen took her hand and ran with her toward the approaching vehicle.

Chapter 14

Brycen waited with Drury in the trees surrounding Melvin Cummingses' dock. All was quiet for now. No boats approached, none they could see. Special agents lurked nearby, out of sight, armed and ready to pounce.

The sound of a motor reached them first.

He moved so that Drury had to back against the tree, careful that they stay hidden, and even more careful to protect her. Still listening to the approaching boat, he felt her watching him. When he looked down at her face, her rapt gaze and stunning beauty arrested him. She had her hands on his chest. His body lightly against hers, he grew aware of every point that connected with hers.

Now was not the time for passion to sweep him away. He cleared his throat. "When we move in, you stay here, okay?"

"Okay." Her gaze moved down to his lips.

Hearing the boat draw closer, he pressed his mouth to hers for a quick kiss, a promise for later. But that only heated into more. Instead of letting go and heading for the dock, he held her against him and kissed her longer, deeper. Her breaths touched his face and she answered his need.

The boat grew louder and he had to draw away. Staring into her eyes, he stepped back, his feet reluctant to comply.

With her breathless and sultry, backing against the tree and making the sight much more tortuous to bear, he glanced over at the dock and saw the boat floating toward the boathouse. A three-man crew worked to dock the vessel, one of them going down below.

When a line of women emerged from the hull, FBI agents swarmed the dock. Brycen left Drury at the tree and ran with gun drawn toward the boat.

The two on deck started firing and the agents took them down. The captain ran from the wheelhouse and the one who'd disappeared below took one of the women and held a gun to her head. The woman screamed and pleaded in Spanish.

Brycen moved along the back to the boathouse, hurrying to the front on the water side. At the end, he peered out and saw many of the women had ducked for cover on the boat. Two made it to the dock and ran toward him.

The agents shouted for the man who'd taken the hostage to drop his weapon.

Brycen covered the two women running toward him, aiming at the man with the hostage, whose attention remained on the dozen agents on land. He guided the two women to stand behind him, out of sight from the boat.

"Go to the trees," he whispered to the women. He

could see Drury peeking out from the tree. When she saw the women, she waved for them to come to her.

The women began to run toward her.

Brycen covered them again, the man shouting he'd kill the hostage if he wasn't allowed to leave on the boat. He stood at an angle to him, the hostage blocking a clear shot.

The agents wouldn't have much of a better shot with the slope and curve of the shoreline. Some crouched behind rocks or trees while two had made it to the boathouse. Brycen heard them rush in and take cover behind the walls.

The man began backing up with the woman. He dragged her into the wheelhouse, keeping an eye on the agents. Restarting the boat, his gun moved away from the woman's head briefly and his arm and shoulder leaned out of the wheelhouse door on Brycen's side.

Not hesitating, he took the shot, hitting the man in the shoulder. He yelped and the impact threw him backward. The woman screamed and ran from the wheelhouse while agents rushed to the boat.

Before the man could fire his gun, he had four pistols aimed at him.

Brycen boarded the boat, seeing the face of the first gunned-down man. Not Dexter Watts.

The next man was still alive, leaning against the bow, holding his bleeding lower left abdomen. Not Dexter Watts. The man in the boathouse wasn't Dexter, either.

The women, there were four on the boat, clung to agents and spoke rapidly in Spanish, obviously overwhelmed by their rescue, one of them outright sobbing in the arms of an agent. He soothed her and spoke her native language, rubbing her back.

"Nice shot," an agent said to him.

"He didn't see me."

"Watts isn't here," another agent stepped over and said.

"There are two more women up there." Brycen pointed. "I'll send them your way."

He wouldn't explain he'd head back to Anchorage and continue his search. Leaving the agents to clean up the mess, he jogged back up the slope toward Drury and the two women.

They each had long dark hair and brown eyes and wore dresses they must have been in for days.

"Gracias, señor," the taller one said.

"They don't speak English," Drury said, wrapping her jacket around the shorter woman.

Brycen removed his and gave it to the taller woman. Then he pointed up the slope through the trees.

"There are people with cars waiting up there. They'll take care of you," he said, putting his hand on her back and guiding her in that direction.

"Gracias," they kept saying over and over.

He followed them with Drury toward the Cummingses' house. When he arrived, he was surprised to see agents had Melvin Cummings in handcuffs. He must have just arrived, ready to meet the crew of the boat and lock up their fresh shipment of slaves.

While Drury took the women to the shelter of a van, Brycen went to the agents holding Melvin.

"Where is your wife?" he asked Melvin.

"I don't know, man."

"You must know."

"I don't. I swear. I wouldn't hurt her."

Brycen gave him a sardonic frown.

Melvin noticed and shook his head, standing between the two agents with his hands behind his back. "I wouldn't kill my wife. She figured out who Watts was and he wanted her dead. Tried to off her when I left on a fishing trip. She ran. Watts said if she came back that I was to let him know or kill her myself. I haven't seen her since."

"What about Noah?"

"Noah saw Watts when he answered Evette's call. He ordered him dead. I had nothin' to do with that."

"Watts killed him?"

"He didn't personally kill him. One of the men you killed did. At the hospital? They did the killing for Watts."

So Noah's killer was dead. Somehow that fell short of satisfying Brycen's need for justice.

"We went over this with him, too," the agent on the left said. "I think he's telling the truth."

"Where is Watts?" Brycen asked Melvin.

"He was supposed to meet us here. I don't know where he is. Someone might have tipped him off."

"Who?" The mysterious caller who'd contacted Drury? Why would he tell Watts about this raid after helping them try to catch him? That made no sense.

They'd captured all but the most wanted.

Brycen showed Junior how to fly BayMax and handed the controller back. Junior took it and still struggled, so Brycen got down onto the floor with the boy. Sitting behind him with his legs wide on each side, Brycen took the controller. They'd played with dual screens, he playing Hiro and Junior playing BayMax.

"Like this. Watch."

Junior looked down at Brycen's hands as he moved the knobs and pressed one of the front buttons. Then he looked up at the left screen.

Putting BayMax back on the ground, he let Junior take over.

"Easy." Junior lifted BayMax and the big red hero flew up over the platform of green and crossed the space of abyss to the city.

"Lower him down," Brycen said.

Junior let go of the button and BayMax landed on the ground. From there, Junior ran the character along a street, turning a corner and running some more.

"You got it."

Junior's light laughter lightened his heart. He lifted his own controller and played Hiro on the other screen, finding a bridge and running across.

"Trouble." Junior pointed at Brycen's side of the screen.

Brycen triggered the nanobots and cleared the opposition.

Junior laughed louder.

Brycen chuckled, feeling it down deep. He'd only imagined what this would be like, spending time with a child…his child. *His child*…

Drury stood before a chair folding laundry. She looked from her son to Brycen. She must have done that a lot while they played the game. Disconcerted he'd thought of Junior as his own, her warm smile almost made it worse. Almost. But then he noticed her. Slender and shapely, long dark hair shining with health. Beautiful. Sexy. The memory of kissing her just before they freed those women took over.

He fell back into the floating wonder of being a part

of a family. He'd never felt this way growing up, the way Junior must feel with him playing a game. Brycen's father had played with him, but the love hadn't been there. Love for a son had been there, but not an overriding love, a family love.

What the hell was he thinking?

Love?

Seeing Junior absorbed in playing BayMax, Brycen rose to his feet, giving the kid's head of hair a tousle. Drury finished folding the laundry. There wasn't much, only what they'd packed to come here. She didn't have to do his laundry, and he'd told her that, but she enjoyed the work. Something about household chores gave a person a sense of basic accomplishment. One of those necessities of survival.

"All right, Junior, time for bed," she said, leaving the folded clothes to get her son away from the game.

"Aw," Junior complained.

"Turn it off. Come on."

Junior did as he was told. Putting the controller back on the TV stand shelf, he walked toward the stairs. On his way he smiled up at Brycen with sleepy eyes that had focused on a TV screen too long. When he leaned in and hugged him, Brycen froze with the unexpectedness of it. Then he put his arms around the boy.

"Sleep tight, little man," he said.

Junior laughed. "I'm not a little man." He ran off, a happy kid bounding up the stairs.

Drury raised her eyebrows as she passed Brycen and he wasn't sure her pleasant smile conveyed all she felt about his interaction with her son.

He waited for Drury to tuck her son in, turning the TV to a network channel, not particularly caring what he watched. He had too much on his mind. Noah's murder. Dexter Watts. But mostly Drury and her son.

After several minutes, she finally came downstairs. "He was all wound up."

He smiled a little as she came to the sofa and sat next to him.

"He's pretty taken by you," she said.

"Yes." He couldn't feel bad about that, either. Junior needed someone to bring him out of his grief, to move on without his dad. The good in doing so, however, might come with a price.

She faced the television, which neither of them actually watched.

"After you find Dexter Watts, what will you do?" she finally asked.

Although she asked in a nonchalant way, her question was anything but nonchalant, or insignificant.

"I have to go back to Chicago. To my show."

"It's that important to you?" she asked.

Was she fishing for a reason for him to stay? "I worked hard to build it to what it is now. I can't just walk away from that."

Slowly, though a sign of agitation, she rubbed her hands over the jeans on her thighs. "What about what you left here?"

"I left negativity behind when I moved away from here."

She stopped rubbing and angled her head as she looked at him. "Did you? Was it all negative?"

He turned away. He saw where she headed with this, what she intended to make him face. His show gave him a positive outlook and something good to take with him into old age. He'd have no regrets there. He had too many in Alaska.

"Working on *Speak of the Dead* is the best thing that's ever happened to me. I made a good decision going into that."

"I agree, your show has done you good. But you ran away from Alaska and haven't dealt with that yet."

"I didn't run. It was time to go." Nothing made him feel good anymore. His job had led to Kayla's death. Her family despised him.

"All right. You had nothing left in Alaska to keep you here. But you liked what you did here, didn't you? Your job? Your career?"

He had. Moving here from Colorado had felt right. His career had felt right. He hadn't made a mistake. Where had he made a mistake? He had never wondered before. Of course, he had regrets. He regretted marrying Kayla. He hadn't felt right standing before the pastor, a feeling he'd shoved away, rationalized away. Kayla had beamed delight and utter happiness and love. He had not felt her level of joy. He'd felt anxious.

"I regret marrying Kayla." He said it out loud, needing to. Her family had not driven him from Alaska, his decision to marry her had. Had they not married, they wouldn't have been driving that road. The accident wouldn't have happened.

"Because you didn't love her or because you don't believe in marriage?' Drury asked, cautiously.

He'd always told himself he'd loved Kayla. But now, in this frank, non-confrontational talk with Drury, he realized he hadn't loved her, not enough to marry her. "Neither. I thought I loved her enough. Deep down, I didn't love her and I married her anyway because I knew that's what she wanted. And on the way back to Anchorage, the accident happened. She died."

"You only just now realize you didn't love her?"

"Only just now, I admit I didn't." He looked at her. He hadn't been able to face the truth until now. Admitting he didn't love her after she died because one of his cases had gone bad would have been awful. It had dawned on him shortly after her death, and plagued him long after.

She studied his face as she considered his confession. Then she put her hand on his knee. "Brycen, do you see why your theory on marriage is flawed? You married Kayla when you knew you didn't love her."

"I didn't know it then."

"You did know. Your heart knew. You just didn't listen or pay attention to what you felt in your heart. You married her anyway. Marriage doesn't work for people whose hearts tell them something is off. The yin might be right but the yang lacks duality."

Was she trying to convince him to change his mind about marriage? "What about you and Noah? Did you have duality?"

She turned away, sitting back and looking across the room in thought. At last, she turned to him again. "Yes." Then she moved closer on the sofa. "But I never felt with him what I feel with you."

Something went off inside of him, a spark, a sense of intense truth. With her face so close, tipping back, eyes blue as a clear sky, sweet breath warming his skin, instant desire inflamed the spark.

"What's your heart telling you now?" she asked.

He didn't answer. Not with words. His head came down and he touched his mouth to hers, soft at first, then heating into something deeper. He could not satisfy his desire for her. The need he felt surpassed any other he had ever experienced.

His heart clamored with passion, a sure and strong passion that could only come from love. That's what scared him most. And that's what made him pull back.

Chapter 15

"I had a bad dream."

Drury came awake with a start. She lay against Brycen, her arm and one leg draped over him, his arm up along the pillow supporting her neck, his hand precariously close to her nipple. She'd put on a nightgown, if you could call it that. She'd put on one of her sexy ones. And Brycen had put on his underwear.

Junior didn't seem bothered in the slightest over seeing her in bed with Brycen.

Brycen groaned and woke. Lifting his head, he blinked a few times before it registered Junior stood in the doorway. He jerked up onto his elbows.

"Can I sleep with you?" He walked toward the bed.

As Junior crawled onto the middle of the bed, Drury glanced at Brycen and him at her. She had to move over to make room for Junior. Unabashedly, he wormed his way under the covers between them. With a sleepy, content look at Brycen and then Drury, Junior curled toward his mother and closed his eyes.

She put her arm around him and looked over at Brycen as her heart swelled with warm love. He answered her look, equally touched by the power of the moment, by Junior's act of innocent trust. He put his arm on the boy's upper arm and propped his head on his other hand.

Her awe lasted only so long. What would Brycen's leaving do to Junior? All this progress will have been for nothing. Maybe she should have been more careful. Seeing her son react in such a positive way had her cheering, but maybe he'd have been better off going through this tough time on his own, and with her.

When next she met Brycen's eyes, she saw passion. This closeness affected him in ways he couldn't have predicted.

A ringing phone woke Brycen the next morning. Junior mashed to his side, Drury with her arm over her son and hand on Brycen's bare chest, he experienced a quick and strong bolt of longing. What if he ended his show? Could he move it to Anchorage?

The phone rang again, and he realized it was his cell. Picking it up from the side table, baffled over the two questions that had run through his mind, he answered.

"Cage." Beside him, Drury stirred, rolling to her back. The covers slid down and one of her breasts peeked out from the twisted material.

"It's Chandler. We got a lead on Watts. He's staying at the Antler Motel."

"He's still here?" Brycen sat up, reaching for Drury's

nightgown as Junior began to wake, trying to ignore her sleepy but love-struck look.

Pulling the material over her nipple, she looked down and grew more awake as she straightened the gown.

"We're checking now," Chandler said. "One more thing you're going to want to hear. The lead came from Evette Cummings. She called from her mother's house this morning, as soon as she heard Melvin had been arrested."

"Her mother? We spoke with her." Brycen got up off the bed, aware of Drury's glances toward his body.

"I'm hungry," Junior said.

"Okay, get in the shower and get dressed." Drury kissed his nose.

"She hid there," Chandler said as Brycen watched the mother-son exchange, Junior smiling up at her.

"Her mother lied to protect her," Chandler went on. "Evette was too afraid Watts would find her, or her husband would tell him where she was. Melvin came looking for her a few times."

Junior crawled off the bed and walked out of the room as though he'd slept with the two of them many times before.

"How did she hide?" In a bedroom? Where and how had she not been sighted by others or found by Melvin and Watts?

"She never left the house and her family made no secret over how they felt about Melvin. They didn't let him in. Watts sent someone looking, but Evette managed to hide."

"How does she know where he is?"

"She said that's where he goes when he's here. She heard Melvin talking to him. It's his secret place. Melvin didn't know she heard them talking. After he started smacking her around, she began to pay attention to what he was doing. Eventually, she got caught."

And that's why she'd run.

"We have a team ready," Chandler said. "Checking guests at the hotel. Watts would have used an alias."

"All right. I'm on my way." He'd drop Drury and Junior off at her parents first. Drury didn't need to go with him and he definitely didn't want Junior there.

Disconnecting, he went into the master bathroom and started the shower. By the time he stepped in, Drury followed. Her naked body took over his attention.

"No morning kiss?" she said.

He slid his hand around to her lower back and pulled her against him. Kissing her, he wondered why they kept doing this. The only good thing was Junior couldn't see them.

"Who called?" she asked against his wet mouth.

"Chandler. They found Watts."

She jerked back. "Really?"

"I'll drop you and Junior at your parents' and meet the team."

"You want to drop me off, too?" She kissed his mouth. She sped up his breathing, her slick skin sliding against his, her nipples hard.

"Yes. It's over. Watts will be arrested."

"The case is closed." She kept kissing him, more fervently now, as they both drew closer to the time when he'd have to leave.

He didn't want to call this farewell sex, but he had a strong feeling Drury needed the same. He had to return to Chicago. Even if he came back to Alaska, he couldn't do that overnight.

"I'm afraid to ask, what about us?" she breathed.

He lifted her and pressed her against the back shower wall. "Wrap your legs around me."

Kissing her to stop her questions, he found her softness as she hooked her legs around him. He entered her with the urgency he felt, the confusion over how he felt *for her*. Kissing her, making love with her, took him away from the conflict.

He kissed her as he moved, gently bobbing her up and down against the wall, warm water at his back and misting her. She dug her fingers into his wet hair and leaned her head back as he ran his tongue down her neck to her breasts. He held her while he caressed one breast. Treating the other to the same taste, he went back to her mouth and kissed her harder.

Unable to slow the craving, he thrust quicker. Her audible breaths heightened the building ache for release. He stopped a groan as he watched her peak, the sight and friction sending him to the same soaring cloud.

Drury flew the toy plane between the two front seats of the car Brycen had rented since his had incinerated, a black Volvo that in one way fit him and in another didn't. Sleek and stylish and safe, but not as masculine as a truck or SUV. A girl car, her dad would say. She supposed she got that outlook from him. Her dad had a plane and drove a big truck. Her mother often teased him about how he stereotyped based on the vehicles people drove. She'd bought a big Cadillac SUV just to prove a point. Girls could drive big vehicles, too. He'd come back with, "Yeah, but only a girl would pick a Cadillac."

Her parents often played around like that. And she

used to, as well. Flying this toy plane was the first time since Noah died that she'd done anything like this.

"Vrrrroommm," She twisted to fly in front of Junior's face.

He giggled and flew his superhero after her.

"Okay, kids, we're here," Brycen said.

Smiling, Drury flew the plane in front of his face and he just looked over at her as though she'd gone coo-coo. With a laugh, she got out and joined her son on the driveway, walking with him toward the door as he continued to fly his superhero.

She took the doorknob and found it locked. "Hm. They must not be home yet." She dug into her purse for the key she had.

"Where are they?" Brycen asked.

"They said they were going to go out for breakfast. Must have hit the church crowd." It was Sunday.

When she had the door open, she turned to Brycen to say goodbye.

"I'll be right back," he said, leaning in for a kiss, pressing soft warm lips to hers and giving her a whiff of his cologne.

He moved back and met her eyes, the fire of yearning for more burning.

She didn't think he'd planned to kiss her, just automatically did before going. Like a husband. Like a father. She felt part of a family again. What a wonderful, welcome gift.

"Ew," Junior said, looking up at them.

Brycen grinned down at him. "Watch your mother for me, Partner."

Junior smiled big. "I will."

To Drury he said, "Don't wreck your plane while I'm gone." He tapped her plastic toy plane in her hand.

Laughing softly, full of joy, she watched him walk back to the Volvo, appreciating his butt in jeans beneath the hem of his leather jacket. She sighed wistfully. She could do this the rest of her life.

The last thought came unbidden and she quickly put it away. Best to not start hoping he'd stay and be a family with her. When would he say goodbye? When he returned, after arresting Dexter Watts? Should she prepare Junior?

"Mom." Junior tugged on her sleeve.

She followed him inside and closed the door to a quiet house. Putting her purse on the front entry table and handing the plane to Junior, she found a note her mother had left.

This came for you.
Mom.

Drury lifted an envelope, one a card would hold. Opening the top, she slid out the card. It was from Avery.

I wasn't sure how to get in touch with you and Brycen. I would like to apologize for the way I treated Brycen when I first saw him. I've had to live with what losing my sister did to my father. She was always his favorite and I often struggled with being second. I guess that's why I went along with his bitterness for so long. I could see he was hurting and wanted to help, but I see now that I felt obligated to agree with him. Maybe in some way I did this to win his love.

You were kind when you could have been justifiably angrier than you were. We probably don't deserve your or Brycen's forgiveness, but I'd like to try to earn it. I've spoken with my father and with my mother's help, we've managed to make him see what an ass he's been. The time has come to put our bitterness behind us.

We would like to meet Brycen and try to establish more friendly terms. I don't expect he'll want to become close friends, but if we could at least part ways amicably, I think this would go a long way to heal my father, and maybe ease Brycen's mind some. Would he be willing? I thought it best to approach you first, since I expect Brycen won't initially want anything to do with us.

Avery.

She had left her phone number.

Drury wasn't sure how long Brycen would be apprehending Dexter Watts. But meeting Avery and her father would do Brycen good. Would he be angry if she interfered? He might not ever want to see or talk to Kayla's family again.

Junior's toys clattering to the hardwood floor preceded his high-pitched scream.

Drury pivoted, her pulse flying as she saw a well-dressed man with a gun. He stood behind Junior, one hand grabbing his arm and the other pressing a gun to his head.

All the blood left Drury's head. At first light-headed with a bolt of fear, she felt aggressive protectiveness quickly taking over.

"Let go of my son."

"Mommy...?"

"It's okay, Junior." What could she do? What did this

man intend? Though she hadn't seen a picture of Dexter Watts, he had to be that man.

"Junior," Dexter said. "I didn't know this was your mommy. She's been kind of a pain in my side lately."

"If you hurt her, my partner is going to get you," he said.

"Your partner, huh? Would that be my even bigger pain, Brycen Cage?"

"He's not a pain!" Junior stomped his foot down on Dexter's.

Dexter didn't even wince. He gave Junior a jerk. "Hold still, kid."

"What do you want?" Drury moved toward him. If he'd come to kill her, he'd have done it by now. Why the drama first?

"Junior? Do you want your mother to live?"

That was the last thing Junior needed to hear. She watched, helpless, as his eyes rounded with stark fear. "You can't take my mommy away!" Junior yanked against the grip on his arm.

Drury stopped. "I'm not going anywhere, honey." What if this terrible person succeeded and killed her? Brycen, too? She could not allow that.

"Can you ride a bike, Junior?"

"Yes." He looked up at Watts.

"Go get on the one out front and ride it to the Antler Motel. Do you know where that is?"

"Let go!" He pulled harder.

Dexter released him and he ran to Drury, who hooked her arms around him, relieved beyond measure that Dexter hadn't harmed him.

"There's a bike in the front, Junior. It looks like it's yours."

Her parents did keep a bike here for Junior, and he rode it enough to be familiar with the area. He didn't go into town, but the Antler was on the outskirts of town. She didn't care if he didn't find it. As long as she knew he was safe—away from here and Dexter's gun—she'd feel a lot better.

And she'd find a way to deal with this disgrace to humanity.

"Go get on it and give this to Brycen." He handed the boy a folded piece of paper.

What was that? What did he have planned? He had something planned, and it involved Drury.

Before Brycen entered the motel office, an agent emerged from there and intercepted him. The tall, sophisticated-looking black man put away his phone. "Detective Cage?"

"Yes."

The agent tucked away his phone inside his suit jacket. "Watts isn't here. He hasn't checked out and is scheduled to stay through the weekend. I just received word that we're going to wait for him to return. You're welcome to wait with us, or someone can give you a call when we've apprehended him."

He wished someone would have called to tell him. He didn't like leaving Drury.

"Is anyone looking for him?" Were they really just going to sit here and wait? Odds were Watts knew his cover was blown and he'd fled.

"Yes. We've got some agents trying to locate him, but he uses several aliases. We're doing our best."

At least they hadn't discounted the possibility that Watts had gone on the run. "Have someone call me when he turns up." He'd rather not waste time hanging around a motel Watts most likely wouldn't return to.

"Will do."

Brycen started to turn back for the Volvo.

"Hey, Detective."

Brycen stopped and looked back at the black agent.

"When Chandler took Melvin's statement, Melvin said Watts was pretty upset over what happened to the Tennessee House and that nobody messes with his business and walks away. Watch your back, all right?"

He didn't need to be told, but he appreciated the agent's concern. "Thanks." With a lift of his hand in farewell, he walked to the car and drove toward Drury's parents' house.

They'd have to wait until either Watts returned to the motel or the FBI found him and made an arrest. Spending more time with Drury both enticed him and stirred up worry over leaving. He was sure she felt the same. For Junior, but also for themselves.

As he turned onto the street where Drury's parents lived, he spotted a boy riding a bike. His legs pumped frantically, as though he was late to get wherever he was going.

And then he recognized Junior's jacket.

He pulled to the side of the road and rolled his window down.

Junior saw him stop and braked. He jumped off his bike and ran over to Brycen, who checked the road for cars. Crazy kid!

"It's Mommy!" Junior yelled. "You have to help her!"

Chills raced from his scalp down his spine. Something had happened to Drury?

Junior ran to the passenger door and opened it himself, climbing in. While Brycen pressed the gas, he dug out a piece of paper.

Brycen read as he drove. All that was written was an address. That and a warning not to bring anyone else or he'd kill Drury before he arrived.

"The man told me to ride my bike to give this to you!" Junior breathed fast. "He has my mommy! Is he going to hurt her like he did my daddy?"

"Not if I can get to her." And he had to. Not only for Junior, but for himself. He could not lose another woman because of his line of work. It didn't matter that Drury had contacted Kadin.

He felt so much for her. Making love with her this morning…he could almost believe in marriage.

Watts forced Drury at gunpoint into the trunk of his car and drove for about thirty minutes. When the car stopped, she contemplated fighting. He'd tied her hands, so that might be tricky. When he opened the trunk with his pistol aimed at her face, her decision became clear. She'd have to wait for another opportunity.

He hauled her out of the trunk and on her feet. She saw a house on a large plot of land. The nearest house from here was probably two miles down the road. She could make it there if she could get away.

"Move it." He shoved her.

She stumbled into a walk toward the house. A large brick Colonial with black trim, it spoke of money.

"Is this your house?" she asked.

"Just keep moving."

It must be. "You earned a lot of money off the suffering of innocent people."

At the door, he glanced back as he got out his keys.

Drury rammed her elbow back and into his sternum. He bent forward with a grunt and she turned to run past him.

Except he tripped her with his foot and she fell down onto the concrete slab of the front porch. Her shoulder hit hard and hurt like mad. She stifled an all-out yell and struggled onto her knees.

Watts grabbed her by her tied arms and pulled her up, putting her face right up to his. "Try that again and I'll beat you."

She moved her head away from the stench of his breath. "When's the last time you went to the dentist?"

He put the key in the door and pushed it open, his biting grip stinging as he yanked her inside and kicked the door shut. From there he took her down a hallway to a master suite.

He shoved her forward. "In there."

She entered a walk-in closet big enough to be a small bedroom.

Unfastening the cuffs, he said, "Put everything in those drawers in the duffel bag."

Glancing back, rubbing her wrists, she saw he pointed to the built-in drawers and a duffel bag on a bench before two low shelves of shoes.

"Where are you going?" More important where would he take her? She didn't know what the note read he'd given to Junior, but it must be directions to meet somewhere, presumably to kill both her and Brycen.

Watts ignored her, sitting on the bench, holding his gun over his forearm, not really aiming at her.

"The FBI knows who you are," she said, throwing items from the first drawer into the duffel bag. "They're going to catch you."

Without responding, he merely met her glances as she packed.

"Why bother with me and Brycen when you have bigger problems than us?" she asked.

"You're the reason I have those problems," he said. "First your husband and his meddling, and now you and that detective…"

"Why did Noah go to the coffee shop? Did he follow Carter there?"

"Carter got sloppy. He talked too much to Pulman and held meetings with Melvin there."

So that was how Noah had ended up at the coffee shop. He'd been suspicious of Carter and must have seen him with Melvin, maybe also talking to John Pulman. And then the call for help had come in from Evette. He'd gone alone because he'd seen Carter meet with Melvin. And then he'd seen Watts—a most-wanted human trafficker. Had he known when he went to the coffee shop? Had he connected the Tennessee House by then? If not, he'd been close.

Noah must have noticed the falsified report and begun his own investigation. He should have told someone, especially about the report. But then he might not have discovered Carter's involvement with Watts.

"You told Carter about Noah answering Evette's call for help alone?" she asked.

Watts scoffed. "Carter. What a waste he turned out to be. Yes, Carter was another mistake I made. The first was not killing Melvin's weak, ugly wife before I started doing business with him."

His business? Carter's protection for a fee? Help in keeping law enforcement from sniffing out his trail?

Drury couldn't resist saying, "She couldn't take the beatings like a real woman, huh?"

His expression, empty and cold, didn't falter. "You have a smart mouth."

Closing one drawer, she opened the next and crumpled some shirts into the duffel bag. "Where is Carter?"

"Hopefully his useless bones are scattered all over the mountainside after the bears ate his stinking corpse."

Sickened, she stopped and looked back at him. He'd murdered Carter?

"I paid him to keep the cops off my back and he drew them in like flies. He got what he deserved."

"Did all those innocent people you promised jobs deserve what they got?"

He didn't respond immediately. He couldn't deny he'd stolen the dreams and hopes of innocent people. Maybe for an instant he felt brief empathy. She doubted that.

"Finish packing. We have a plane to catch."

A plane? Drury took her time packing. She had to do whatever it took to avoid getting on a plane with him.

Brycen didn't have time to drop off Junior anywhere safe. He had to get to Drury. The address would take him to a pretty nice neighborhood. From the satellite image of the place on his phone, the lots were spaced far apart and backed to a heavily wooded area. There was also a dirt swath in the back of the house, indicating a private landing strip. The photo showed no planes on the ground, but that had to be Dexter's escape plan—fly somewhere remote, kill Drury and Brycen and disappear.

"When we get to where we're going, I need you to do exactly as I tell you, okay, Junior?"

Junior looked over, more worry marring his face than should for one so young.

"You stay in the car with the doors locked and don't get out or let anyone in unless I say it's okay, got it?"

He nodded.

"I'll get your mother and bring her to you. You have to trust me on that."

"I trust you."

Brycen felt a moment of uncertainty. What if he couldn't bring her back? What if Dexter had killed her already?

No.

That could not be. He floored the pedal as he reached the two-lane highway that would take him to Dexter's hideaway. The navigation screen told him he was almost there.

"Hurry up," Watts said.

Drury put a pair of jeans in the bag and went for another, packing them one at a time to give Brycen more time.

Impatient, Watts stood and pushed her aside, throwing the rest of the jeans in the bag.

Drury made a run for it. She darted out of the closet and into the hall, running as fast as she could to the main room. There, she skidded to slow down. The front was too open. There were trees in the back. She ran for the back door. It was locked, so she flipped that up just as Watts banged her over the head with his gun.

She fell. Getting onto her hands and knees while the room spun, she tried to crawl away.

"Stupid woman." Watts grabbed the back of her shirt

and lifted, throwing her into the room. She slid on the wood floor and hit the side of a chair.

Watts aimed his pistol at her.

Drury's only thought was of Junior.

The sound of a helicopter made Watts straighten and go still. Then he ran to the back door and swore.

Drury stood and ran down a hallway, going into the first bedroom and shutting the door. There was no lock. Through the window she saw a man get out of the helicopter with an automatic weapon.

Watts started shooting at whoever it was. The man jumped to the ground from the chopper and fired his weapon. He missed Dexter, but it was enough to stop him from shooting.

From another room in the house, she heard glass breaking.

Brycen?

She went to the door and cracked it open. Watts appeared in the hallway from the main room just as Brycen came out of a bedroom down the hall. Brycen fired his gun.

Watts dove back into the main room, behind a wall for cover.

Drury went into the hall and rushed for Brycen, who took her hand and pulled her behind him. She wanted to wrap her arms and legs around him and kiss him everywhere for making it here.

Outside, a fierce explosion vibrated the house.

Watts could be heard swearing in the main room.

Brycen ran after him.

Drury made it to the room just as Watts left the house firing his gun.

Brycen followed. Then he stood on the patio and

aimed, firing once. Drury stepped out onto the stone patio and saw the stranger climb into the helicopter. A plane Watts must have intended to use to escape was engulfed in flames. The energy from the explosion blew her hair slightly.

She looked closer at the stranger. It was the man from the airport. He gave them a salute and lifted up into the air.

Brycen watched with her.

She saw Watts lying on the ground, gun still in hand, facedown and blood pooling from the gunshot wound to his head.

She covered her mouth, seeing the stranger who'd helped save her and Brycen fly away.

"His sheets must be too dirty to stick around for a chat," she said.

Brycen turned to her.

"That's what he told me at the airport when he came to warn me."

He turned back to the retreating helicopter. "That chopper doesn't have any identifiers on it."

"I wish we knew who he was." But she had something more important to do. "Where's Junior?"

"In the car."

"You *brought* him?" She went back into the house and ran to the front door.

Brycen kept up with her.

She saw her son in the passenger seat. As soon as the boy saw her, he clumsily opened the door and got out, running to her.

Swooping him up into her arms, she kissed his cheek. "You're a sight for sore eyes, Noah Jr."

"Your eyes are sore?"

She laughed and almost cried she was so happy. Finally it was over. Noah's murder was solved. For good now. She could bury him and put that part of her life behind her.

Now she just had to figure out her future.

Chapter 16

A few days later, after closing out the case with Deputy Chandler, Brycen packed his bag and left it on Drury's bed. All he had to do was say goodbye to Drury and Junior. He could stay a few extra days, but what good would that do? Drury had asked him to stay through lunch. He'd share that with them and then go.

He entered the living room and saw her end a call from a new client who'd just booked a flight to go skiing somewhere remote. With her silky blouse that fell to her waist above a beady-pocket pair of skinny jeans, long dark hair draping over her shoulders, her beauty magnetized him.

"Hi," she said, blue eyes flashing with awareness.

"Hi." They'd been on awkward ground like this ever since he saved her. He slept with her while he closed the case, but they hadn't made love. He sensed her putting her guard up, preparing for the inevitable. And he found himself doing the same thing, uncertain whether he'd made the right decision to leave.

The doorbell rang and he watched Drury go and answer it. Was she expecting someone? When he heard voices and the door closing, he stood from the sofa. Junior was in his room catching up on homework.

He stood in the threshold between the living room and the entry and saw Kayla's father and sister enter behind Drury.

What the hell?

Drury approached. "Sorry, Brycen, I didn't think you'd agree to this. It wasn't my idea. Avery contacted me. They want to make peace with you."

"And you took it upon yourself to arrange a meeting?" He tried to quell his anger. Meeting with Kayla's family didn't bother him; her sneakiness did.

She backed up as Avery and her father stopped before him.

"Thank you for seeing us," Avery said. "We didn't come to tell you to get lost. In fact, we came to apologize. You didn't tell us you married Kayla the day of the accident."

"You didn't give me a chance."

Mr. Jefferson lowered his head. The man had anger-management issues and it must cost his pride a hefty load to come here. Brycen had to give him credit for that, but he still had a lousy attitude. He'd make peace, but he'd never consider Brycen worth his attention.

"Would you like to take a seat?" he asked.

"No. This won't take long," Mr. Jefferson said. And then when he must have realized how pompous he sounded, he added, "We won't take up too much of your time, is what I meant."

"We hope you can understand why we treated you the way we did," Avery said. "Kayla told me about your… your views on marriage…" She glanced at Drury, who stood behind the kitchen island with her hands on the counter.

Did Avery see something between Brycen and Drury?

"We thought…" Avery continued, "well, we thought you'd…string her along. We thought you were stringing her along. And then she died. And the way she died…"

"You don't have to explain," Brycen said. "It must have taken a lot for you to come here." He looked pointedly at Mr. Jefferson, who finally met his gaze like a guilty party.

"There's one thing I don't understand," Avery said. "Why didn't you tell us you married her? I know you think we didn't give you a chance, but why didn't you tell us?"

He could have told them. And he probably should have. He probably should have told Drury everything, too. Even Kadin Tandy himself didn't know everything. He knew about Kayla, and maybe even the marriage, but he didn't know the most terrible thing about Kayla's death. He'd thought he'd spared them the anguish. When instead he'd drawn it out. He'd also created a burden on himself he could never shed.

Thanks to Drury, he had this chance to ease the weight. Avery and her father might have difficulty sorting through what he had to say, but they needed to know.

"Kayla was pregnant," he said.

He heard Drury's sharp inhalation.

Avery's mouth opened as though she tried to say something but couldn't.

Mr. Jefferson stared at him, an empty man made even emptier with the news.

"I didn't tell you because I knew you were already hurting too much," he said.

"Oh my God," Avery breathed. "How far along?"

"Not long. Eight weeks."

"Oh," Avery breathed again. Tears welled in her eyes. She put her hand on her father's arm.

"I didn't tell anyone because it would have been too painful," Brycen said, looking back at Drury. "I'm sorry."

She gaped at him, startled. But then she said, "No. It's all right, Brycen." Walking around the island, she came to him and he faced her as she put her hands on his chest. "It all makes sense now. Why you left Alaska. Why you had a hard time warming up to Junior. Why you left the CPD. I'm so sorry you had to go through that."

"You and Junior have helped me finally get past it," he said. "Junior especially." He smiled with a wry laugh.

"He can be quite the charmer." She smiled back.

He looked over at Mr. Jefferson, who still stared as though he'd received the shock of a lifetime. If Brycen were a cruel man, he'd say he had it coming. But he only felt sympathy for the man.

"I'm sorry," he said again. "I don't know if telling you back then would have been any better."

"No." Avery shook her head numbly. "It wouldn't have mattered. It's terrible. But you were right in telling us."

"That's why you married her," Mr. Jefferson said. "For the baby."

Brycen took Drury's hand and faced the two. "That

was part of the reason. I believed Kayla and I would make it as a couple. I wanted to marry her."

He didn't lie. He wouldn't say he didn't love Kayla. He didn't need to add to the hurt.

"I think we should go now," Avery said. "Daddy?"

Mr. Jefferson nodded and began to turn.

"Mr. Jefferson?" Brycen said.

The man looked back.

"I hope you can find a way to get past your regrets and be happy. Kayla would have wanted that. She wouldn't have wanted you to think she didn't love you. She did."

Moisture gathered in the older man's eyes. "Thank you." He didn't move for the door yet, and his daughter kept her hand on his arm. "I'd be honored to see you in town. I'm sorry for the way I've treated you."

He talked as though Brycen had decided to stay.

Instead of responding, Brycen addressed another issue he had just discovered a few minutes ago. "I received a call from Deputy Chandler. Someone tried to attack another woman at the pub where Cora works. He was arrested and confessed to also attempting to attack Cora."

Drury beamed a smile toward him with the good news. Cora no longer had to worry about looking over her shoulder.

"That is fantastic news," Mr. Jefferson said, a man starved for good news. He looked at Avery. "We should go see her."

Avery nodded. "Thank you, Brycen."

"You don't have to thank me. Just promise me you will both move on with your lives and be happy."

"Yes. We promise to try."

Brycen watched them go to the door and leave.

"Brycen—"

He faced Drury and put his finger over her mouth. "Yes, you should have told me you invited them here. But it's okay. I can finally close that chapter of my life."

She looped her arms over his shoulders. "You're such a good man. How am I ever going to let you go?"

He kissed her. "I'll stay awhile if you want me to."

She kissed him this time. "No. You go back to Chicago. You have your show, and Kadin offered you a job with DAI."

Even if he did want to stay, he had a life in Chicago he couldn't just walk away from.

"We could see each other," he said.

She ran her finger down his cheek and over his lower lip. "That's awfully tempting, but if you want to see me, I'd like you to do so only if you have faith in us and our future."

As in, she wouldn't be with him if he put a condition on their relationship, and she viewed his belief that love didn't last as a restriction. Funny, he could almost agree with her. But he wouldn't. Not until—and if—he was sure.

Drury stood behind Junior as Brycen put his bag down in front of the door. Junior hadn't said much since he'd gone in his room and told him he was leaving. She had her hands on his shoulders to let him know she was there for him.

Brycen went to Junior and crouched before him. "You be good for your mother. Keep up on your schoolwork and don't get into trouble. No picking your nose or farting during class."

Junior laughed. "Nobody farts in class."

"Oh, trust me, they do. You just haven't smelled one yet."

He squealed with a laugh this time.

Brycen put his hand on Junior's arm. "You're a special kid, Junior. I'm lucky to have met you. I'm going to miss you."

Junior's humor faded. "You said I was your partner. Partners stick together."

"Yes, they do." He looked up at Drury and she felt him thinking of her as his partner—a very different kind of partner.

She couldn't believe he'd walk away from this, from what they had together. But she kept telling herself he had to find his own way back to her. She wouldn't have him any other way.

"Hey," Brycen said. "If it's okay with your mom, maybe you could come to Chicago for one of my shows over your school break." He looked back up at Drury. "I could introduce him at the end of the show."

"Really?" Junior jumped up and down and tipped his head back to see his mother. "Can we, Mommy? Can we, please?"

Drury wasn't so sure that'd be a good idea. If her son had to get used to not having Brycen around, what would it do to him to have to say goodbye for a second time?

Then again, maybe by then Brycen would have come to his senses.

Not one to shy away from a good adventure, she said, "Sure, we can do that."

"Yeah!" Junior jumped against Brycen for a big hug. He hugged him back.

"Okay, kiddo. I've got a plane to catch and your mother said she wouldn't fly me." He winked at Drury.

"Liar. My plane wouldn't make it all the way to Chicago." She gave his forehead a playful shove. "You're just chicken." And she didn't mean of flying.

Chuckling, he stood. "You're the one who won't have a long-distance relationship with me."

"You don't meet up with my standards," she said. Although she was teasing, she meant every word.

Leaning forward, he kissed her, a soft warm touch at first.

"Ew." Junior wiggled out from between them. "Why do you keep doing that?"

Brycen put his hand on her waist and kissed Drury with more purpose. She didn't stop him. Junior would just have to be uncomfortable. But when the kiss heated up and broached on inappropriate groping, she withdrew and put her forehead against his.

"Can I call you?" he asked.

"No." Looking up, she made sure he could see she wouldn't bend.

"Can't blame a guy for trying."

She stepped back. "Come back to us, Brycen." Touching her lips, wishing she could save the feeling, she watched him contemplate her.

"I'll send you the information on the show."

Drury couldn't allow herself to be angry with him. She did think he was making a mistake. But he had to make his own decisions and she wouldn't help him stay away by agreeing to a long-distance relationship. She wanted him here.

With each step closer he came to Chicago, Brycen felt emptier. Moreover, he felt Drury tugging him back to her. Now at the Ted Stevens Anchorage International

Airport waiting for his flight, he couldn't stop thinking of her. When his phone rang a jolt of excitement zinged him with the hope that Drury called.

It was Kadin.

"Cage."

"You sound disappointed to hear from me."

"I thought you were someone else."

A few seconds of silence passed before Kadin said, "Ah, Drury Decoteau, huh?"

Brycen sat up from his reclined position on the airport gate chair. "What?"

"I've seen her picture. I've met her in person, too. She's hot… Not as hot as you, honey."

Brycen pictured his wife with her hands on her hips, admonishing her husband for noticing another woman was hot.

"Yes, she is pretty hot." That was all he'd volunteer.

"Did you sleep with her?"

"You called for something?" Brycen said, steering his too-perceptive temporary boss back to business.

"Yup, you did." Kadin chuckled. "You're right, it's none of my business, especially if I'm going to be your new boss."

"I'm my own boss."

"Working for me is like working for yourself. Have I interfered in your investigation?"

"No." The man wouldn't stop until he had his way. "Why don't you get to the point, Kadin?"

He chuckled. "All right. Deal. You're on your way back to Chicago and I was hoping to plant a bug in your ear to consider doing your show from Anchorage."

"I've already told you—"

"I know what you told me. You told me no the first time I came to you with an offer."

"Are you saying I'm—"

"I'm saying I could help you relocate. DAI would benefit from having a detective in Alaska. You can keep your show if you want, but I'm betting you're ready to put that in the archives."

The boldness of the man!

"Just think about it."

He'd asked him the same thing last time. "Why do I have the feeling I'm wasting my time flying home?"

"You aren't. Well…you are, but you'd have to go back and get your things anyway." He chuckled. "Little does Drury know, she's helping me out."

"How so?" Brycen had to ask, hearing the call to board his flight.

"You may as well give in now. You're in love and that isn't going away."

How could he make such an observation? He hadn't even been here. "I'm not in love."

"No? I denied it, too. I didn't realize love doesn't happen according to your plans or expectations. What you think is love doesn't even come close to the real thing. You have to experience that kind of love before you make any assumptions."

"I'll think about your offer." Brycen disconnected before Kadin could go on about him and Drury.

He reluctantly headed for the plane. Reaching the passenger boarding bridge, he stopped and looked back. Once he got on this plane, he'd be gone. He'd be far away from Drury and Junior, away from a life with them.

Something strong compelled him to walk out of the terminal and go back to them.

But he did have unfinished business in Chicago. He'd have to go back anyway, whether he decided to stay or not.

Was he actually contemplating a life with Drury and Junior?

She wouldn't take him unless he offered a lifelong commitment. Could he do that in all honesty?

You have to experience that kind of love before you make any assumptions.

Strangely he felt as though he had…with Drury.

Chapter 17

Drury followed the security guard backstage. The show was about to begin.

"Excuse me, ma'am," the guard said, stopping at the threshold of a hallway. "Mr. Cage requested to speak with Junior before he brings him onstage. He plans to introduce him at the beginning, then return him to you so that you can leave with him. He wasn't sure you'd want him to watch a murder story."

"Yes, he told me that. Not that he wanted to talk to Junior, though. Alone? Why alone?"

The guard shrugged as he shook his head. "He only told me to bring the boy. I can't bring you both."

He had his instructions.

"Mommy?" Junior said, like a question. He'd been so excited all the way here. He couldn't wait to see Brycen again.

"All right. I'll wait here."

"Come with me." The guard led Junior down the hall.

Brycen paced inside his dressing room, in a suit, ready for the show, nervous as hell. The guard opened the room door and Junior came running in.

"Brycen!"

Lights from his dressing table reflected off Junior's thick black hair. He wore a suit and tie, looking adorable, brown eyes happy and excited. Brycen crouched and took the boy into his arms for a hug. "Hey there, little man."

"I'm not a little man!" Junior laughed as he drew back.

"Have you been good?"

Junior nodded. "When are you coming home?"

That he asked was a good sign.

"Well, that's why I asked to talk to you alone, Junior." He had his hands on the boy's arms. "I need to talk to you about something very important."

"Are you going to catch another bad guy?"

"No, not today. Today is extra special. I want to ask your mother something, but I need to get your okay first."

Junior waited wide-eyed.

"You know how your mom and dad were married, right?"

"Yes."

"Well, how would you feel if your mom and I were married like that?"

"You mean, you'd be my daddy?"

"That's up to you. We can be friends or I can be your next daddy. Your real daddy will always be that, but I'd always be there for you in kind of the same way." He felt he was babbling. His nerves had him twisted up inside, second-guessing. Was he making a mistake abandoning his conviction on marriage?

"I want you to be my daddy."

Junior spoke with such sincerity that Brycen's heart mushroomed with love.

"Are you sure?"

"My daddy would approve. He'd like you. And he wouldn't want me to not have a daddy. Plus, Mommy's been mad a lot. I think she misses you."

He held back a radiant smile. "Good. Because I miss her, too. I also missed you." He tapped Junior's nose. "Okay. I have something fun planned and I need your help. It's a surprise for your mother. A big surprise."

Drury spotted Brycen and Junior leaving the dressing room. Junior was chatting excitedly about a new video game and Brycen was looking straight ahead at her. Seeing Junior so happy thrilled her, but hot sparks inundated her with the sight of Brycen, so incredibly handsome in a suit. But the man inside was what had her heart in such a pitter-patter.

She clutched her purse, white to match her dress. She hadn't been sure what to wear, so she'd dressed both herself and Junior up. She was rewarded with Brycen's roaming gaze and resulting fire in his eyes.

"Drury," he said in a deep, raspy voice.

"Hello, Brycen." Was her face flushing?

"Right this way." He guided her to the stage.

"You want me out here, too?"

"Yes."

"You're part of the show, Mommy!" Junior almost yelled in excitement.

She stepped out onto the stage to the applause of a

crowd. A big screen showed the title of the show, and a commentator narrated a trailer of today's program.

"Cindy Wilson didn't know she'd met a killer until it was too late. Did her boyfriend commit the crime or did someone else have motive." The deep, rich sound filled the studio through top-of-the-line speakers. "Find out today on *Speak of the Dead* with Brycen Cage."

"Have a seat," Brycen said to her. "Junior, you stay with me."

He faced the crowd, who still applauded. "Good evening, ladies and gentlemen." He waited for the applause to fade.

Junior stared in amazement at the crowd of faces.

"Today's show is a little more special than others," Brycen said. "We told you we'd start with an introduction. Here he is, my partner, Junior Decoteau." The crowd cheered and applauded. "Junior helped me solve a case recently. The case isn't one I'll be sharing with you, out of respect for the family. But Junior here is going to help me with something else." He looked down at Junior as though sharing a secret.

What were these two up to? Drury gripped the arms of the chair.

Junior smiled back up at him. "I'm ready."

The crowd "awed," and murmurs of "how cute" and "how adorable" spread.

Brycen turned to Drury.

What was he doing? She watched him approach her.

"Drury, Junior and I had a talk in the dressing room. I've got his approval to do this."

Drury held her breath, fleetingly seeing a sea of faces in the audience.

"Now," Brycen went on. "I know I've expressed

some pessimistic ideas on marriage, but meeting you has changed my opinion." He knelt before her and took her left hand.

"Oh my…" Drury had to breathe faster. "You aren't…"

"Drury Decoteau, will you marry me?"

The crowd erupted in awe and surprised delight.

Junior dug into his jacket pocket and produced a ring box.

"Junior." Tears stung her eyes. He'd approved this.

He handed the ring to Brycen.

"As you can see, I've had time to plan this." Brycen held the ring before her hand.

It was a beautiful white gold ring with duets of round stones between a delicate rope pattern.

Her jaw had fallen open. She had not anticipated this at all. She lifted her eyes.

"You've changed your mind?" she asked.

"Yes. I love you. I'm sure of it."

She covered her mouth along with a chorus of "aaaw-wws."

She started to cry, not sobs, just tears of pure happiness.

"Mommy, don't cry. You're supposed to say yes."

She laughed and said, "Yes!" Then flung her arms around Brycen.

"Hang on there, tigress. I haven't put on the ring yet."

Laughing some more, wiping tears as the crowd now cheered and applauded, she held out her hand.

He slipped on the ring and she admired it for a while. Then she looked at Junior and then Brycen. Her new family. Nothing could make her happier.

* * * * *

For a moment longer she just gazed up at him and looked nothing like the fierce protector who had been ready to shoot to protect her child.

He wanted to protect her. And Emma. He wanted them both safe and able to grow and blossom as he knew they would. He'd never felt the urge this strongly in his life.

Except with her.

He couldn't stop himself; he reached for her. She came into his arms easily, and he realized with a little jolt she was trembling.

"Jolie?"

"I'm scared," she whispered.

"They're gone, whoever it was," he assured her.

She leaned back again to look at him, gave a tiny shake of her head. "Not that. You."

He went still. "You're scared of me?"

Again the small gesture of denial. "Of how I feel about you. How you make me feel."

Making her feel was exactly what he wanted to do right now. He wanted to make her feel everything he'd felt, he wanted to make her move in that urgent way, wanted to hear the tiny sounds she made when he touched her in all those places, wanted to hear her cry out when she shattered in his arms.

On some vague level he knew she was talking of deeper things, but that reasoning part of his brain was shutting down as need blasted along every nerve in his body.

"I think we should check on Flash," he breathed against her ear.

He felt a shiver go through her, hoped it was for the same reason he was practically shaking in his boots.

"You think he might be getting in trouble out there?" she whispered.

"I think I already am in trouble."

"No fun getting in trouble alone," she whispered and reached up to cup his face with her hand. He turned his head, pressed his lips against her palm. And read the longed-for answer in her eyes.

He grabbed a blanket from the storage chest at the foot of the bed. Last time he'd been picking straw out of uncomfortable places. He supposed she had, too, but she'd never complained.

Jolie never complained. She assessed, formulated and acted on her best plan. It struck him then that she was exactly the kind of person he preferred to deal with in business. No manipulation, no backroom maneuvering, just honest decisions made with the best information she had at the time.

Like she had made four years ago?

Don't miss
COLTON FAMILY RESCUE by Justine Davis,
available October 2016 wherever
Harlequin® Romantic Suspense
books and ebooks are sold.

www.Harlequin.com

Love the Harlequin book you just read?

Your opinion matters.

Review this book on your favorite book site, review site, blog or your own social media properties and share your opinion with other readers!

Be sure to connect with us at:
Harlequin.com/Newsletters
Facebook.com/HarlequinBooks
Twitter.com/HarlequinBooks

JUST CAN'T GET ENOUGH?

Join our social communities
and talk to us online.

You will have access to the latest
news on upcoming titles and special
promotions, but most importantly,
you can talk to other fans about your
favorite Harlequin reads.

Harlequin.com/Community

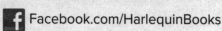 Facebook.com/HarlequinBooks

Twitter.com/HarlequinBooks

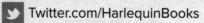 Pinterest.com/HarlequinBooks

THE WORLD IS BETTER WITH

Romance

Harlequin has everything from contemporary, passionate and heartwarming to suspenseful and inspirational stories.

Whatever your mood, we have a romance just for you!

Connect with us to find your next great read, special offers and more.